THE HIGHER HILL

THE
HIGHER HILL

GRACE CAMPBELL

COLLINS
70 BOND STREET
TORONTO

THE HIGHER HILL

The fifteen illustrations in The Higher Hill
were designed and engraved on wood by
Franklin Carmichael, R.C.A., O.S.A., who
planned the entire book and directed its
typography.

In Love and Pride
this Book is Dedicated to
Grant and Roy

CHAPTER

I

THE ROAD was like a chasm slicing deep into the forest, with a far brightness at the top of it and, on either side, a dim green world of leaves. At the bottom of the chasm a *calèche* moved along behind a stout little black mare whose hooves raised puffs of dark loamy dust that hung for an instant in the still air and dissolved slowly.

In the *calèche* rode Dougall MacKay and his daughter, Felicity. She was blue-eyed, bright-haired, seventeen, and her face was at the moment illumined by an inner excitement. Dougall looked at her out of the corner of his eye, and the curve of her cheek, so soft and young, moved him. He thought with a little quiver of amusement of the grand title of the school to which she was on her way. "The Misses Fraser's Seminary for Young Ladies." Well, it was the best the country had and would regularize the education he had himself given her.

9

A man's education it had been. And manfully she had mastered it, with an ease and an eagerness that had astounded him. Every once in a while, he mused, our race throws up something special in the way of minds; and here it is, and I have fathered it, and God help me if I know what to do with it.

He flicked a fly off the mare's black haunch with a curl of the long *babiche* and looked sideways at his daughter.

"Perhaps you've noticed," he remarked carefully, "that the girls around here have not studied the things you have. Does it make any difference between you?"

She shook her head, and her curls danced beneath her blue bonnet. "No. There are so many other things to talk about."

"Such as?"

She laughed suddenly, a clear bubble of sound. "Oh— clothes, and boys, and whom we'll marry."

"Marry!" He looked at her in dismay and touched Pegi, the little mare, with the whip. High time he was getting her into a boarding school. Yet, her mother had married at the age of seventeen, and probably her grandmother also. He might as well face it—this motherless bairn of his had all but grown up.

She turned and looked at him soberly. "Father, when did you first meet my mother?"

Dougall was silent for a moment. Then, "It was in a boat," he began slowly, the picture taking form before him, "coming up the St. Lawrence. After the war she and your grandmother came to Halifax from New York to meet your grandfather who was in the Royal Yorkers. I was a junior officer under him. We came up the St. Lawrence in open boats."

He paused. The rigour of that journey took hold on him again. The rigour and the bliss. So cold it was, and the children crying in a huddle of misery. Allison Munro, that fine woman who was now Felicity's grandmother, sat holding another's sick child in her arms, shielding it with her plaid, while against her knee crouched her own young daughter. Allison, cool and courteous even in the stress of the time, looked out over the huddled forms with a sort of bleak tenderness. There was staying power in her. But the composure of her face broke when a long shudder shook the girl sleeping against her knee.

Then he, Dougall, had come stepping over the recumbent forms with his scarlet soldier's cloak in his hands, and laid it over the sleeping girl. He eased himself down beside her and braced her body with his own. She never wakened, but her mother leaned towards him.

"Thank you, sir," she said softly.

The long night passed. The moon came out and shone down wanly on the cold, wide water, and on the pure outline of that quiet face. Once she turned and laid her head trustfully against him and was again asleep. That, he had never been able to forget. But of that he could not speak, even to Felicity.

"I met her then," he went on. "But I lost her again. Then, when I came here from Montreal, I found her in Martintown. And we were married."

11

"And I was born and she died," finished Felicity. "I'm hardly worth it."

"She would not say so."

Clear sky now showed ahead of them in a notch in the trees. Then the woods thinned out and fell away, and they were in the long clearing that stretched on either side of the South Branch River.

Pegi's hooves drummed smartly on the bridge, and they looked down into dark water spangled with water lilies. On a log three mud turtles sunned themselves; then when the shadow of horse and carriage fell across them, one after another they up-ended themselves and slipped awkwardly into the water. Felicity's bubbling laugh rang out.

"After all, she's yet a child," thought Dougall comfortably.

The road wound along the river to the east, with farmhouses on either side, and fields of stooked grain, or half-cleared meadows where sumacs held up red velvet clusters of bloom, and wild grapes trailed over the stumps.

Thought Dougall, "It's a rich and fruitful land that our harried clansmen have found. Long may they keep it!"

They now entered the village of Williamstown. A covered bridge took them over the Black River. They turned eastward down the long street, and there, on a trim green lawn shaded by elms stood the house of the Misses Fraser.

A boy came running out of the side door to hold Pegi's bridle. Felicity felt a quiver of nervousness as she climbed down. But her father's presence reassured her, as always. Fine he looked, in his cloak of navy broadcloth lined with tartan, fine and tall and master of the situation.

12

In a tiny box of an office they met Miss Jemima Fraser, head mistress. She moved to greet them in a rustle of black silk, but there was nothing frivolously feminine about her. She was tall, and her eyes met Dougall's levelly.

"So this is Felicity," she said, and Felicity dipped a curtsey.

Miss Jane came in, fluttering, and blushed when Dougall bent over her hand, her faded prettiness blooming into a sudden, fleeting youth.

"My sister," Miss Jemima explained, "looks after the fine arts and the deportment—music, embroidery, poetry, French and drawing. I guide the girls down the sterner paths of learning. Show Felicity to her room, Jane," she suggested.

She and Dougall sat down on opposite sides of the table.

"If you will tell me how long your daughter has been at school . . ."

Dougall's eyes had a flicker in them. "She has never been at school."

"Then she is quite unlettered?"

"Not exactly. Since she was quite small I have taught her. Her Latin and Greek are fairly creditable. She knows the standard English authors. In mathematics she is not so advanced. She has some French. As for music, she plays a little on the spinet. Not very much. But she dances"—here the careful casualness of voice and face broke—"she dances like a sunbeam."

"I see." Miss Jemima rested her elbow on the table and her chin in her palm. "I see. A strange bird has flown into our cote of pigeons. As for the Latin and the Greek, perhaps

13

I had better consider her proficient in them." A companionable grin lighted up her plain face.

"But you will find many gaps in her training. She has, I think, the makings of a scholar. I should like you to make of her an accomplished young lady."

Miss Jemima tapped her fingers on the table. "Do you mind if I ask what you have in view for her? For a girl, you have given her a strange and special training."

"I taught her what I myself knew. There was nothing else I could do."

"I see. Of course you must know she is a particularly lovely girl. She is likely to marry soon."

A shadow struck across Dougall's face. "I hope not. Not too soon. Her mother died when she was born."

Then Miss Jemima rose and held out her hand. "We'll do our best for her, my sister and I."

Dougall felt sure that she would.

*   *   *

Another beside her father bore the fortunes of Felicity on her heart that day. In the stone house by the river side, from which Dougall and his daughter had not long since gone, Allison Munro sat at her spinning wheel and thought about her grandchild. Delicately she fed the white rolls of carded wool to the wheel, and the small zooming sound of the spinning filled the air like the humming of bees. It was a sound made for brooding and unhurried thought.

The door opened and Kirsty, her serving-maid, came in with a tray, and on it tea and oatcakes and cheese.

"Late it will be before he is home. So have you now a bite."

14

Allison smiled at her and ate and drank. And Kirsty lifted the tray. Her broad red face glowed in the firelight with affection and concern.

"Sure, now! You mustn't be grieving for Felicity."

"I'm not. Truly, I'm not." She assured herself as well as Kirsty. Nevertheless, she was aware that the small girl-child laid in her arms so many years ago was now grown out of her need of her. And she felt curiously desolate of spirit.

No one had ever been dearer to her. Indeed, her affection for Felicity had its roots in her remote past. And she remembered that past as she turned again to her spinning.

She remembered her early home in the Highlands and the dark day of the Battle of Culloden. She remembered men fleeing across the heather, and Finlay, her brother, carrying her father up the hill to their house, his hair falling over his brow, dark and shiny with blood. And she remembered Finlay hiding by day in the hills and coming back stealthily in the dark of the night, whistling a throstle call beneath the window. She could see the eight-year-old child that had been herself, creeping in her bare feet down the dark stair and coming on her mother and him in the lighted scullery. Her mother with tears on her cheeks was packing bread and oatcake and roasted fowl and bottles of wine.

"For *him*," whispered Finlay, with the sudden dark flicker of a smile on his face.

"God keep him then," cried his mother. "And you, too, my own bairn."

Then Finlay looked up and saw his sister, and she ran and leaped into his arms. He rubbed his chin on the top of her head. "You heard, Alsoon? You'll not tell?"

15

"I'll never tell," she promised proudly. And she never had. To this day. From her, at least, no one ever learned that young Finlay Grant had been one of those who brought food to and kept guard over Prince Charlie in his shelter in the hills.

There was yet a darker picture. One that every so often she had to call up out of the hidden places of her mind.

This was a few months later. It was summer now in Glen Moriston, and she and her mother, on their way home from a neighbour's, came on a little glade in the forest. And there, beneath a great beech tree, lay Finlay. He was naked but for his kilt, and his back was criss-crossed with wet, red welts. Blood oozed from his side. They ran to him, and his eyes opened and that strange flickering smile of his shimmered over his drawn face, like sunshine on dark water. He caught at his mother's hand.

"I didn't tell," he whispered. "Rather, they could have killed me."

As a matter of fact, they had. In two weeks he was dead. At seventeen. But really, for her he had never died. Nor had he grown old. And he was alive again in Felicity. The smile that had lighted up his dark young face was the same she saw every day on Felicity's fair one. There was the same sudden illumination, the same shining sweetness.

So, for her, Felicity was set apart. There must be for her feet some fair, high road to travel. Through her, she felt in a vague and mystical way, God was making it up to Finlay for his young life so soon cut off, in that his spirit was alive again in one of his own blood. Many an old hope and dream of the broken clans was now coming to fruition in this rich, peaceful land. Felicity was part of that fruition.

*   *   *

As for Felicity herself, she was at that moment in a light-hearted mood, with little thought of the hopes and dreams of her elders for her.

Supper was over in the Seminary for Young Ladies, and prayers as well. A chapter of the Bible had been read, each taking a verse in turn. After that, they knelt by their chairs and Miss Jemima offered up a short, business-like prayer, as if she thought God, like herself, had a lot on His hands and she had no intention of wasting His time. Then they all gathered about the spinet while Miss Jane's slim fingers danced over the keys.

Arms entwined, they sang heartily, and with a fine disregard of pronunication, in French, and then yet more heartily in English. Till dusk filled the corners of the room, and Miss Jemima lighted the candles on the mantel.

Then, without, there was the sudden rattle of wheels.

"It's Meron," cried someone, in a voice that crackled with expectation.

The door was flung open, and a great dark girl stood there with a wicker basket in the crook of her arm. Her face lighted up in a superb wide smile that broke into laughter.

"Bless you all," she cried, and her voice was rich and deep and exciting. "And me that glad to see you!"

The girls surrounded her. Miss Jane rose too.

"Curtsey, Meron," someone whispered.

That careless, ready laugh rang out. "Me, with a bushel basket in my arms? Here, Miss Jane, are the rowan berries I promised you."

17

"My dear child, I do thank you. But why did you not give them to Louis?"

"Because I wanted to show them to you. Look!" She moved the basket and the berries slid about in a moving red-gold mass. At one side was a little pile of bright red clusters with leaves attached.

"These are to hang in your rooms, my darlings. To bring you luck!"

She tossed them to this one and to that, and the girls, laughing, caught them and tucked them in hair or bosom. All at once she saw Felicity.

"For you, too," she cried, and tossed her a spray.

"Felicity is your new roommate," explained Miss Jane as she introduced them.

"A good influence you'll be," grinned Meron. Then, turning to the rest, "Do you know who brought me? My handsomest brother!"

"Och, Meron—not Hughie!"

"Hughie? No, not Hughie. Peter—that's who. Miss Jane," she turned with sudden dignity, "may I bring in my brother to meet my friends?"

In a moment she was back. A sudden hush fell on them. In that roomful of young and fluttering feminity Meron's brother, Peter, was like a primeval force. Tall and dark, slim and lordly, he towered over Miss Jemima who came in with them and presented him.

At each name he bent courteously.

Felicity came last. She gave him the sweeping, slow curtsey her grandmother had taught her, and as she rose from it their eyes met. His were suddenly intent, and hers had the shy shimmer of a smile in them.

"Felicity is to be Meron's roommate," explained Miss Jane brightly.

"I understand you are once more about to leave this part of the country," put in Miss Jemima.

Then Felicity heard for the first time his voice, a rich, warm voice that had a curious, heart-stirring quality.

"I am going to the far west again."

"Fur trading?"

"I am in the employ of the fur company, but I have been with Simon Fraser exploring in the mountains near the sea."

"What of that wild river he traced?"

"The Tacouche Tesse? I hear they are to call it now 'The Fraser,' after him. I was on that trip."

His eyes met Felicity's and surprised in them a sudden look of concern. A little flush ran along his cheek bones. His glance fell on the cluster of rowan berries she still held. He stepped closer and put out his hand.

"May I have these for luck?"

Felicity hesitated a moment, flushed, then laid them in his palm. His fingers closed briefly, warmly over hers.

"For luck!" she repeated. "Will you be long away?"

"Not longer than I can help."

Their eyes met, and for an instant held. Then he turned to Miss Jemima and to Meron, and in a moment he was gone, and the girls gathered again about the spinet.

Miss Jemima's brief glance flicked ironically over Felicity.

"Not to be married for a long time, so says her father.

19

The Latin and Greek seem not to have made much difference. They took better on me."

Feeling envious and rueful and amused all at once, she crossed the hall to her office and took out a heavy leather-bound account book.

"Five pounds tuition," her finger ran along the column. "Seven bushels of potatoes and three pecks of buckwheat flour against the board of one, Nancy MacKillop. Wages of Louis Lalonde, minus board and keep . . ."

The glow of the candle lighted up her good plain face as she added and subtracted busily. A burst of song came from the other room. "*Malbrouk s'en va t'en guerre.*"

Miss Jemima smiled tolerantly. "They're excited," she thought. "Meron back, and the new girl, and the big MacAlpin, all in one evening. We're not going to be dull, I think, this session."

★

★

CHAPTER

II

EARLY IN OCTOBER Felicity spent a week-end at the home of Meron, her roommate. David, the youngest of the MacAlpin brothers, came for the girls, and the three of them drove along the road that edged the South Branch River. It was a warm and windy day. The trees were in full colour, crimson, mahogany, old gold and copper, threaded with the dark green of the pines. The air was rich with the smell of autumn, of wild grapes and dry leaves and smoke.

David was sixteen, a quiet dark lad with quick blue eyes. He was shy with Felicity, and turned his gaze to his driving. Meron plied him with questions.

He grinned. "You'd think you'd been away a long time. Things haven't changed much."

"I'm not so sure. Have you cut the corn?"

"We have. Look! Here's Duncan MacFarlane."

A battered sulky came rattling around a curve in the road

behind an old gray horse that trotted briskly along and switched impatiently at the continual light tickle of the whip over his bony haunches. The driver, ancient like both horse and carriage, nevertheless sat youthfully erect on the hard seat. His head was bare and his curly gray hair moved in the breeze. He was a good-looking old man who had been handsome and romantic in his youth, it was plain. Even yet there was pride in the set of his shoulders, and his eyes were blue and unfaded and full of humour.

"*Tha mi gu math*, my fine young folk."

He greeted them as they passed with grave courtesy; then a flicker of interest acknowledged Felicity's presence. His voice was full of the music of the Gaelic, and his words were well spoken.

"Who is he?" asked Felicity.

"He's a cobbler. Not a hard worker, but he enjoys life, so he does."

The road now dived into the deep gloom of a grove of pines. The ground was a rustling carpet of dry needles, and the air was so aromatic with the cool, exciting odour of evergreens that the nostrils quivered to it. Then the trees thinned out. A cow-bell jangled, and the smoke of dwellings rose, and the road wound between grassy meadows and fields of corn with ripe pumpkins gleaming goldenly among the stooks.

"I can see smoke from the chimney," cried Meron. "See! That's Tulloch Ard."

"*Tulloch Ard*," echoed Felicity. "The high knoll."

Meron nodded. "Yes. Really *Tulach Ard*, but everyone says Tulloch."

24

Beyond they could see a still higher hill, crowned with trees.

David touched up Shanlan's black flanks and the horse broke into a trot. He turned to Meron: "Have you, then, been lonesome?"

She laughed and pushed her bonnet back. "It's better at home. More exciting."

Up a gravelly slope they went. The horse's hooves sent back small showers of earth and stones. Then the *calèche* turned into a lane, dark-shaded by hemlock and pine, and came out again into sunshine, and there before them was the house of Tulloch Ard, with a plot of grass in front of it, and behind it, four great maple trees standing so close they touched, and so were one great crimson banner of colour.

The squared logs of the house were weathered to a silvery gray. Stone chimneys rose at either end. Across the front ran a narrow verandah, along the length of which was a flower-bed, gay with sweet-williams and pinks, candy-tuft and nicotine. West of the house was a little turning-green, well rutted by wheels. Here David pulled up and Meron sprang eagerly out. Felicity let David help her ceremoniously down.

"Mathair!" called Meron in her full rich voice, and hurrying from within came another Meron, except that white streaks were in the dark hair, and crinkles at the corners of the eyes that were gray and clear, not gentian blue.

"So it's back you are, Meron *mochree*. And this will be Felicity."

She drew the girl into the circle of her arms and kissed her. Felicity was lost in the embrace. She had an impression of strong, friendly arms, a broad, soft bosom, and a clean fragrance that she did not know.

"Come away now and put your things upstairs. Meron will show you."

Meron's room was at the west end of the house. It was slope-ceilinged and whitewashed, with a window to the south and to the west, and a yellow-painted floor that caught up so much of the light that it was reflected in sunny patches on the white walls. There was a high bureau with a swinging mirror, and a washstand with a blue pitcher and bowl, and in one corner a bed, very high and plump, with a feather tick and yellow woven coverlet.

Meron punched it with an experimental fist. "They've filled the under-mattress with new straw. Fine and high we'll sleep tonight."

Felicity poured water into the blue bowl. Burying her face in the clean, coarse linen towel, she paused and sniffed.

"It's sweet-mary," said Meron. "Didn't you smell it off mother? She has a big plot of it by the garden fence and she puts it between the sheets and towels and among her clothes."

Meron sat on the window-sill and watched Felicity combing out her light brown curls and setting them with her fingers.

"Boys-oh!" she exclaimed, "you're a pretty thing. Wait till Hughie sees you."

Then, before Felicity could answer, she went on in pride and complacency, "And wait till you see Hughie. Come now down to supper."

Downstairs the room seemed full of tall men and laughter and deep, resonant voices. There was Big Rorie MacAlpin himself, six foot two, and broad accordingly, with a shock of curly, iron-gray hair, and a beard to match, and Meron's own blue eyes. He patted Felicity on the shoulder with a great hard hand and looked down at her with such welcome and good will that she broke involuntarily into delighted laughter. David hovered smiling in the background. And then there was Hugh. "Wait till you see Hughie," Meron had said. He was worth seeing. A fair bright head among all the dark ones. Gray eyes, clear like water, and dancing. Not so tall as the others, but slim and lightsome.

"Sit in now," urged Mrs. MacAlpin. "Starved you must be with the long drive."

There was a steaming savoury stew with vegetables and dumplings on a big blue platter; there were mealy brown potatoes, bursting their jackets; there were scones and sweet butter for them, and golden squares of johnny cake drowned in maple syrup. All fell to in a workman-like way.

"Do they feed you well at school?" Rorie MacAlpin looked up at the far end of the table.

"Well enough. But not like this."

"I never get enough," put in Meron gloomily, and they all laughed.

"You'll hurry now with the milking," said Mother MacAlpin. "There'll be a few in tonight, I've no doubt."

"There will that. We met Duncan MacFarlane," observed David.

They laughed again and trooped noisily out. Felicity thought she had never been in a place where there was so much loud and hearty laughter.

Meron put on a coarse blue apron that quite covered her,

27

took a pail from a bench behind the woodshed, and Felicity followed her to the barn. In the fence corner a red cow stood looking contemplatively into space, with a half-chewed buttercup dangling from her mouth. Meron sat down on her three-legged stool, laid her head firmly against the smooth red flank, and twin streams of milk sang sharply against the bottom of the pail. Then presently the hard ringing sound changed to a soft whirring as the milk rose higher and made white foam in the pail, and the bland smell of it floated out on the cool air.

Felicity leaned against the fence and watched. Evening primroses bloomed near, and mulleins with their furry leaves and tall stalks and creamy, close-set blossoms. The sun was low in the sky and long shadows wavered over the short-clipped grass. In the level yellow light the colours were richer and more mellow than in full sunlight. Meron in her blue apron, leaning against the red quiet cow, sang an old Gaelic milking song.

"*Sil a bho, sil am bainne*—Let down, O cow, let down thy milk."

Her voice was soft and deep. Felicity felt pensive, watching. For thousands of years had women milked their cattle in the gloaming in every pastoral country in the world. It was simple and strong and good. It was like an old poem, or a painting. Her thoughts grew tangled and confused.

Hughie appeared at the barn door, whistling. He came and sat on the fence. "Do you want any help?" he called to Meron.

"No. David and I can finish. He doesn't like to milk," she told Felicity. "So we humour him."

28

Hughie smiled at Felicity. "I'm the lazy one, you see. Unless I like what I'm doing." His eyes smiled into hers. "You're clever, Meron says."

She shook her head. "Meron is too kind."

His gray eyes rested mockingly on her. "Clever, I'm sure. And smart enough to hide it."

She laughed. "Then we understand each other."

He plucked a pale primrose flower, blew the petals back about the powdery stamens, then laid the blossom in her hand. "We'll always do that, you and I, understand each other."

"Might it be uncomfortable?"

He nodded gravely. "Very. For me. But you'll see. It's true."

"What are you talking about, and you so serious?" Meron turned her head, scowling. The red cow had without warning flicked her with the long lash of her tail. She got up.

"There, you besom!" she said and slapped the smooth flank with her open hand, and the cow moved indignantly away. "I was done anyway."

The milking over, the girls hurried up to the bedroom. Meron lit a fat candle and they held it for each other, and tilted the mirror to see better.

Felicity put on her best dress of pale blue cashmere, pin-tucked and with a fichu. She looked young and innocent in it, with her pink cheeks and her round white forehead and the shimmering bright sweetness of her smile.

Meanwhile, Meron buttoned herself into a yellow linsey, snug in the bodice and full-skirted. She was a dark and handsome lass as she stood preening herself before the small

29

mirror. Suddenly her hand dived deep into her pocket and held up a crumpled leaf.

"Mullein. I'll loan it to you whenever you like. When you feel yourself pale, give your cheeks a rub. Brings out the colour lovely. Stings, of course."

"You don't need it. Not now, anyway."

And Meron didn't. She was flushed and taut with excitement.

"Is anyone special coming tonight?" asked Felicity on a sudden thought.

Meron flashed a bright, enigmatic smile. "If anyone does, I'll let you know."

The big room downstairs was ready for company. On the wide stone hearth, flames curled rosily around the maple log and sent out welcoming warmth and light. On the mantel stood a row of tall pale candles, and more were on the table that was now pushed against the wall.

Mother MacAlpin was sitting in her own high-backed chair, busy with her knitting.

"With a family of boys," she remarked, "the socks keep me busy. Though two there are away, and me not able to mend or knit for them." Sombreness settled down over her.

"Two?" inquired Felicity diffidently.

"Yes. Peter in the far western mountains, and Evan for many years trading in fur on the plains. God keep them. Good boys both. But venturesome. All mine are." She looked bleakly into Felicity's eyes for a moment, then the bleakness broke in a wide, rich smile. "But that's the way I like them. Venturesome."

Hughie joined them. He had made himself fine. He wore

a green kilt and a loose shirt, open at the throat and with no stock. His slim, muscular knees gleamed in the firelight as he leaned against the edge of the table whistling idly, his bright appreciative eyes on Felicity.

He was a handsome lad, and he knew it, but he was lovable, too, and it lightened the heart just to look at him. His mother's eyes played over him with a richness of affection that was like a mantle wrapping him round.

In half an hour the big room was full of people. Duncan MacFarlane was there in his white linen shirt and his decent black jacket and breeches. Beside him was Mairi MacDonell; "Dark Mary of the Songs," they called her. She was an austere woman in her middle years. Life had not dealt easily with her, it was plain. But her eyes were steady and unflinching, and there was a fine, bitter pride in her face.

Beside her, and in complete contrast, was her niece, Ceit —Kate, in English—or "Little Katie," as everyone knew her. She was red-headed, fine-boned and dainty, composed in her manner. "A complete little body," Mrs. MacAlpin called her. Felicity liked her at first sight.

The door opened and Meron was suddenly still. A stain of red crept up over her cheeks.

"Fergus," said someone in a low voice, and Felicity looked well at him as he entered. He was a dark lad, dark of eyes and hair and brow.

"Come away in," cried Rorie heartily and motioned him to a chair.

They made room for him, though there was perhaps a little restraint in their welcome. But Mairi at least looked at him with eyes that were warm and friendly with affection.

31

"Sit by me, lad," she cried. "Did you bring your fiddle?"

He shook his head. His eyes drifted warily towards Meron and away again.

"Then it's yourself, Rorie," said Duncan.

"Well now, just to start you off." And Rorie tucked his fiddle under his chin, lifted his bow, and a light sliding melody slipped from the strings, turned to a strathspey and quickened into a reel that set their toes tapping. Then he paused and laid it across his knees. While good friendly talk, news of the countryside, passed from one to another, and tales and old stories.

Then said Duncan, "Sure, we've not had a song from Mairi."

Rorie laid the fiddle down. "I like best your singing without any other music at all."

Mairi looked around at them with the assurance of one who knows her worth, and with kindliness in her eyes as well.

"I'll sing you first of the beginning of the year," she said simply.

And she did. With freshness and delight she sang in Gaelic of the green hills in springtime, and the red and white calves gambolling on them, and the young lambs snuffing the daisies, and girls in white dresses and cherry-coloured ribbons coming down the glen on Sunday mornings, and the light soft sunshine over all, and behind them the blue hills of the Highlands. It was a scene out of the happy days in their past, and though the younger ones knew it only by hearsay, yet they felt it true by instinct and knew it in their blood and bones.

When she paused they all looked at her with soft and

friendly eyes for the sweetness she had showed them out of the old, good times.

Then her long fingers began to beat on her knee, and her face was sombre, and there was no lightheartedness at all in her voice when she sang. Trouble had come to the glen. It was a Jacobite song. It was a song of the defeated, the fugitive, the dispossessed.

> *"Over the hills and far away;*
> *It's over the hills and far away,*
> *Over the hills and over the sea,*
> *The wind has blown my plaid from me.*
>
> *It blew my corn, it blew my gear,*
> *It left me neither kid nor steer;*
> *And blew my plaid, my only stay,*
> *Over the hills and far away.*
>
> *But though it's left me bare indeed,*
> *And blown my bonnet off my head,*
> *There's something hid in Highland brae;*
> *It hasna blown my sword away."*

It was bleak, and it was angry, and there was a threat in it. The knowledge of that sword hidden in the bracken, and the dark, sweet thought of revenge, was in it.

Then she lifted her voice and sang an old, old song they all knew. The lovely swelling melody of it rose and fell. Sweet and sad, the very honey of woe it was—*"Fear a bata, oh my boatman."* There was pain, yet there was something limpid and joyous in it, too, as if love and loneliness reached out past all barriers to a far, fair joy to come.

They were still when she stopped. Rorie rose and threw a log on the fire and the sparks flew up. "That was fine music, Mairi. Like the grand pibroch, it goes deep into a man."

She smiled. "Let's have a reel now and be happy."

Rorie handed his fiddle to Fergus. "Give us Tulloch-gorum."

Then Hughie pushed back his chair and stepped out in the clear place in the floor and danced. He danced as effortlessly as the play of a sunbeam on water, his feet tapping lightly and truly, his face quiet.

"Oh, lovely, lovely," breathed Felicity in her own mind.

They were all still, watching. His strong knees flashed in the intricate measure, his sleeve fell back from his arm as he flung it up, and every movement had the lift and beauty of a line of verse. His body was fluid, was light as air, was given over entirely to the music. The firelight limned him against the dark walls, a flying figure of utter grace.

When he finished, there was a spatter of hand-clapping.

"Hughie, lad," said old Duncan. "You dance as your uncle used to on a market day in Inverness, when we and all the world were young."

Hugh nodded to Fergus. "It was good fiddling."

And Fergus smiled his rare smile. "Better on the pipes, though, is Tullochgorum." And he continued to play, lightly and easily, filling the gaps in the conversation.

Duncan leaned towards Rorie and said behind his hand, "Look you now, could it be you've run short? Sure the boys could slip over to my place."

34

Rorie spoke softly under the music. "Thank you for the thought, Duncan, but a full keg have I myself. Nevertheless, this young girl is yet a stranger among us."

Duncan nodded his courtly gray head. "A proper thought."

Then Rorie's elbow nudged him. "But what would be the harm for you and me to slip out and sample it?"

In the woodshed, Duncan drew his hand over his mouth and smacked his lips. "The best *usquebae* I have tasted forever more." And Rorie lifted his mug with, "*Slainte*, and God bless you, and here's to us all."

When they came back in, food had been set out on the long table—oatcakes, and curly-cakes, and scones, and strong hot tea, and cold and creamy buttermilk. Chairs were drawn in, and "Take hold now, do!" cried Mother MacAlpin hospitably.

The three girls served, and they all ate and drank in friendship and good will. When they had cleared the table, Meron and Felicity and Katie came out into the full light of the fire again and stood for a moment, arms entwined, all of them of an age, one dark, one fair, and one ruddy.

Suddenly old Duncan reared himself out of his chair and raised his glass to them. "Three of you alike, and all bonnie, and your lives and your loves twisted together like a tangled skein for the knitting."

"What do you mean?" cried Meron.

He put down his glass and interlaced his fingers. "Your fates are like that."

"But how do you know?" in Katie's crisp, pretty voice.

"How do I know?" he answered deeply. "I bring it up

out of the knowledge that is in the bottom of my mind. That's how a man knows anything. But—here's to you, anyway! And when you're old women, you'll all be friends."

"But not before?" cried Felicity, laughing, yet in consternation, and their arms tightened about each other.

Fergus's black eyes flicked over the three of them, and a smile played momentarily about his mouth.

Up in the bedroom later, Felicity and Meron undressed slowly, still too quick with excitement for sleep. At the window Felicity leaned and looked down into the soft black night. Meron knelt beside her. Below was the roof of the porch.

"Once I climbed down there," she offered suddenly.

"Really?"

"Yes. To go to a dance." A pause. "With Fergus."

"They wouldn't let you?"

"No. He's wild, you know," she stated in pride and simplicity.

"But you like him?"

She laughed a low, rollicking laugh. "Don't I, though! Yes, he whistled from the rowan grove and I climbed down. One night last summer. His horse was up the road a bit. We went to a dance in Glen Falloch."

"Did you have a good time?"

Meron's mouth curved and her eyes brightened. "Best I've ever had." Then, fixing Felicity with a hard stare, "But mind you, there was nothing wrong in it. Nothing at all."

"Exciting, though," thought Felicity. "Would you go again?" she asked.

Meron laughed and went to the mirror and shook her

hair over her face. "No," her voice came muffled. "I'd be afraid. But I'm glad I did it once."

The next day the girls went down the slope and up the higher hill to the west to pick what was left of the grapes. It was again a wind-swept sunny day, and from the height the whole countryside lay spread out, the shorn fields, the tossing bright trees, and the river winding blue between them.

On the very crown and summit of the hill was an open space, green and smooth, surrounded by and enclosed in the heart of a grove of rowans. The trees with their slim and airy grace were nearly hidden by the massed, red-gold clusters of fruit, that made in the sunshine an almost unbearable great brightness. It was like a flame or the last supreme high note of an anthem. It was beautiful and breath-taking.

Beyond were the grape vines, climbing over the rail fence and draping with borrowed green an old thorn-apple tree. These were wild grapes, bearing their small purple bunches lightly and casually on strong vines.

As Felicity picked, her fingers purpling, her eyes were on the rowan trees. The very grass beneath them was different. Fine and soft it was, like hair, and spangled with strawberry leaves, fall-reddened.

"I've never seen a place like this," she said seriously.

"Like Tulloch Ard?"

"Like this higher hill."

She could not put it into words, but this grove of red rowans, with the small green lawn enclosed within it, seemed beautiful and meaningful to her as no other place had ever been. She gathered it in with her eyes, as if to make a picture in her mind.

37

Meron spat out the seeds of a grape. "Bitter, aren't they? But they make good wine." Then, looking at the bright tossing trees, "Father wanted to cut them down. But Peter said, 'Leave them be.' So Mother won't have them touched."

"Peter," thought Felicity. "Where is he now?" She was reluctant to ask.

Meron sighed. "I wish he'd come home. Mother frets. All those mountains! And winter coming on!"

★

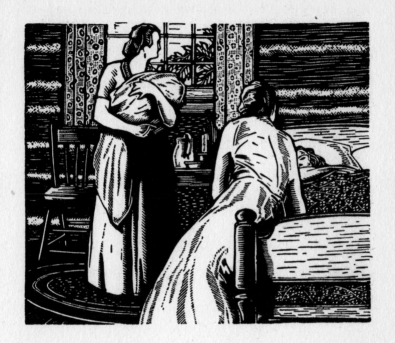

★

CHAPTER

III

IN THE MANSE STUDY at Williamstown the fire leaped and crackled on the hearth, and the ruddy light of it washed over the room and lighted up the faces of the three men who had just come in.

"Sit down, Dougall, sit down," cried John Bethune, the minister. "You've a good hour to spare. Let the horse have his oats, and we'll have a crack by the fire."

He lowered himself stiffly into a worn leather chair. "My joints are giving out," he remarked as if it were an affair of no importance.

"You should take more care of yourself, sir," offered the younger of his guests, Gavin Scott of Montreal.

Dougall MacKay laughed shortly and laid his hand in a brief affectionate gesture on the minister's knee.

"He doesn't know how. By day and by night, riding over

our wretched roads, rowing up creeks into the back country, tending the sick."

The minister tapped out his pipe against the hearth. "It's a big parish," he observed mildly. "And why should I spare myself?"

His clear eyes rested on Gavin. "We'll miss you, lad. It's been like having one of our own boys back to have you with us, and loath we are to hand you over to Dougall."

"It has been a great pleasure to me, sir," said Gavin with formal courtesy, but there was warmth in his voice. "I'll tell your sons in Montreal that you are well, if over-busy."

"Tell John," continued the minister, "to send me that new poem written by a namesake of yours, an Edinburgh attorney, 'The Lay of the Last Minstrel'."

"I'll send it myself by next post."

"That's a good lad." The Reverend John leaned his head against the high back of the chair. He looked like a saint, or a scholar, who had once been a man of action, and some of the fire and energy had been carried over. Violence there had been in his life, war and imprisonment, friends turned to enemies, and a new life to be made in a raw, hard country.

Thought Dougall MacKay, "I can understand him better than Gavin does, because I, too, knew war in my youth."

As for Gavin, Dougall looked keenly at him. Born to an interval of peace, he had had what any man would crave for his son, an ordered, easy life. School and travel and a not too demanding career in law. Yet he was not soft. He had a serviceable, square-built body, near-sighted friendly eyes, and the indefinable air of a man of means and leisure. He had also, as Dougall knew, a strong and original mind.

42

The minister turned to Dougall. "I saw Felicity last week. Of course I see her always on Sundays. But this time I was calling at the school." He paused, and Dougall's eyes flicked over him with parental impatience.

Mr. Bethune continued thoughtfully. "Quite a remarkable young woman! Her eyes. Her smile. Then when her interest is aroused, her complete absorption." He sighed. "Too bad she wasn't a boy."

"Why?" asked Gavin.

The minister took a few pulls at his pipe. "A waste of brains."

Dougall rose. "Night falls early," he observed. Already from the windows the brightness of the day was fading.

"Christmas weather, this. Are you well wrapped, with plenty of robes?"

"Plenty, sir," Dougall assured him.

*   *   *

They called at the school for Felicity. She came directly out, blue-eyed and rosy in her dark cloak and her bonnet and stole of gray squirrel. Gavin she had not seen for three years, and she had been then a child. Now she greeted him as a young lady.

Fur robes lined the seat of the carriole and were tucked well around them. Felicity sat in the middle, for warmth, and was silent except for the light lift of her laughter from time to time. She was excited, and her excitement was like a light within her. It shone through in her eyes and in her voice. It was enough that she was going home and that it was Christmas Eve, but here also was this fine friend of her father's coming to spend the holiday season with them. A man out of another world, he was. She tilted her bonnet and stole a look at him, and met his eyes fixed on her in an intent and steady regard. Her own eyes dropped, and then she raised them again and flashed him her bright, shining smile.

They passed the church and the Red Tavern and were soon out of the village and on their way. It was cold. Specks of frost sparkled in the air. Snow lay everywhere. Every fence rail, every twig, carried its burden. The spruce branches were weighed down with it. Then a little wind rose and sifted it off in fine swirls and eddies. There was a bite in that wind.

"Cold?" inquired Gavin.

Felicity shook her head.

But he shifted his position and laid his arm along the back of the seat, so that when she swayed a little with the movement of the sleigh she felt his solid strength beside her. She sat looking down at her small mittened hands, and in an inner stillness she knew that his mind was on her. Words were superfluous. By an older and subtler means of communication she was aware of an intentness in him, an excitement of mind and sense. She thought of Hughie at Tulloch Ard and the feeling of understanding and comradeship she had with him as they, young and light-hearted, had tried out their bright words and laughter on each other. This was different.

Then she thought of Peter, whom she had so briefly known. That was different too. She sighed suddenly, overcome by the new complexities of life. Then turned her mind to what her father was saying.

"It grieves me to see that the minister is now showing his years."

44

"He has lived a strenuous life, I gathered from his son. He was anxious for me to see his father and report on his health. I'm glad to see you're looking well yourself, Dougall."

Dougall smiled and waved his whip. His friendship with this man ten years his junior, whom he saw only at long intervals, was curiously satisfying. They shared the same tastes and had, as well, some experiences in common. When Dougall had been with the Royal Yorkers stationed for a time in Montreal, Gavin had been a hero-worshipping boy, and that had been the beginning of a friendship that had grown with the years and only throve on separation.

"I'm hoping you won't find it dull in the countryside." He frowned thoughtfully. "In summer the river's a great highway—*voyageurs*, *bateaux* of all kinds on it. But with winter we den up."

Gavin laughed. "It won't be dull."

They were now in the woods, and the long shadows of trees slanted across the road. Rabbits bobbed over the snowy ridges and squirrels chittered from the branches. The sun was a dull red behind the dark tree trunks. Night was coming on.

But the bells jangled cheerily and the carriole slid along over the snowy road, and presently they came out on the river and turned west. And now the wind did come with a great swirling sweep across the wide St. Lawrence and buffetted them and sifted through their garments and chilled and tightened the skin.

But there ahead of them was the long, low, stone house, and Felicity's heart quickened at the sight. As they looked, the windows blossomed into yellow light.

"Kirsty's lighting the candles," she exclaimed happily.

Then with a swerve and a sweep they were inside the lane and before the house. And old Bateese was running out with the lanthorn, and there was grandmother herself silhouetted in the open door, and the black dog was barking madly, and she was home.

She ran in quickly, and the warmth and light enfolded her. She was caught in her grandmother's arms and kissed and held at arm's length. And Kirsty patted her and took her cloak and threw an entirely unnecessary log on the fire in her enthusiasm. Not till then did Felicity remember Gavin who was now in the doorway and being welcomed in his turn.

It was Christmas Eve, and that night after they had eaten they gathered around the fire and talked in a leisurely way, till Kirsty brought in the silver tray with the pound cake and elderberry wine. Gavin lifted his glass to Felicity.

"Why Felicity?" he enquired smilingly. "In a sea of Mairis and Pegis and Floras and Kirsties. Why a New England name on as Highland a lass as I've seen?"

Allison and Dougall exchanged glances.

"I'll tell you," she said. "In the days that followed the Revolutionary War, my daughter Barbara and I were making our way to a place where we might join my husband, and we were greatly helped by a kind young woman who sheltered and cared for us. Her husband was away in the army fighting against our men. But she was in need of comfort as we were, and we were just three women together in a bitter time of war. While we were with her, her baby was born and Barbara washed and tended it and thought there never was so sweet a bairn. So this kind young woman, lying there and looking up at Barbara who knelt by her, said, 'I'll call her Barbara after you, and if you ever have a daughter call her Felicity for me, and there'll be a little friendliness between us and our people, though we may never see each other again.'

"And so it was. When Barbara's daughter was born here she named her Felicity."

"Sometime you may meet that other Barbara," suggested Gavin softly.

Felicity's eyes turned on him. "Do you think so? How I should like to!"

Dougall sat still, his face in shadow. For how short a time had his Barbara lived to fill his world with love and brightness!

Allison rose. "Felicity and I will leave you now. There's no use telling you not to sit up late. I know you will."

Felicity took a candle and followed her grandmother up the wide, curving stair. She shaded the light with her hand, and the glow of it shone rosily through her fingers and up into her face, highlighting it. The two men followed her silently with their eyes, then smiled at each other and pulled their chairs closer to the fire.

*   *   *

Kirsty was waiting in the big bedroom upstairs. She had thrust the long warming pan between the sheets of the feather bed and was moving it about.

Felicity went through to her own little room and undressed swiftly. Shiveringly she slipped into her long-sleeved, high-necked white flannel nightgown, thrust her bare, pink feet into padded slippers and came back into her grandmother's room. Kirsty was rubbing her mistress's back, and

47

the air was full of the penetrating smell of liniment.

"Lie still now," she admonished, and with her strong red arms and her expert thick fingers she kneaded and chafed the tired muscles, then snapped down the nightgown and covered Allison up as if she were a child.

"Tired herself out, so she did," she grumbled. "With all that shining and polishing."

Felicity wrapped herself in a plaid shawl and sat down in a low chair by the bed. Close by stood a small table and on it a leather-covered Gaelic Bible, a candle and a curiously shaped glass-stoppered bottle. This she uncorked, held for a moment under her nose, then passed it to her grandmother who took it and bathed her forehead and the lids of her closed eyes. It was an aromatic camphor dissolved in alcohol, and was astringent and cooling. As long as she could remember, her grandmother had performed this nightly ritual.

"Why?" she now asked curiously.

"It soothes and settles me for the night. Now tell me, did you have a fine time at the school?"

Kirsty drew up another chair, pulled her knitting out of her pocket and prepared to listen. All through her childhood this had been the time of day that Felicity liked best, when the three of them, her quiet austere grandmother, Kirsty the stout and buxom serving-maid, and she the child among them, had talked and laughed together, relaxed and easy at the end of the day.

So she gave them her news. She told them of the school and of the Misses Fraser and of the girls and Meron and her visit to Tulloch Ard.

"Duncan MacFarlane," smiled her grandmother. "The

48

old rascal! I knew him well once. And Mairi MacDonell. The man whom she was to marry was killed. He was a wild one, but she was heartbroken. He has a nephew, I hear, as like to him as another pea in the same pod."

"I met him too," cried Felicity. "At Tulloch Ard."

"But did you eat well at the school?" demanded Kirsty. "Did you clean up your porridge plate in the mornings, and did you wear your flannel petticoat at all, at all? Well I know you didn't, you the proud thing!"

"You'll be cold, girls," put in Mrs. Munro mildly.

Felicity laughed and kissed her grandmother, and in a moment was snuggled in her own bed, exploring gingerly the icy regions untouched by the warming pan. With the skill born of practice she curled her toes in the hem of her long nightgown and pulled it down around her feet. Then the warmth of the feather bed enclosed her and she was asleep.

Dinner on Christmas Day was a festive occasion. The best linen graced the table, and the silver and the pewter had been polished to a lovely sheen. First came a savoury Scotch broth, rich and smooth and steaming hot in the big blue tureen. Then a plump and crackling, roasted, stuffed young turkey with a platter of pink sliced ham and a saddle of mutton for support. There were potatoes, too, and carrots cooked in cream, and a sauce of wild cranberries, and scarlet rowan jelly, and crisp pickled cucumbers, and savoury small apples, both tart and sweet, and brown with spices.

Then Kirsty proudly bore the pudding in, with blue flames licking round it, and mince tartlets and shortbread squares with hot green China tea completed a fine sustaining meal.

Afterwards Gavin brought out gifts. For his hostess he had a silk shawl with a wide shimmering fringe. It was not black, nor even gray nor purple, but a blue-green aquamarine shade that caught the light like the underside of a wave. He laid it across her shoulders and they all exclaimed in delight. Her delicate pallor, her eyes, were lighted up by it. Colour glowed in her quiet, proud face.

"My dear boy, I do thank you," she smiled. "Especially for the colour. Black is very wearisome when one is old."

Then Gavin looked at Felicity. "I didn't know what you'd be like, now that you are grown up. But I thought you might like this."

He held up a small oil painting, richly framed. A bit of shore line and waves coming tumultuously in. Dougall stuffed his pipe in his pocket and came and studied it close, and then at long range.

"That's good," he exclaimed. "Who did it?"

"Du Longpré. You like it?" he enquired of Felicity who stood looking at it, the colour coming and going in her face.

She nodded, then remembering her manners, she came over to him. "Thank you very much," she said earnestly. "You couldn't have given me anything better."

The picture was placed on the mantel above the big fireplace, and Felicity came again and again to look at it from every angle. There was such an intentness in her gaze that Gavin enquired of her, when they were for a moment alone, "What particularly interests you?"

"Oh," she exclaimed on a breath of despair. "How it's done. That's what interests me."

She stood looking at it with the flush deepening in her

cheeks. "You see, we painted a little with Miss Jane at the school. I brought one home with me. I was wondering"— she paused, and it came out with a rush—"if I worked hard for years, if I could some day paint. Really, I mean."

He looked at her with understanding, even with a little pity. "Go, bring me your painting," he said.

When she brought it he set it on a table on the far side of the room from the Du Longpré, and stood back a little.

It was a rowan grove on a windy hill. There was motion in it, and much high colour, with a bank of massed maples and oaks in the background. But the rowan trees—in his mind he gave them their English name of mountain ash—*were* the picture. Light and proud and graceful, bearing their ruddy clusters aloft, they gave an impression of wildness and freedom.

Gavin felt a sharp relief. This he could with sincerity praise. His pleasure was in his face as he turned to her.

"Do you mean," she faltered, "that it's even a little good?"

"I mean more than that. So Miss Jane taught you. I fancy you have already learned all she knows."

"So she says. But she thought the colours were too bright. She said a soft mistiness over all would help. But they really were that bright."

"You painted from life?"

She nodded absently, her eyes still on the picture. "Well, from memory. It's the grove at Tulloch Ard where I spent a week-end."

She sighed deeply. "I should know more about drawing. I can see that."

Dougall came in.

"See what your daughter has done," cried Gavin.

Dougall looked, and felt in his heart a little twinge of jealousy that she should have shown it first to Gavin.

"Aye, indeed!" He examined it critically.

Felicity slipped her arm in his. "It's the only one I brought home. The rest were daubs. But this one I liked a little."

"I like it a little too," confessed Dougall, smiling at her.

"I'll show it to grandmother," she cried, and carried it off with her.

Dougall led the way into his study. It was a book-lined small room, with a tall window that looked out over the wide, frozen St. Lawrence. The winter sunlight streamed in and touched the brass-mounted globe in the corner, and a brace of old swords on the wall. Gavin tapped the basket hilt of one.

"From Culloden," remarked Dougall grimly. "About all my people had left to bring out of Scotland with them."

Gavin shook his head. "Sad, those old wars. Sad and senseless."

"But as inevitable as doom."

"Yet senseless."

"No. A man has to stand for his loyalties, or else life has no meaning."

"The trouble is he is often too dead to know if it has or not."

"He may be just as dead the other way, and live to be ninety. But that's not what I have on my mind. Do you think she has any talent?"

"Undoubtedly!"

"Real talent?"

"One can't say yet. She has facility, and feeling, and a sense of the dramatic. But there's something else. She has a mind and a spirit looking for an outlet. It may as well be painting as anything."

Dougall gave him a sharp glance. "You've put your finger on it. She has a keen, relentless mind, and a restless spirit." He looked moodily into the fire. "And born a woman, and into the backwoods at that."

Gavin placed his long fingers on the globe and twirled it. "God forbid that she be less a woman, but she need not stay in the backwoods."

CHAPTER

IV

IN EARLY FEBRUARY another visitor arrived at the stone house by the river. It was Elliot Todd who was with his driver en route to Kingston. He carried a letter for Dougall MacKay, and was moreover glad of a chance to break his journey.

Travelling on the ice of the St. Lawrence was speedy and pleasant, but had its dangers nevertheless. Their sleigh had broken through by the sedgy shore near St. Zotique and, "If it hadn't been for Edouard," said Elliot, "one of our faithful nags would have drowned."

Old Edouard spat deprecatingly into the fire. "Sure, for a long time we know how to save a horse in the river."

"With a rope around his neck?" inquired Dougall with interest.

"*Oui*. Always I carry a rope. If a horse fall in, I pass it quickly round his neck an' pull ver' tight. His breath, it stops. He floats. We pull him out. But take the rope off queek, or he'll be dead anyway."

"I've heard of it," observed Dougall.

"Well, I hadn't, and I'd not have believed it. There the brute was, plunging and kicking in the water. At any minute he might have disappeared under the ice. Then in ten minutes he was up and on his way, as good as ever. Snorting a little, that was all."

The letter for Dougall was from Charlotte Scott, sister of Gavin.

"My dear Mr. MacKay," she wrote in her even, slanting hand. "My brother has just been informed that a friend of ours, Mr. Todd, is travelling to Kingston by way of the St. Lawrence and will be passing very close to your home, and so can deliver this letter more speedily than if I sent it by post.

"The reason for my writing is to invite you and your charming daughter to visit us in the near future. Gavin enjoyed so much the Christmastide he spent with you and thought you might in your turn take pleasure in a little stay in Montreal, breaking as it would the long winter. As it happens, there are a few social events in the offing which should interest your daughter Felicity. A ball at the Chateau St. Antoine is a pleasure definitely promised us, and soon.

"You will know the location of our home from the memory of days gone by. And rest assured, my dear Mr. MacKay, that we are earnestly hoping for the pleasure of a prolonged visit from you both.

"Believe me,

"Yours most sincerely,

"CHARLOTTE SCOTT."

Dougall stood for a while with the letter in his hand, recalling in his mind the writer. She was a few years older than Gavin, fair like him, with the same near-sighted, brown eyes. Strange, she has not married, he mused. And kind of her to invite us. Kind, indeed!

Beneath the flow of his thinking there lay a pool of speculation into which he dipped briefly, but did not bring his findings up into the open spaces of his mind. That the reason for the invitation was Gavin's interest in Felicity and, on Charlotte's part, a desire to see her in a possible future setting, was all decently smoothed over in his consciousness, and the prospect lay before him, a pleasant and profitable and broadening experience for his daughter, and for him a renewal of old friendships and a former way of life.

Preparations for the visit were at once made. Felicity came home from the Misses Fraser's Seminary. The girls had been wide-eyed with vicarious excitement.

"Not much like a visit to Tulloch Ard," Meron said, watching her pack.

"If I have half as good a time!"

She felt uneasy about the trip, yet eager. Who wouldn't be? Her fingers trembled a little as she folded her clothes neatly and swiftly and laid them in the big portmanteau. At home she repacked them again and wondered wistfully if they would be fine enough.

"Your father will have to speak to Miss Charlotte," her grandmother broke in on her thoughts, "about getting a fine new gown for the ball and what you may need to go with it."

Felicity came and sat on the arm of the older woman's chair and leaned against her. "I'm a little scared," she said.

"Why so?" Her grandmother gave her a kindling look. "It isn't as if you came of a race of ghillies."

It was a clear and frosty noonday when they set out, with the sun so bright on the wide snowy surface of the river that it hurt the eyes. The horses snorted with excitement, as if they sensed the beginning of an adventurous journey. The carriole, lined with robes of bear and buffalo skin, slid smoothly over the hard, wind-swept snow, a little moving box of warmth and comfort.

Their first stop was at MacPherson's Hostel at Pointe Mouille. It was crowded and Felicity had to sleep with the innkeeper's daughter. But the bed was clean, and as soon as she sank into its depths her lids closed over her eyes and she was asleep.

Then, after an early breakfast of porridge and fried pork and flapjacks drowned in gravy, to which they both did fair justice, they set out again, and that night they dined well and slept soft with cousins at Beauharnois. So, on the morning of the third day they angled across Lake St. Louis and climbed the steep bank and were at once in the heart of the city.

They went first to the Mansion House and took a room and had a meal sent up, and tidied themselves before going to their host's. Felicity laid off her flannel petticoat and the warm clothes she had worn for the drive and donned the blue poplin and stole and bonnet of gray squirrel. Dougall had his broadcloth cloak well brushed, the one with the brave tartan lining, and they were ready.

The carriole and horses were brought, and they drove along Notre Dame Street between rows of well-built houses and shops.

"It's a fine, friendly city," observed Dougall, "and easy to live in. And just now growing so fast that it's bursting its bounds and spreading out over mountain and meadow. See the new lamp posts."

Felicity looked and marvelled. Tall wooden standards and, at the top, sheltered by glass cages, kerosene-fed lamps. Wonderful!

Past the Recollet Gate they made their way and into the St. Antoine suburb. And there on the first lift of the mountain, in a pleasant rural setting of trees and shrubs, rose the square-built stone house of Gavin Scott and his sister, Charlotte.

A stable boy came for the horses, and Dougall and Felicity were ushered into a wide, panelled hall where Charlotte and Gavin greeted them warmly.

In a pleasant rose-hung upper chamber Charlotte and Felicity lingered for a while. Felicity unpacked the big portmanteau and hung her clothes on scented hangers, and told Charlotte what her grandmother had said about the fine gown for parties.

"Good!" cried Charlotte heartily. "There's nothing I'd like better. We'll go to the drapers in the morning."

So they did. In the big carriole, half buried in robes, and with the coachman on the high front seat. There Felicity watched the bolts of silks and satins unrolled till they came to one all shimmering and iridescent with shaded soft colours, and she and Charlotte looked at each other in complete agreement.

The next day a plump little French dressmaker came and went gaily to work. She and Charlotte thumbed over patterns and surveyed Felicity with measuring and impersonal eyes, turned her this way and that, and snipped and pinned and fitted; and the party gown was well on the way.

Then in the afternoon Gavin's big carriole was brought to the door and they drove about to see the sights of Montreal—the new jail, the court house with the great iron fence before it, the Chateau de Ramezay where the Governor lived, and Beaver Hall, with ranks of tall Lombardy poplars on guard about it.

The city was full of life and colour. Gaily painted red or bright blue *berlots* flashed by and carrioles were everywhere. Countrymen in blanket coats bound with *ceintures flechés* padded about in their high moccasins, short black pipes in their mouths. Clerks dashed importantly from one office building to another. It was cold and the smoke from chimneys went straight up. In the carriole, they sat two by two, facing each other, their faces ruddy from frost.

"Have him drive around by the MacTavish house," suggested Dougall. "I've not seen it."

Just beneath the abrupt slope of the mountain, on a site that commanded a wide, sweeping view, stood the unfinished stone house of Simon MacTavish, former head of the North West Company. The place was of great size and magnificence, with wide circular wings abutting each end.

"The dining-room was round, arched overhead and practically all windows," observed Charlotte meditatively.

Felicity's eyes were on the vast unfinished building. "Did he die too soon?" she asked in an awed voice.

"He did. Just that. He's buried behind the house. That slim shaft on the height above is his monument."

It seemed strange and sad that stone and mortar should so endure and man be so frail. Life was not long, though it seemed so. So, one must live while one may. She sighed, and Gavin's hand closed on hers beneath the fur robe. She let it lie for a moment, then gently extricated her fingers.

In a week came the ball at the Chateau St. Antoine. By that time Felicity had already made some friends. She had driven over with her father when he went to pay his respects to La Baronne de Longueuil and her handsome Highland husband, Captain Grant, in their pleasant home on St. Helen's Island. They had seen the McGills of Burnside and the McKenzies of Terrebonne, and on Sunday they went to St. Gabriel's Church to hear the Reverend John Somerville. A Scottish regiment was quartered at that time in Montreal, and the officers and men occupied a block of pews and made a brave splash of colour as they marched out, their kilts aswing.

So, when the night of the ball came, Felicity no longer felt strange or unsupported. Not with Charlotte taking her capably in hand, and Gavin her escort, and her father keeping a watchful, affectionate eye on her. And she was upheld by the new gown.

She had been a little doubtful when she tried it on. "You can see through it," she exclaimed.

"*Misère*, and why not?" demanded the modiste. "Beneath will be the flesh-coloured slip."

Felicity looked at her.

"But you must know that the clothes of a fashionable lady should be fragile enough that they may all be put in her pocket. It is the mode. Regard the portraits of the beauties

63

of France, Madame Recamier, and *toutes les autres*. There, you are now beautiful. Is it not so?"

Charlotte nodded. "You are indeed, my dear," she said sincerely.

Felicity stood looking at herself in the long mirror, at the tiny high-waisted bodice, the little puffs for sleeves, and the long beautiful length of fabric that was the skirt.

"Alas for Kirsty and the flannel petticoat," she thought, feeling her slim hips.

The ballroom at the Chateau St. Antoine was an enchanting sight. Mrs. MacGillivray, a pretty, dark-haired woman, the daughter of MacDonald of Garth whom Dougall knew of old, received them cordially at the foot of the great staircase with her husband. Felicity could see the officers of the Scots Regiment who had been at St. Gabriel's on Sunday, and the "*petite Baronne*" as well. The long room was rich with colour and movement, and the great candelabra spilled down a soft yellow radiance over all. At one end was a raised dais where the musicians were.

"This is where we have our private theatricals," explained Gavin. "You've not seen me in grease paint and wig. Perhaps next fall you'll come down for the play we put on in October."

"We?"

"Our company of amateur actors."

His hand was under her elbow, and they took their place in the pretty, formal pageantry of the Lancers.

"She dances like a sunbeam," Dougall had said once of her.

Gavin found it so, and the young Scots officers, and Elliot Todd who had brought them Charlotte's letter and

64

who was, it seemed, Charlotte's special squire. Felicity felt herself carried along on a wave of delight—the music, the dancing, the radiance, the pervasive sweet perfume of hot-house flowers, the laughter, the compliments, the good will. Never would she forget this ball at the Chateau St. Antoine.

It was morning when they got back to the stone house on the first lift of the mountain. For but a little while Felicity lay in her rose-hung bed, a smile on her lips and her eyes bright behind the closed lids, till her thoughts drifted into dreams.

Not so quickly did sleep come to Charlotte. In her own fine warm room, hung in cream and old-gold, she stood by the window and looked out. She saw the sleeping city and beyond, the wide frozen river, and above, the dark blue sky where the stars were now fading out and a pearly light coming in the east. Her forehead was cold against the glass, and her heart too felt cold and tired.

For many years she had known Dougall MacKay, this friend of her brother's. He had been for her, when a girl, a dashing figure of romance. As a young widower her heart had gone out to him in pity. Then, his very unawareness of her and his complete constancy to his dead wife, added to his appeal. But that was many years ago. And she was now nearing forty.

She thought of Elliot Todd for whom she felt a luke-warm regard, and she knew that all she would ever feel for him, married or not, would be that lukewarm regard. Which did not seem enough.

"So, like many another old maid, I am full of good works," her bitter humour continued. "The Ladies' Benevolent Society. The Orphans' Aid. This household that I keep running smoothly. And all of it I'd give for that lucky disposition of features, that smile of Felicity's that goes straight to a man's heart."

"Nevertheless," she concluded, as she drew aside the old-gold hangings of the bed and saw that the warming pan was within, "at least I have comfort."

A warm drink, carefully covered, stood on the hob of the little fireplace. She sat for a while sipping it thoughtfully; then she went to bed.

Another incident occurred during the visit that was as memorable for Felicity as the ball at Chateau St. Antoine, but in a different way.

Said Gavin, "Come with me to the shops today and we'll get oils and canvas and the tools you need for your painting. Then we'll visit an old artist I know, near the Seminary."

The artist, who was old indeed and his fingers getting a little stiff, lived in a high narrow house on Notre Dame Street, and the walls of his rooms were covered with pictures. He peered over his glasses at Felicity.

"So you want to paint, eh? Pouff! You'll be married."

"Need that prevent her?" put in Gavin softly, and M'sieu Barbin cackled and rubbed his hands.

"Look around, Mam'selle. Just look around."

While she looked, Gavin and M'sieu talked, and before they left, M'sieu made a proposition.

"Spend one day with me, Mam'selle. One whole day. My housekeeper, she will feed us at noon. Not ver' well, but good enough for *les artistes* whose mind and soul rest on higher things. *Oui*, one whole day. You watch me work. Maybe, work a little yourself."

So Felicity spent a day in the studio of M'sieu Barbin. And that she never forgot.

The light streamed in from the high uncurtained north windows. Canvasses stood about the walls, and on an easel stood a large, partly done landscape. M. Barbin puttered about.

"See, here is the sketch. And here the unfinished work. Now, sit there and watch. But not talk. Pliss!"

Felicity sat and watched. In a minute M. Barbin had forgotten her existence. He scraped paint on his palette, he chose his brushes, he used them. He stood back, he exclaimed in anger, or disgust, or approval; he ran at the picture again. Then he stood off again and snorted.

"Bah!" he said finally. "It goes not well. Today is not my day for landscape. Look. You paint." He shuffled among canvasses and brushes.

"But what shall I paint?"

"Something you 'ave done before. Just a sketch. I'll not watch you. Me, I make a sketch too."

So Felicity painted. She painted the rowan grove on the hill. What else was there clear enough in her mind? And when she saw how little attention he paid to her, she settled diligently and happily to work.

At noon the housekeeper brought up steaming bowls of soup and a plate of rolls and, pushing some brushes out of the way, spread a cloth on a corner of a table. Felicity, ravenous, enjoyed every mouthful.

"*Bon!*" cried M'sieu. "You eat like a good working man. Now *à travail encore.*"

When the afternoon light was beginning to dim a little he threw down his brushes. "*Alors*, now we see each other's work. Aha!" He stood off and squinted. "Zut!" he cried, and a quiver crossed Felicity's face. "Zut! I say, that you're a woman."

He was silent for a little while.

"You have a vigour. Strange in a young girl! To give you lessons would be for me a great pleasure, Mam'selle." He made a low bow.

"But," shaking her head sorrowfully, "I don't live here."

"I know." And he sighed. "Even if you did. A few lessons, maybe, and then you marry, and *les bébés*, one, two, three, and no more painting."

She flushed and laughed.

"But if perhaps," he went on slyly, "you should marry one man in a thousand, who would care for '*l'arte*,' and not mind that you work very hard, say, between *les bébés*, then perhaps it would be possible.

"Nevertheless," he shook his head gloomily. "Not many women achieve it. Mostly it has to be like Rosa Bonheur— work like a slave, dress like a man, live like a hermit, and *voilà*, a great artist. Now, look at me, what I have done."

Felicity looked and her eyes widened.

It was herself as she had stood before the easel. But not herself of the ball at the Chateau St. Antoine. Her face was thinned down, intent. Her eyes were bright and hard with effort. Her nostrils were aquiver. It was an absorbed and

68

fine-drawn face, alight with achievement, and any beauty in it was incidental.

"Only a sketch, you perceive. I'll finish it later. I'll call it *L'Artiste*. M'sieu Scott, he can get it for you when I am through. And yours I'll keep, Mam'selle Felicity, in the hope that sometime again we paint furiously all day together."

* * *

In June Gavin brought the picture and took up lodgings only a half mile east of the MacKay home. School was now closed for the summer and Felicity was home again.

In the same wide-eyed wonder she had before felt, she looked at this Joan of Arc portrayed on the canvas. There was no hint of the shy smile that was peculiarly her own. Nothing but fervour and the will to achieve.

"Losh save us," cried Kirsty when she saw it.

"I can't see that it's much of a likeness," her father said uneasily. While her grandmother looked long and carefully at it and said nothing at all.

The summer months that followed, Felicity was always to remember as a lovely and light-hearted time. It was the sort of season that should be part of the life of any girl, when she is borne up by the consciousness of beauty and desirability and is not yet much involved emotionally.

Almost every day she saw Gavin. He helped her fit up a small room with a northern exposure as a place to paint. He saw that she had always an abundance of supplies. In every way he aided and abetted her in her ambition.

"How do you know so much about it?" she asked him curiously once.

He laughed briefly. "I should know a little. I haunted

69

M. Barbin's studio all spring. He knew why, too. He'd say, 'Tell her this,' or 'Warn her of that.' We became very good friends."

In the cool of the evening, when it was fine, they went out on the river in the cedar row-boat. This was a restful and lovely time of the day, when they moved lazily along to the liquid light sound of water slipping over the blades of the oars, and the river all about was pale like mother-of-pearl, or rose-stained by the sunset.

In August the white water lilies bloomed, and one evening they pushed their boat into a little cove where there was a matted bed of them.

Gavin parted the flat green pads and pulled up the lilies by their long muddy stems and broke them off short and filled Felicity's lap with them. She bent her face over them. The perfume was halfway between that of a jonquil and a peony rose, but different too, because this was a perfume of the water, not of the land. She touched the cool pointed petals, curving like scimitars of snow around the bright gold heart.

"They're beautiful," she said softly.

But Gavin was not looking at the lilies. "M. Barbin should see you now."

She sheered away from the implied compliment. "I've just thought of the word to describe his painting of me. I look hungry. Hungry for something that I intend to have."

"You need never be hungry for anything, my Felicity," he told her gravely. "Not if I can help it."

He shipped the oars. "You know what I mean. I'm coming to it clumsily, but you know. Ever since I saw you

70

last Christmas! I've spoken to your father. But you, what have you to say?"

She looked straightly at him for a moment. "I don't know," she said simply, and was silent.

"I'm not trying to bribe you," he went on hurriedly, "but with me you could paint. The best masters. Abroad. Yet that's a small thing. Everything I have and am is yours."

"Oh, hush, Gavin. I mean it when I say I don't know. But I'm very fond of you."

"Fond! It hardly seems enough. Yet it might be. Look, Felicity. You've seen me every day for more than a month. Now I'll go away and I'll not come again till Christmas. But I'll write. I'll not let you forget me."

*   *   *

Gavin kept his word. Letters and gifts came by every available messenger, bonbons in silvery heart-shaped boxes, hothouse roses cut in bud and carefully packed so that they were withered hardly at all, and a little water-colour of the house on the St. Antoine Road.

Felicity was aware that her father was deeply pleased. He had for a long time been fond of Gavin. Her grandmother smiled kindly at her but said nothing. Till in an evening hour of confidence, in the corner of the verandah where the yellow roses spilled over the railing, Felicity told her that Gavin was coming at Christmas for his answer.

"That was wise. To wait, I mean, till you were sure."

"You like him, Grandmother?"

"I do indeed. And you?"

Felicity laughed.

"Nevertheless," went on the other, "you are very cool

71

and calm about it. Perhaps girls are different nowadays."

"When you and grandfather were betrothed, were you not cool?"

"I was light in the head from happiness," drily.

"Perhaps I shall be by Christmas."

*   *   *

Summer passed. Felicity went back to school. Then it was October again and November. She was restless that fall. Christmas was coming far too swiftly. The summer had been for dalliance and delight, but now winter was on its way.

She missed Meron, who had not returned after the summer holiday. Something of savour seemed to have gone out of the place with her absence. However, she had promised to spend a week-end with Felicity early in December. She and one of her brothers would come to the school for Felicity and together they would drive on to the MacKay home. Would it be Hughie or David? What if it should be Peter?

At the thought Felicity was for a moment still. Peter! Over a year since she had seen him. At first she had thought of him a great deal; then gradually the picture in her mind had grown faint. It came back now. A long, limber lad, blue-eyed, black-haired, lordly, appealing. She sighed tumultuously. "Why did you go away, Peter?"

Not that it meant anything to her, she reminded herself, whether he came or went. Nevertheless, he had been interesting to meet. Now, Gavin was kind and good and reliable, and had the regard and approval of everyone concerned. While Peter was like a man from a strange far country, unpredictable and disturbing. Might it be that he still had her rowan berries?

After all these months, hardly.

CHAPTER

V

PETER was at that momen nearer than Felicity knew.

On a little headland jutting out into the Ottawa River near Ile aux Chats, two men bivouacked beside an upturned canoe. A roaring fire of spruce boughs threw their figures into bold relief and lit up the woods that lined the shore. With quick, deft blows Peter lopped off still more spruce boughs and laid them overlapping, curling ends up, to make a bed.

The fire burned lower, forming coals. At that, Peter's companion looked up, grinned, and fixed on a small spit two skinned and dressed wild ducks. Then set near the fire to warm, an iron kettle of pea soup.

Jacques divided the soup meticulously, and the two sat on their haunches and drank it, then leaned back against the spruce boughs till the ducks should be done.

"Me, I get a leetle tired of peas," remarked Jacques. "Wait till I get back to Trois Rivières!"

"How many years since you left?"

"Six."

"How long will you stay?"

"I don' know. Maybe a few months. Maybe never go back west."

Peter turned to look at him.

"You put ideas in my head, M'sieu Peter. All along I think, me, I never leave the Nor'-Westers. Like one big familee they are. Never do they forget their own. Because they are *Ecossais*. Fraser, MacDonell, Grant, Campbell, MacTavish, like our *seigneurs* of old. But different too. They share our dangers. Eat what we eat. Sometimes take Indian wife too. But now, when I get near my own country I go a little homesick."

"How came you to join the fur company?"

Jacques got up, examined the spit and sat down where he could turn it. "Well, you see, where I live as a boy it is very quiet, *ordainment*. Then one time some *voyageurs*, clerks of the company, come to the parish. And were they *magnifique!* Beaded buckskin, brass-handled *pistolle*, fine silk kerchief. And the tales they tell! *Ma foi*, our eyes stick out, me an' my friends from the little log farms back of Trois Rivières. Then at the dance the girls no longer look at us. No, the *voyageurs* from the west swing them round and kiss in the corner."

He paused to hold a spoon under the ducklings and catch some of the juice. He smacked his lips.

"So," he continued, "we think, why can not we be

voyageurs too? Our parents say, '*Non, non.*' The *curé* say, 'Stay in your own parish, marry nize girl, raise beeg familee.' And I look at Julie Rose who live the next farm over. An' she very nize. But those tales of the far countrie stick in my mind. So, I go quick to the clerk and I sign.

"Then bye and bye when I am sober again, I go back to him and I say, 'Tear up the paper. I change my mind.' But he stand and look at me and laugh. And laugh some more. 'Boy,' he say, 'you have the build for *voyageur*. Some men, their legs go bowed from too long in the canoe. Your legs, they bowed already.' Then I feel bad. A man's legs, they are, after all, his own business, *n'est-ce-pas?*"

Peter laughed. "They are, by thunder."

"Well, I say again, 'Give me back my paper.' Then he lay his hand on his *pistolle*, an' he say, 'Back out now, and it's jail for you, my fine fellow.'

"So then I say, 'All right, I go.' An' he clap me on the back an' say, 'Jacques, we make a man of you.' An' by gar, he was right. I have seen the world. I have been hungry. I have been cold. I have been in great danger. I have used every bit of strength in my body, and every bit of brain in my head. I belong to the Athabasca Brigade. Come, M'sieu Peter, your duck is now ready."

Peter pulled the meat from the breast with his strong white teeth. "Then you have decided to stay with the Company?"

"*Oui.* I have this minute made up my mind. But maybe not for always. Sometime I go back, in two, three years maybe, and marry Julie Rose. *Non*, she'll be by then *marriée*. Well, I find me noder Julie Rose and settle down. But when I plough the field, when I feed the small pig or milk the red

77

cow, I am not just Jacques Latourneau, *Fermier*. I am Jacques Latourneau, *Voyageur*, who has been to the ends of the world and back. My soul, she has been expand, see?"

Peter looked into the lean swarthy face before him and saw friendship there and reliability. "I'll miss you, Jacques," he said.

"Me too. The men of the Athabasca Brigade, we do not forget. Not those of us who went down the Tacouche Tesse together."

Peter's eyes had in them a reminiscent gleam. "In my dreams I sometimes see those mountains."

"*Misère*, I don't wonder. But it was the river that gave me the big scare. Alive, it seemed. Saying, 'Hish, hish,' and flinging off your hand. So sweeft. So wicked. And the high black cliffs meeting over our heads. Was it those terrible high mountains that made you leave the Company, M'sieu Peter?"

Peter shook his head. "No, it was not. To explore with Simon Fraser, that was fine. But to trade in furs all the rest of my life, that for me is not so good as a farm among my own people. I saw that in Fort Chipewyan after I had been for a while home in Glengarry."

Jacques sighed gustily. "Every man to his own place. And, as I said, Julie Rose was ver' nize."

That night Peter on his bed of balsamy boughs looked up at the high stars and thought that he had not told Jacques or anyone the real reason for his return.

When he had left his home for the west, he had gone by swift canoe right through to the far northern post of Fort Chipewyan with letters from Montreal. There he had spent a long, white, lonely winter. Then spring came, late, as always in the north, and the trading-post came to life. The brown skin tents of the Indians dotted the lakeshore. Bales of fur were made ready for the long canoe trip to Rainy Lake, not to the Grande Portage where the other brigades went, but to Lac La Pluie, which was quite far enough when you came from Chipewyan on Lake Athabasca.

When Simon Fraser arrived at the post, Peter, who had served under him on that memorable first trip down the river which now bore his name, was glad to see him. That night they sat up late, and it was, "Do you recall this?" or "Do you remember the day we climbed the precipice by sticking in our dirks?" Or "When the Indians threw the big stones down at us?"

In the morning Peter, walking by the shore, saw an old Indian whom he had previously known, and crossed over to sit a while by the flap of his tent.

"Ho, Oroneeka!"

"Ho, my brother!"

Nearby sat the mother and the daughter of the family. They were making moccasins, and the girl was embroidering on the toe a wild-rose design of coloured fibres. The deer-skin was very fine and soft and almost white.

"Where do you get the pattern?" Peter asked curiously of the mother.

The girl's bowed head came up and her black braids were tossed back. "I show," she said.

She took a piece of birch bark, folded it twice, then bit into it with her sharp teeth three times. Unfolded, there was the pattern of a full-blown flower.

Peter laughed. "Pretty fine," he said.

She laughed too, and a rose stain came up over her brown cheeks. She lifted the moccasin. "Maybe I give to you," she added a little breathlessly.

"Fine," said Peter again, and turned away. There had flashed into his mind a sudden vision of Felicity, her bright hair and her shimmering sweet smile and her candid eyes. That was when he decided to come home.

And not too soon. The same day Oroneeka sought him out.

"Brother, I would speak."

"Good."

They sat on a pile of squared logs that would yet be a fur-press. Sat in silence for a while, as Oroneeka smoked and Peter looked out over the island-dotted lake, and slapped at the mosquitoes that settled on his wrists.

Oroneeka spoke. "My girl good girl. Fourteen years. Much better for her here than up-country with Indians. You take my girl?"

Peter felt his forehead hot. He answered gravely, "Your girl very good girl. But I go to my people. No more do I trade for the Company. I go far and I do not come back."

Oroneeka bowed gravely. "My heart grieves, brother."

From his pocket Peter took a clasped knife and held it out on his palm. "Will my brother take this? And may hunger be far from the flap of his tent."

The Indian examined it gravely and thrust it into his pouch. "My thanks, white man," he said, and they both rose and slowly and in silence walked towards the fort.

There Peter sought out Simon Fraser.

Fraser looked keenly at him. "You've thought well of it? You're a trained man now."

Peter was for a moment silent. Then, "I'm sure," he said.

Fraser sat, knees wide, elbow on one, and chin in his hand. His dark eyes peered kindly up at Peter.

"A girl, lad?"

"Only a hope."

Fraser laughed and rose. He was a big man and broad, with dark fire in his eyes. Peter, looking at him, remembered days of peril, following that tawny wicked river through cracks in the mountains and over roaring rapids, when he, Simon Fraser, had held them with the power of his will, playing out his anger like a goad, filling them all with his own burly courage. His hand now came down hard on Peter's shoulder.

"Well, good luck to you. You're a good man on a portage, as well I know, or on a long pull with the paddle. We'll miss you. And look you, my mother lives at St. Andrew's back of Cornwall. Will you see her and give her news of her wandering son?"

"I will that," Peter assured him warmly.

*　　*　　*

So here he was, almost on the last lap of his journey. This time he had not come by swift canoe but with the Brigade, and heavily laden with bales of beaver and bison and muskrat pelts. By Portage La Loche they had come, and the Churchill and Lake Manitoba, and so on to Rainy Lake. There Peter left the Brigade and with Jacques alone went on to the Grande Portage.

It was midsummer now, and he spent nearly a month

81

waiting for his brother Evan who was expected in from the Assiniboine. Finally he came, and a week they had together. Every detail of his dark silent brother's appearance, and everything he told him, Peter stored away in his memory to tell his mother.

"Will you not come out for a visit even?" he asked.

Evan shook his head. "You had better not say anything about it, but I have taken a wife. A chief's daughter."

Peter looked at him gravely. "It can happen."

"She's a good girl," Evan went on, "and faithful. But I'll not be going back."

So it was a long good-bye Peter said to his brother, and his heart was for a while heavy after it.

Again he set out by the familiar fur-trader's route that took them eventually down the Ottawa.

"We'll be lucky," Jacques grumbled, "if we don't make the last of our journey on snowshoes."

"The Ottawa never freezes over till St. Andrew's Day, they say. And this is but the first of the month."

Nevertheless a hard frost did come, and the leaves drifted down and the colour paled and the light darkened on the hills. The purple haze that had veiled the horizon lifted, and the air was sharp and clear. Little ridges of ice formed by night at the edge of the shore. The sunshine, when it came, was thin and cold.

But still the Ottawa flowed on, dark and swift between the cold hills, and even when a light snow drifted down and fell hissing into the water, still ice did not much form. Their paddles plunged tirelessly and presently there was the spire of the church at Ste. Anne's. Soon they were in Montreal.

They made their way first to the Company headquarters, then their business finished, Peter took leave of Jacques. They stood, hands firmly clasped, for a moment.

"Some day we meet again," said Jacques.

Peter watched the short, sturdy figure with the astonishingly bowed legs till it was lost in the crowd. Then he found an outfitter's shop on St. James Street and bought clothes for himself. So that when he turned homeward all that he had with him that had come out of the west was a great buffalo hide to be made into a sleigh robe, and a couple of fine beaver pelts.

The stagecoach took him in two days' travel as far as Lancaster, where he left his baggage to be reclaimed, and set out along the road to Williamstown, then up the South Branch to Tulloch Ard. It was night when he neared his destination.

The walking was good. The ground was hard-frozen beneath a film of snow. The moon rode high above flying clouds. A wind whistled through the bare branches and sent the fine snow sifting across the road in little scuds of white. It was, on this November night, a hard, iron-bound country to which he had come back. But his heart lifted to it. It was his own, as no land of prairie or mountains could ever be. Stuff of this firm earth, and of these frozen streams, was his body formed. Their elements sang in his blood and were the strength of his bones, shin bone and thigh, lean flank and wide shoulder. Physically he was at home.

When he came to the base of the hill below Tulloch Ard he dug his feet into the snowy incline and breasted the slope, and there was the house, its windows bright with candlelight. He stood for a moment beneath the last big pine of the driveway and looked.

They were all there. His mother was there, her lips moving to count the stitches as she turned the heel of a sock. Meron's black head was bent over her mending, and Hughie leaned forward to stir the fire. David sat with his father's violin in the crook of his arm, plucked a note and listened, and tried a little run of melody, then laughed and handed it to Rorie himself, who tucked it competently under his chin.

Then Peter strode over to the door and pushed it open. And they all flung aside what was in their hands and sprang up and welcomed him. They crowded and clung about him, and took his jacket and his fur cap and his gauntlets, and drew him to the fire and gave him the best chair. Rorie threw another log on the fire and Meron hurried for food.

Peter sat there in the glow of the great, golden, hard-maple blaze, and they plied him with questions. Here, too, he had that strong sense of being where he belonged. There was a likeness and a tie that bound together those of his family. A certain blueness of eye, a high squareness of forehead, a length of limb, and a challenge in the lordly look they turned on the world. They were the house of Rorie, of the clan of Alpin.

*　　　*　　　*

On Sunday morning Peter went with his father and mother to the church in Williamstown. In the same boxed-in pew that he well remembered, he sat and looked up at the alert, worn figure of John Bethune, minister, and at the patriarchal white locks of Archie Alec MacGregor behind the precentor's desk, and he felt as if he were again the small boy he had been, sitting awed and silent by his mother in this same high-roofed solemn place.

Then his eyes sought and found the pew where sat the girls of the Misses Fraser's school. At the near end was the uncompromising straight back of Miss Jemima herself; then came a row of bonnets, a blue one, a black, a brown, one with cherry-coloured ribbons. Which? The blue one turned, and there was the remembered curve of a cheek, and his heart began to thud steadily and he knew.

Not much of the sermon, either the Gaelic or the English part, did he hear. When they rose for the psalm, and Archie Alec struck the bright tuning fork for the pitch and lifted up his mellow old voice and they sang, Peter found that, standing, he could see very well into the pew of the Misses Fraser. He could see the slim, blue-clad shoulders of Felicity and the light brown curls at the back of her neck.

Finally the service was over and the people made their way in decorous slowness to the door where Mr. Bethune stood in his gown and bands, and gave each as he passed a firm grip and a kindly word.

Just outside, Peter waited till Felicity came. He stepped forward then and touched her elbow.

"I've something to show you," he said.

She turned swiftly, and a bright flush touched her cheeks.

"You're home again," she breathed.

"Home again." And they stood there in the cold sunshine, looking at each other, while people passed to one side or another.

From his pocket he took a small chamois bag and shook

out on his palm a few withered dark red berries, and smiled at her as he did it.

"My rowan berries! Did they bring you luck?"

"At least they brought me back. May I come to see you?"

"When?"

"Any time. Now I must go."

On the way home his mother said, "So you know Felicity."

"Yes," he answered briefly, and waited.

"She's a friend of Meron's," she went on in a thoughtful voice, "and has visited us. We all liked her."

Peter said nothing, but he turned a little and a quiet glance, yet significant, passed between them.

When they got home, Meron had just piled the big blue platter high with chicken pot-pie. Peter remembered the endless meals of whitefish at Chipewyan and the strips of dried salmon they ate along the Fraser, and thought how fine it was to be here in this high homestead of Tulloch Ard. And finer still the prospect of seeing Felicity soon. His heart beat high with exultation.

But the next day came the trouble at Glen Falloch. If trouble one might call it. Along about midnight old Rover set up a shrill barking, and the sharp beat of a horse's hooves sounded on the frosty ground. Then came a sudden brisk pounding at the door.

Peter pulled on his trousers and stumbled down the stair, his father following. A cousin stood there, Jimmie Black Alec MacFarlane from the King's Road. One eye was black and nearly closed. There was a reckless light in the other, and in his voice a high carrying note of excitement.

"There's been fighting in the tavern at Glen Falloch. My brother Ranald's hurted bad. We need help," he said, and waited.

The same excitement flared in Rorie's eyes and voice. "Give us time to get dressed, lad. Then we'll hitch up the sleigh."

"Good. I'm away now for Alastair John Grant and his sons." He swung his leg over the high back of the roan mare; there was a clatter of hooves and he was away.

Rorie was up the steps, three at a time. Peter followed. At the head of the stair stood his mother, a candle in her hand. In the far bedroom he could hear David up and dressing. Hugh was away at his uncle's in the next concession. Peter met his mother's eyes. In the upflung light of the candle her face was bleak and withdrawn. He felt, all of sudden, abashed.

"Have I not got one man grown out of this foolishness?" she asked bitterly. Then her face changed. She came near to Peter, laid her hand on his arm and motioned with her head towards the bedroom where Rorie was.

"Take care of him, Peter. He's too old for such a frolic. And look out for David too."

"Must he go?"

She made a hopeless gesture, then laughed. "If I were a man I suppose I'd go too. Being a woman, I have more sense."

Their eyes met. Hers were full of anxiety and rueful laughter, and into his mind came the feeling that he and his mother were of an age, contemporaries; and his father younger than either of them.

Yet when they were speeding over the frosty road to Glen Falloch, with the forest black on either hand and the stars speckling the dark blue sky above them, Peter's own blood began to tingle. He glanced sidewise at Rorie who sat, feet braced, a line taut in either hand.

"What's wrong with the MacIntoshes?"

"Nothing's wrong with them." His father's voice was cheerful. "Good people."

Peter gave a short bark of laughter. "Then why this present jaunt?"

"Why? When my own mother's sister's grandson is in trouble, and comes for help, would you have me stay in my bed? The MacFarlanes and the MacIntoshes have been at outs before. And the Grants will be in it. There's a prayer they used to say in the old land, 'From the wild Grants and the MacAlpins, good Lord, deliver us.' It sticks in my mind they may say that prayer tonight in Glen Falloch." His voice was rich with laughter. He shook out the reins over the backs of the horses and they leaped forward.

"They'll have been drinking," conjectured Peter.

"Och aye," agreed his father in the same hardy, cheerful voice. "They'll all be full."

He was right. But one man was sober enough. Ranald Black Alec had a broken wrist and a shoulder out of joint. He lay in a back room, moaning softly.

Rorie had a look at him and felt the shoulder with strong probing fingers; then with a "Brace yourself, lad," and a sudden wrenching pull he had it back in place. Ranald's white face ran with sweat, but he was at once easier. A stick of fire wood was hastily splintered, and with torn strips of his shirt and the improvised splints his wrist was bound.

Then they turned to more urgent matters. Just in time. Their opponents had returned with reinforcements, and the battle was resumed. There in the forefront was red-headed Murdie MacIntosh, whose quarrel with young MacFarlane had been the cause of the trouble.

"Where is he now?" he called out in a high, whinnying voice. "Where now is Jimmie Black Alec who was going to break my neck to me?"

"He'll be here in good time, lad," Rorie called out cheerfully. "Will we do for now?"

Peter stood between his father and young David. The youngster's face was white with excitement and his blue eyes blazed. The MacIntoshes came on. Peter swung and feinted and parried with right good will and, when he could, edged himself in front of his brother and kept one eye on his father who needed no help from him at all.

"Bloody their noses to them, Davie," counselled Rorie, "then one good clip to the jaw!"

They were outnumbered, and it was hard going. David's breath began to come in long sobs. Then there was a roar from without, "*Creag Ellachaidh!*" and it was Alastair John Grant and his six big sons, and with them Jimmie Black Alec.

"Ach, there you are," cried the MacIntosh, and Jimmie Black Alec put down his head and bored through the crowd.

"Keep them apart, or there'll be somebody hurted," muttered Rorie.

So Peter bore down on the redoubtable Murdie who, it turned out, was a good man with his fists. It was not long before Peter's right eye was no good to him, and there was a warm trickle down the side of his face. Then MacIntosh pushed in to get under his guard and Peter dipped suddenly and sent him over his shoulder in a flying-mare.

"Boys-oh!" came admiringly from David.

The struggle went cheerfully on, and gradually the intruding clan was pushed nearer the door. But in the back of Peter's mind was an uneasy prickle of anxiety about the man who was piled up in the corner behind him, and now quiet.

When he could, he broke away and bent over him.

Then suddenly the prone figure catapulted into action, hurled itself on him, hard head into his stomach, and they both went down and rolled over together. Then Peter was on top and held the struggling shoulders flat, and red-headed Murdie grinned up at him.

Peter grinned back. "So you were only resting."

"Och, sure. Resting and waiting."

"Get you up then. Your friends are now outside."

But when Murdie tried to stand, he could not. His ankle.

"Give him a dram," cried Rorie, then went over to the window, now devoid of glass. "You've left something behind," he called.

"What, you old deil?"

"A man, just. Two of you come, and two of us will bring him."

So the door was opened, and Peter and Alastair John's oldest son, Alec, took each an arm and helped the disabled warrior. His friends were there to receive him.

"Losh, it's Murdie himself," cried someone. "We clean forgot you."

Then Peter shook Murdie by the hand, and so did Alec, and Rorie called out, "Well, good night, boys, and no hard feelings," and someone answered in a friendly way, and some could not find it in their hearts to do so.

As they drove home in the pale winter dawn, Peter's blood began to cool. He thought suddenly of Felicity. How was he now to go to see her, with a black eye and one side of his face a bloody pulp? He felt the eye with wary fingers.

"A slab of beefsteak will fix it," his father advised.

Peter smiled at him. "As for you, sir, I believe they never once got in past your guard."

"I got a skite on the lug once, that's all."

"When you heaved him over then," cried David pridefully, "will you teach me that, Peter?"

"The flying-mare? Sure. Some day on the barn floor."

But he was thinking to himself, "Beefsteak and cold presses and all, it will be a week before I'm presentable. And what if she learns of this night and is not pleased with it?"

★

✳

CHAPTER

VI

FELICITY walked home from church on the Sunday she met Peter with a small tumult in her heart. Only by a conscious effort did she keep her face and voice serene and casual. For something within kept whispering, "Peter! Peter!" in amazement and delight.

"How did you come to know him so well?" asked Nancy MacKillop when they were getting ready for bed.

"I don't know him well," countered Felicity, yet how false and foolish seemed the words even as she spoke them. She felt she had known him forever.

"Well," said Nancy, taking firm hold of her forelock and winding it up into a twist with a strip of white cotton, "he's a grand-looking fellow, but think of living in Montreal!"

"Montreal?"

"Och, I know about your beau from the city. A fine, big house you'd have, and servants. Ho hum!" She sighed

95

gustily and rolled into bed. "Just give me the chance."

Felicity blew out the candle, pushed back the heavy curtains from the windows, and slipped between the covers, but left a little ridge of feather tick between herself and the warm largeness of Nancy. She lay straight and still, her eyes shut, and breathing evenly. Nancy was in a mood for talking, but with no encouragement in a little while she heaved herself over on her side and was soon asleep.

Then Felicity opened her eyes and watched the moonlight slanting in across the foot of the bed. Through the window she could see a square of dark blue sky, a few pin-points of stars, and the black-pointed tip of a fir tree.

She liked the quiet of the night-time. Then she could be entirely alone. At home it had been easy to be alone. But not here. All day she was surrounded by the chatter and companionship of girls. Only before she slept did she have a while when she could lie still and be by herself. And tonight she wanted to think of Peter.

In her mind she saw him as he had appeared suddenly at her elbow. Tall and lithe, and full of vitality. Blue eyes and black hair, and an ardent, arrogant face that had in it, for all its pride, a queer, recurring flicker of tenderness. He was like no one she had ever known. No wonder she had not been able entirely to forget him.

And he was coming. Perhaps tomorrow. "Soon, soon," his importunate eyes had said. So she must be fine to receive him. What would she wear? Not her dark blue linsey school dress, surely. And not her best, lest the girls suspect. She would wear her frock of lavender wool. It made her blue eyes violet and gave her a delicate and romantic air.

So the next day she took the lavender frock from her chest of drawers, shook it out and slipped it down over her shoulders, while Nancy exclaimed, "Well, for losh sakes, you're dressing up."

"This! I'd better wear it before the moths get it." But she had an uneasy feeling that Nancy was not deceived.

All day, at every step on the porch, her heart skipped a beat. Every time the dog barked she paused and listened. Then she thought, "He'll probably wait a little, for appearance sake."

The next day she again wore the violet dress and was again expectant. Tuesday, Wednesday, Thursday passed, and still he did not come. Every morning she curled her ringlets carefully over her finger, and she even retrieved a dried mullein leaf from her trunk and put it in her pocket, lest her cheeks should be pale when he came.

By the end of the week a slow anger took possession of her. She scoffed at herself and tried to think there was no occasion for anger. But she knew better. There was. Something had passed between them that day on the walk before the church. By an older language than by word of mouth he had spoken, and by quick leaping glances that were full of promise and intent.

Now she thought, "If I meant nothing to him, I'll forget about him. I'll think of Gavin instead, whom I have this week entirely forgotten. Gavin, so kind and solicitous, so dependable and safe and wise."

So she went over in her mind all the pleasant summer days they had spent together. But her mind was a traitor to her and would not stay where she bid it.

"Why doesn't he come?" she asked herself desperately, angrily, and she was not thinking of Gavin.

Then it was Sunday again, and from the corner of her eye her glance flicked over the MacAlpin pew. Rorie himself, and his wife and Hughie. Where, then, was Peter?

So engrossed was she with her private conjecturings that not till the minister was well on in his sermon did she give heed to him. Then he startled her into attention.

"Woe unto you, wine-bibbers and revellers, and you who would lift up your hands against your neighbours in drunkenness and brawling."

He leaned well over the pulpit. His eyes were dark with wrath and his voice was stern, like a prophet of old. It was the voice of their conscience and of their church, and it was no uncertain trumpet.

Felicity wondered. But she was not left long in ignorance. When the girls gathered for the noonday dinner they were full of it, and later when they sat around the fire in the common room.

"A tavern brawl, mind you. And Meron's father and brothers in it!"

"Drunk. One man had his shoulder put out."

"And a sprained ankle. Windows smashed."

Felicity felt her heart sag as she listened. So that was it. Anger and humiliation fought in her mind and whitened her face. A tavern brawl! That did not belong in the life of Felicity MacKay. Indeed, it did not.

"Och, it's terrible." Nancy folded her thick hands piously. "They should make an example of them."

Then another voice broke in. It was Miss Jemima herself.

She looked at her flock in distaste. "You weary me," she said coldly.

"Oh, but Miss Jemima, it's true. It is indeed. Everybody knows it."

"Some of it is, no doubt. And if it all were, what is it to you that you act like spiteful old women?" She rose and brushed down her skirts. "Sometimes I despair of the lot of you."

She walked disdainfully out of the room. She thought, "Once in a while I'm tired of being an old-maid schoolmistress. I should have been a man."

The next morning she came into the small classroom where Felicity was alone, working at her easel. Felicity rose and dropped a curtsey.

"Have you ever noticed the colours there are in snow, Miss Jemima? Blue and violet and even pink?"

"You have, evidently." She squinted thoughtfully at the picture. "I'm not much of a judge, but I think that's pretty good."

"Do you really?" Felicity's eyes lighted. Today the colour came and went in her face. She was fine-drawn and tense, and ready to start at a shadow.

Miss Jemima laid a quiet arm on her arm. "Don't be intolerant, Felicity."

The girl was still for a moment; then she looked soberly up into the other's face. The older woman gave her a friendly grin. "I'm inclined to be intolerant myself, so I can't stand it in anyone else. Anyway, what's a tussle in a tavern?"

Felicity laughed outright at that, in a sudden revulsion

of feeling. She took up her brush again, but her hand trembled, and she laid it down ruefully.

Miss Jemima swept up a sheaf of papers from her desk and smiled at her. "Come with me and help me add my accounts."

* * *

That afternoon Peter came. First he paid a ceremonial call on the headmistress herself, asking permission to take Miss Felicity for a small drive in the bright of the afternoon. And Miss Jemima give him that permission.

Along the river-road east of the town they drove, the horse's hooves kicking up a feathery dust of snow.

"Warm?" asked Peter.

She nodded, bright-eyed.

She stole a brief upward glance. Beneath the eye nearest her she could see a faint discoloration and some small abrasions. Her eyes gleamed. "Did you hurt your face?" she asked innocently.

He laid his hand along his cheek. "Why, so I did!" he exclaimed.

Then their eyes met and they both broke into laughter.

"You should be more careful," she cautioned, still with the thread of laughter in her voice.

"Och, sure, I'll be careful. From now on." He was suddenly serious.

She sighed happily. And the whole incident, so painful before, was wiped out and forgotten as if it had never been.

So it was Peter after all who took Meron and Felicity to the MacKay home for the long-planned week-end. During the drive Felicity was filled with quiet excitement which grew as they neared her home. But she had not foreseen one thing. She had not foreseen that when they did arrive, not only her father and grandmother would be there to greet them, but Gavin Scott as well.

There was a brief silence then. Felicity's colour flamed.

"Why, Gavin!" she cried, and gave him her hand.

With a little catch at her heart she watched his meeting with Peter. Each was wary of the other and showed it. Peter stood taut and tall, and his movements as he stepped forward were smooth and easy like a man ready for any eventuality. Gavin's eyes looked out measuringly through half-closed lids.

It was Meron who saved the day. She exerted herself. Her deep, exciting voice was rich with laughter. She was full of anecdotes. She found Felicity's grandmother charming and let her admiration be known. She had no shyness at all. She radiated friendliness and good will. Over the supper table she told of life at the school and of her family at home. The names of Hughie, David, Peter, slipped in and out of rollicking tales till they had a picture of a household given over to dancing and fiddling and the strong laughter of men.

"Don't you ever do any work at your place?" smiled Dougall quizzically.

"Whiles. Between times. Enough to clear three hundred acres and plough and plant and reap it and raise enough to rear four big boys and a frail body like me."

Peter spoke little. Sitting opposite, Felicity refrained carefully from looking much at him. But her grandmother's eyes rested on him with interest.

"Are you home for good from your journeyings?" she asked.

"Ma'am," he assured her, "I hope so."

"Your mother will be glad." Then, with a flicker of fun breaking through her austere graciousness, "And some others beside, maybe."

His eyes met hers then and he saw friendliness there, and it warmed him. But when he turned to Dougall at the other end of the table, he realized that his host now sensed the possibilities of the situation and had become quiet and wary.

They left the table and grouped themselves about the fire, and Gavin sat down by Felicity. "I came sooner than I had expected. Because I had a message for you from M. Barbin."

"Yes?"

"It is," he spoke slowly, trying to hold her eyes. "It is that he is greatly pleased with your progress. 'Beyond my most wild hopes,' were his exact words when he saw the last oil you sent him. He asks you seriously to study with him. 'I will make her great,' he said, 'because she has in her the seeds of greatness'."

He waited, and she looked at him, blinking a little. "Why, that's splendid, isn't it?" She tried to fill her voice with feeling, but she knew and he knew that it was no longer important to her.

Dougall took up the thread, ostensibly addressing himself to Meron but in reality to Peter. "Did you hear that?" and he repeated it.

"Losh!" cried Meron fervently.

Felicity's cheeks burned. She stole a glance at Peter. He

sat very still, his eyes bright and hard. He had been given a "No trespassing" warning, and he proposed to ignore it.

Meron again came to the rescue. She leaned to look out of the window. "Did anyone ever see such a moon?" she asked dreamily. A great silvery ball rolled high in a sky that was empty of clouds, and the light was so bright that the shadows of the trees were sharp against the bright luminosity of the snow.

"Do you mind the times, Peter, when we used to go down the hill at Tulloch Ard on the bob sleighs?"

"We have sleighs," cried Felicity.

"Then why don't we?"

That, in the end, was what they did. The four of them, Gavin and Peter, Felicity and Meron, wrapped themselves well against the frosty night, found two sleighs in the carriage shed, and went tobogganing down the steep bank and out over the wide, shining surface of the frozen river. At first they conscientiously changed partners after each descent, but later, as by mutual consent, Peter and Felicity were more often together.

Once when the two coasted far out over the ice, and the sleigh finally swirled and skidded to a stop, they rose and stood side by side in a white, moonlit world that seemed empty of all life but their own. Silent and a little solemn, they looked at each other. Then on a sudden, warm rush of feeling, Peter bent his lordly black head, and Felicity lifted her face, and in a moment they were walking up the hill again, their hands tight-clasped but not speaking.

"We'll race you down," called Meron.

So the two sleighs set off abreast from the lip of the hill

103

and shot down the snowy slope. On a sheet of clear ice at the bottom they swerved close; there was a sudden crash and Gavin was thrown clear and lay still.

In a moment Meron was beside him. She gathered his head in her arms and glared up at Peter. "Do you have to kill him as well?"

Gavin was not dead. He stirred and opened his eyes, then rolled over and was on his feet.

"Are you all right?" the three asked in the same breath.

He laughed shakily and sat down on the sleigh.

"Let me give you an arm back to the house," offered Peter.

"Not at all." But his breath came jerkily. So they sat with him for a little while, then walked back to the house together.

After Peter and Gavin had left, and Felicity and her guest had gone up to bed, Allison Munro sat before the fire and held out her hands to the mass of red embers that had been a maple log. She pulled her shawl closer, her turquoise shawl that Gavin had given her nearly a year ago. Poor lad, she murmured in her mind.

She was waiting for her son-in-law, Dougall, to come and talk to her. The glint that had been in his eye when he went out told her that such was his intention.

Here he was now, back from his nightly inspection of the stables, stamping his feet and blowing out his lanthorn, and letting in some of the cold, fresh winter night. A fine, serviceable man was this son-in-law of hers, and at the moment greatly disturbed in his mind.

"Will you have a warm drink, Dougall?" she asked.

"Thanks, no. Tell me, what did you think of tonight?"

"A friendly evening."

"Tut! You know what I mean. What's got into Felicity? She'll lose Gavin if she flaunts that long MacAlpin in his face."

She sat still, looking into the fire.

Dougall smote his two hands together in impatience. "Well, don't you see what she would be throwing away? A fine home, a cultured gentleman for a husband, and a chance that is one in a million to be a fine artist. Can you sit still and let her?"

He stamped restlessly about the room. "She's gifted and she's beautiful. If anything should come from this attraction she seems to feel for the MacAlpin, what would be before her?"

"What is there before any woman who lives with the man she loves?"

"Loves!" echoed Dougall bitterly. Then, looking levelly at her, "I believe you're for him."

Allison rose and took her candle. "I have come now to an age when ease and comfort do not seem to me so important. In my own life the hard times were the best times, as I look back. Gavin is kind and good, and if she took him I'd be happy. But Peter is a man with love and hate and pride and fierceness in him. She will choose as she sees fit." She turned and went up the stair.

But Dougall sat late about the fire, lost in unhappy and resentful thoughts. Nor was he much comforted on the Monday following.

It was on that day that the Reverend John Bethune of

Williamstown took his saddle to the shop on the south side of the river to be mended.

"You'll need a new girth, sir," Long Alec the saddler told him. "Will you wait?"

"I'll do that." He wandered to the back of the shop. "I see you keep your chanter handy."

"Aye. A bit of a tune between jobs."

"Mind if I try it?" He puffed his cheeks and his fingers moved lovingly over the stops. Slow and stately was the music he played, such as might belong to a service in the kirk. Then with a hitch to his shoulder he broke into a light, ranting tune with grace notes twinkling through it.

A shadow fell across the doorway. "God bless the work, and you hard at it."

"Och, your Reverence, is it you?" Long Alec cleared another chair and swept it forward for Father MacDonell.

Priest and minister exchanged greetings. "And was it you at the piping that drew me to the door and within it?"

"I was having a little pull at the chanter. Will you try your hand?"

Father MacDonell waved it away. "The good Lord forgot to put any music in me. Play on, man."

But John Bethune laid the chanter back on the mantel. "Fine roads we're getting in the country now. You'll be busy."

"You, too, my friend. Wearing yourself out, they tell me."

Bethune smiled. "We've big parishes, both of us."

"Aye. And full of lusty men with troublesome high spirits."

106

"Were you thinking of the trouble at Glen Falloch?"

"I was."

"Any of your flock in it?"

"Well now," reasonably. "Did you ever know of a good fight that didn't have a MacDonell in it?"

The minister laughed, then frowned. "I spoke to my people about it. And there sat big Rorie MacAlpin, that old reprobate that I like nevertheless, looking back at me with a smile in the deep of his eye till he nearly put me out of countenance."

"I can just see him." Father MacDonell's own fine gray eyes were alight with laughter. "Now here comes a man of yours that I covet. A scholar and a gentleman. He should be a Catholic."

"Not if I can help it."

"I've just been threatening to convert you, Dougall MacKay."

Dougall slapped his snowy cap on the door jamb and made a friendly obeisance to each. "You're two hundred years late, Father."

"More's the pity, then."

"Just the same," put in the minister, when Dougall had been installed by the fire, "I want to thank you for comforting poor Teenie MacFall in her sickness. When I saw her, she told me you had prayed fine over her."

"Och sure," agreed the priest comfortably. "I know a lot of good Protestant prayers."

"Another thing." Mr. Bethune hitched one knee over the other. "Do you think that together we could do anything about the whisky that floods this land?"

The priest cast a humorous glance over his shoulder. "Don't be nervous, Alec."

"I don't mean a man's private jug. It's this swilling of liquor at raisings and bees, these taverns full of roistering and quarrelling."

"It's cheap," put in the priest gloomily. "You can get drunk for a shilling, and dead drunk for fifty cents. And the result is a tavern brawl such as the MacAlpins were in."

"The MacAlpins?" echoed Dougall.

"Did you not know of it?" The priest looked at him keenly. "Och, it was just a little hooraw-boys. Nothing at all, at all."

When they were alone, Dougall turned to the minister. "Will you tell me of it, sir?"

Mr. Bethune told him briefly.

"You mentioned it in the sermon?"

"I referred to it here, not in the kirk at Summerstown, where you were. There was no occasion."

So Dougall came again to the school and asked to see Felicity in the little parlour. When she came down he told her what he had heard and she listened quietly, her face never changing its look of dutiful attention.

"Did you know this?" he demanded in sudden harshness.

"Oh, yes," she nodded. "And I talked it over with Miss Jemima."

"Aha! What did she say?"

"She agreed with me. That it wasn't very important."

There was an explosive silence. Then Dougall rose and came over to his child, and she got up and stood looking gently up into his face. She looked sweet and pliable and innocent.

"Felicity!" His voice was husky. "What has happened between you and Gavin? And what is there between you and Peter?"

She considered gravely. "Nothing really between Gavin and me. And as for Peter . . ." Then she paused, and the colour flooded her face and her eyes lightened. "I don't know."

"You're happy?"

Again that shimmer of joy across her face. She nodded.

CHAPTER

VII

IN FEBRUARY, on St. Valentine's Day, Felicity and Peter were married. Long before, Dougall had withdrawn his objections, seeing plainly that opposition was of no avail. So he hid in his heart his deep inner hurt and his misgivings, and was courteous and gracious to Peter. Peter was not entirely deceived, but he, like Felicity, lived these days in a state of strong inner happiness that filled the mind against all else.

Once, it is true, Felicity looked around at the paintings she had during the summer completed, and she remembered the message from M. Barbin, and she frowned thoughtfully. So, when Peter next came, she showed him all her canvasses, and he looked at them with such wonder and delight that her self-esteem rose mightily.

"I can still go on with it after we're married?"

"You can paint all day long, if you like," he told her fervently. "Why not? Mother and Meron are there."

The fourteenth of the month came—a bright jewel of a winter's day.

It had been a beautiful morning. Felicity was always to remember it as she saw it, looking out early from her window. The sky, a light blue. No clouds, nothing to flaw that measureless expanse of pale and lovely colour. It seemed immensely high, as if the bounds of heaven were no longer there, and angels might come dropping down with lifted wings and meekly folded hands. Beneath that blueness was a hushed and crystalline world. Frost lay like silver on the grass, on rose bush and on lilac tree. The elms stood up stiffly, as though encased in glass.

Then the long rays of the sun slanted up over the horizon and smote the ethereal, pale world and the still trees. A little breeze came out of the east with the sun, and all the branches moved and twinkled, and the day began. But never was the sunshine warm enough to melt the icy splendour. The mystical bright beauty remained.

For the marriage ceremony, Felicity stood beside Peter between the fireplace and the window. The sunlight and the firelight flashed over her in white and yellow lances of light. Her gown was of champagne-coloured velvet, very soft of fabric, shading into brownness in the tuckings and puffings but shimmering creamily in the light.

The words of the ceremony she heard through the sound of blood pounding in her ears. She was aware of her own voice making the responses clearly, and she wondered at herself. Was this Felicity MacKay becoming Felicity MacAlpin? Her eyes veered slightly and she saw her father's face, her father's unhappy face, and her heart contracted. In

114

a flash it came to her how selfish she had been in his disappointment, how blind in her own happiness.

So, when it was over, and Peter's kiss warm on her lips, she turned swiftly to her father and buried her face for an instant on his shoulder. And his arms closed strongly, reassuringly about her.

The house seemed now full of MacAlpins, good looking, high-spirited, vigorous, from Rorie himself to David, the youngest, watching everything with shy bright eyes. Strangely enough, Dougall felt drawn to David. He said to Rorie,

"Lend me your lad some time when work is slack. I've a three-year-old waiting for a good rider to break him in. We might even take a trip down river."

Rorie regarded him gravely. "The lad will be honoured."

Mrs. Munro did not go with them to the Welcome Home at Tulloch Ard. When Felicity came down the stair, cloaked and bonnetted, her grandmother took her briefly into her arms.

"A *beannachaid* for every year of your life, *m'eudail*, and may there be many of them."

Then they were away, Peter and Felicity last of all, in the big *berlot* lined with buffalo robes.

All at once they were in a world of their own. There was no word spoken, no sound but the crunch of the runners, the pound of Shanlan's hooves, and the hoarse sweet clangour of the bells. Peter pulled off the big fur mitten from his left hand, and hers from her right, and he caught her hand palm to palm with his and enclosed the two in the furry warmth again. Then indeed there was no need for speech; an almost unbearable sweet intimacy ran along the veins and quickened the heartbeat.

When the sleigh crossed the South Branch and turned, a wind smote them out of the rose-red west and Felicity huddled into her cloak and Peter pulled the robes well about her. Before them they could see now the other sleighs, dark against the white snow and the bright evening sky. One stopped. A man got out and came plunging back toward them. It was Rorie MacAlpin himself, and as he came he was unwinding his plaid.

"Here," he cried, when they pulled up, and he laid the plaid about Felicity's shoulders and hooded the end of it over her head.

"Oh, but you shouldn't," she protested.

"And why should I not?" in his deep voice. "There now, bless your heart, you'll not come cold to your new home."

Tulloch Ard was well lighted against their arrival. Yellow bars of brightness slanted from every window and lay golden across the snow. For the neighbours had taken possession of the house and were welcoming home the bride and groom.

The big room was full when they came into it, full of friendly faces and hearty voices and warm handclasps. Felicity's eyes blinked against the brightness and the confusion. Then she was gathered into Anne MacAlpin's motherly arms and kissed soundly on either cheek.

All the neighbours were there. Dark Mairi MacDonell and Little Katie, Duncan MacFarlane, the Alastair John Grants and the MacMartins, the MacLennans, the Mac-Gregors and the Frasers. The Rosses as well. Fergus too. And Sandy Ban with his pipes. There was with Katie a new

116

girl, round-faced and dark, with her childish plumpness still on her, Tassie MacFall. All of them came forward to greet the bride and wish her well.

Said Katie, "To think we'll be neighbours!" And Felicity squeezed her hand and returned the light kiss dropped on her cheek. Yet she was aware of a restraint in Katie's manner. Her eyes sought Meron's and met a sardonic smile.

There was a great supper then, and after all had eaten, the chairs were pushed back and Rorie tuned up his fiddle. Felicity saw Fergus move surely across the room, not to Meron but to Katie. So that was it. "Poor Meron," she thought, "even if she is better off without him."

The sets formed. Hands clasped briefly, skirts whirled and dipped, there was the steady sound of the padding of feet, and talk and light laughter. Felicity danced for a moment opposite Hugh.

"I hope you'll be happy," he smiled at her. "We're a big crowd and noisy, but we'd like to be good to you."

"I know it," she told him softly. "Of course I'll be happy."

When next they were opposite, he said, "Have you met Tassie?"

She nodded.

She watched Tassie then. She saw her lift her dark eyes worshipfully to Hugh. There was no restraint or cover in her face at all. Felicity was disconcerted. A girl so unformed, so childlike. Then she caught Hughie's eye and was abashed.

Said Peter in her ear as they took their seats, "Could you pay attention to me for a change?"

She gave him a quick look. "I'm trying not to." He

117

laughed and cradled her elbow in his hand.

Then Rorie put up his fiddle and said, "Call Sandy Ban now for a reel."

Sandy came in, a tall fair man with an icy blue eye and a smile of singular sweetness. He crossed the room and took his pipes out of a box under the settle. "Sure now, I won't deave you by playing here," he said in his high soft voice. "I'll be in the next room and leave you the door open a crack."

So in the outer room, Sandy marched up and down in the slow proud walk of all good pipers, and the music came trickling in and set their toes tapping.

He had scarce finished when someone called plaintively, "Have Hughie do the sword dance." It was Tassie. They laughed good-naturedly. "Come on, Hugh."

So Sandy blew up his pipes again and two claymores were laid out crosswise on the floor, and Hughie danced. Effortless and easy, his feet padded surely and firmly from quarter to quarter over the bare swords, and back again. The rest leaned to watch. A man had to be good, with the swords naked.

Then all of a sudden there was a commotion without. Hughie stopped on a stamp of his feet and stood listening. Then he caught up the broadswords and pushed them aside just as the door swung open, and a great mountain of a man stood there, and behind him a small dark woman.

The man blinked for a moment, then lifted up his voice. "Is this the house of Rorie MacAlpin, my brother?"

Rorie thrust back his chair. "By thunder, it's Angus," he roared, and the two big men were in each other's arms.

They were alike. But, for Rorie's darkness, there was Angus' fair hair. A fairness that had once been red, and was now softened by the years into an indescribable creamy shade that was even a little pink. But his brows were still red and beetling, and his eyes blue, and Felicity thought she had never seen so formidable or so dramatic a person.

He reached behind him and pulled his wife forward. "Rorie, this is Lucretia. Lucretia, my brother of whom I have told you."

Lucretia's small hand was lost in Rorie's big one. He turned to the company. "This is Angus, my brother, whom I have not seen since we were boys. And his wife, from foreign parts."

Angus drew himself up and clicked his heels. His hand came sharply to his brow. "Pipe-Major MacAlpin," he announced crisply, "of His Majesty's Highlanders, and at your service."

Then Anne herself came forward and swept Lucretia into her arms and gave Angus a straight-forward, hearty greeting, and took them away to take off their wraps.

Meanwhile Meron was laying out another supper. "Lucky for us," she grumbled in her mind, "that the neighbours filled the house with food. But where we'll all sleep is yet another matter."

Meron's high spirits had suffered an eclipse since Fergus had danced first of all with Katie. Flaunting his preference in her face, as it were. A black-haired, black-hearted lad he was, and well she knew it, yet she had liked him. She sighed gustily as with great swipes of her knife she sliced the meat

119

from the ham bone and then pounded the potatoes furiously with the wooden masher.

Felicity and Peter—she loved them both, so she did—but she had to give up her room to them, and now here was a strange uncle and a queer foreign body of an aunt, and where now was she, Meron, to sleep at all? And no husband in sight to carry her off, and an old maid she'd be, see if she wouldn't!

Then Curly Mac MacMartin poked his fair head around the door. "It's the Highland Scottische, Meron. Come you with me."

She flung off her apron and laughed and was herself again.

Angus explained his presence to the company. "Twenty years in the service, lads. And would still be in it but for a sword-thrust in the shoulder and a small trouble in the chest. The West Indies, Africa, Spain. Fighting Boney, wherever we could find him."

Dougall MacKay leaned forward. "What effect has Napoleon's blockade?"

"You mean his decree forbidding all trade and traffic with England from the continent?"

Dougall nodded.

"It's hurt the shipping business. Trade passed over to the neutrals."

"Then came the Orders-in-Council!"

"Aye. They slapped the blockade back at Napoleon."

Dougall sighed. "There'll be trouble."

Angus snorted. "There *is* trouble. Britain is now fighting for her life."

"It's good to be on this side of the water," came comfortably from Anne. "You've now left wars behind you, Angus."

Angus moved his head uneasily. "Don't be so sure of that, wife of my brother. Don't be so sure that war won't come across the water. The world grows so small now, and nations so interlaced in their policies, that trouble spreads with a queer quickness."

"I don't like it," cried Anne. "Here we are in our own quiet place, and weary of wars. Let them leave us alone."

"Och, sure now. Away with all talk of trouble on a night like this. Was it the pipes I heard as I drove up?"

"Hughie was doing the sword dance."

"Aye so." Angus looked with interest at his nephew. "There's a light-footed one in every generation. Once in my young days I danced The Fling at the Court of St. James. Two of the Regiment were chosen. Gregor MacGregor, called The Handsome, and myself. His Majesty was pleased. Aye. He told the steward to give each of us a guinea as a token of his pleasure. We left it with the doorkeeper as we passed out. Gregor was for being insulted. But, says I, after all, he's a Sassenach. Never would Prince Charlie have done that. He knew us. A kiss of the King's hand, and what is gold to a Highlander?"

Duncan MacFarlane nodded his head in approval. "A true word you've spoken, fair man back from the wars." He made a little bow in Lucretia's direction. "And was it in Spain you got your bonnie dark-haired wife?"

Angus raised his glass and quaffed it. "Sure. When the regiment was stationed at Gibraltar."

"Where the big rock is?"

"Aye so. And I took her from under the nose of a proud and black-hearted brother." He turned to look pridefully at his wife, and the quick glance she sent back was fierce with affection.

Felicity looked curiously at her. Her eyes were so dark they seemed opaque. Her face was tight and wary. It had even a small suggestion of violence. Felicity felt that something dark and foreign and exciting had come into their lives. She was not yet sure that she liked it.

She looked across at her father then, and the steadfast comforting look in his eyes reassured her. She saw him in a different way tonight. As a person. Before he had been just her father and taken for granted. Now, a woman married and of another name, she looked appraisingly at him, and her heart went out to him in a strong and ardent affection.

Then once again the pipes blew up for a reel, and who but the bride and groom should lead it? Peter rose, that limber long lad, his blue eyes darkling with excitement, and held out his hand to Felicity. And she stood by him in her velvet gown that was the colour of rich cream, and six others stood with them. The pipes swelled out madly, then steadied into the lilting bright beat of the reel.

So, to the skirling of pipes and the tapping of feet, in laughter and friendliness and good will, they danced in the dawn at Tulloch Ard.

★

★

CHAPTER

VIII

THE HOUSE at Tulloch Ard was well filled during the days that
followed. At mealtime the long table was crowded, and huge
were the pots of potatoes that were boiled, and the savoury
meat-pies baked, and the great puffy golden loaves of bread
that every day Anne tapped out of the bake kettles. "It's like
feeding an army," thought Felicity, "and it's like living in
the midst of a fair."

Talk there was, and laughter and jesting when the men
gathered for meals, or about the evening fireside. Rorie and
Angus had not yet explored all the years since their boyhood.
Hughie and David were enthralled by the tales of far places.
Evening after evening Duncan MacFarlane and Sandy Ban,
too, came across the snowy fields to sit late by the fire.

But by day in the house it was not so easy or casual.
Between Anne and Meron and Felicity there was no friction
at all, but Lucretia was a sharp disturbing ingredient. She

asked questions. She laughed softly to herself at the answers given, and the laughter jarred. Felicity, coming happily down to early breakfast with Peter, met the dark mockery of her glance and flushed. Or she murmured innocently as they sat at table,

"Who was the dark lad at the party who danced so often with the small red-headed girl? Handsome he was, don't you think so, Meron?"

It was as if she liked to put her finger on a sore spot and press. Yet in her own way she was at times kind.

When her boxes came and were unpacked, she called the three in. To Felicity she gave a carved ivory fan tipped with curling orange-red feathers. For Anne she had a soft shawl of rose cashmere, and a fine silken one for Meron in barbaric colours of magenta and gold. She showed them her linens and silver and jewellery.

"My brother," she explained, "did not want me to marry Angus. Then when he saw that I was set in my mind he would have kept from me all the things that had belonged to our parents. But I had a chest hidden at the foot of the garden. Then when I left by night I had something to bring. He was angry, my proud Angus, and said, 'Take it all back.' But I stamped my foot at him there on the dusty road in the moonlight and wept and he took both me and the treasure."

She smiled a satisfied small smile and went on. "Since then I've been over all the world with him. And now here we are in this quiet place, and when we find a house nearby we'll end our days in peaceful living."

"And glad we are to have you," Anne assured her.

Lucretia acknowledged the words with her quick nod.

126

She moved her hands lovingly over the smooth surface of a fat silver jug. She chuckled softly. "My brother liked this jug. How angry he must surely have been when he found it gone!"

Felicity's possessions, too, came to the big crowded house on the hill—her books, her paintings, her clothes, her small but fine store of linens. Her pride in them was a little dimmed, set over against the foreign splendour and richness of Lucretia's. But Mathair Anne praised and admired them, more even than she did Lucretia's.

"Mathair Anne"—that is what she now called Peter's mother. From hearing the others she slipped into it naturally, and almost without intention. But it pleased Anne, and it pleased Peter, and she was glad. Life with Peter was to her still, even though the weeks of her marriage now grew into months, a heart-shaking splendour. Just to see him come in at noon with the other big men of the family, his blue eyes seeking her out importunately, left her weak with love for him.

She smiled ruefully at herself sometimes, and at Lucretia as well, who for all her coolness and her mocking laughter was so devoted to her Angus that at times it seemed a little ludicrous. Before he went out she would tie his muffler about his neck in a fierce sort of tenderness, and then would watch for him at the window if he were late, her dark brooding eyes on the lane of white between the tall pine trees. It occurred to Felicity once that it would not make much difference to Lucretia what happened to all the rest if but Angus were safe.

That was when Peter laid open his shin, working in the bush with the axe. He came home with his high boot full of blood, and Felicity's face was pale as they dressed the wound.

Mathair Anne brought clean linen and her balm-of-gilead salve. Lucretia looked at it for a moment, then lifted her hand and let it fall. "Wash it and bandage it. It's nothing, really." And she walked indifferently away.

Peter laughed, though he was pale and a little shaken.

"You'll keep off it," insisted his mother quietly. "Go you and lie on your bed and let Felicity talk to you. Sure, a quiet spell will do you both good."

Two days Peter spent waiting for the wound to heal enough for him to work again. They were good days. Felicity took out her canvas and her paints and propped the easel up beside the bed. "Tell me now about that wild river in the west, and the high mountains, and I'll paint it for you."

So he told her. Told her of the tawny Fraser rushing madly between tall cliffs to the sea, of mountain upon mountain in snowy peaks, of men in puny canoes dashing perilously down swift water, or climbing steep banks, canoe laden, luggage laden, making a portage. Felicity tried to plot it on canvas, but it was too big, too splendid. It was beyond her.

In the end she painted from memory an apple tree in full bloom, pink and white against a spring sky, with young grass under foot. Peter lay and watched her. Gradually she became entirely absorbed, her head bent over her work, the white nape of her neck showing and her clustering light brown curls. He waited for a long time. Then, "Felicity," he whispered.

She swung around, looked at him for a moment blankly, then he held out a hand to her and she climbed up beside

128

him on the edge of the high bed. She outlined his features with a slim forefinger.

"Sometime I'm going to do a very beautiful picture of a handsome man."

"Felicity," he said again, as if that said everything. And for Felicity it did.

* * *

The next day Hughie said, "I hear Dark Mairi is ill."

"Och, the poor soul," cried Anne. "And she alone but for Katie."

"Not now alone," went on Hughie. "Yesterday Katie and Fergus were married."

There was a silence. Lucretia's black eyes snapped with interest. Then Mathair Anne spoke calmly. "We must go then to see poor Mairi, and to put a good wish on Katie in her marriage."

That afternoon Anne and Felicity walked down the west slope and up over the crest of the higher hill. From there the whole countryside was visible, and the smoke from many houses.

"It was different when we first came," remarked Anne.

"It must have been hard in those days."

"It was. Just to keep warm and fed, and to get the big trees torn out of the ground so we could grow our crops! But thirty years have gone, and now it seems to me we have every comfort we could wish."

They found Dark Mairi propped up in the small bedroom off the kitchen. She looked ill, but happy. Katie hovered about, concerned for her, yet her small creamy face was luminous with her own happiness. Presently she slipped out the back door.

Said Mairi to Anne, "You with your house full of men-folks, you don't know what it is for us to have at last a man about the place." She paused, and in an altered, musing voice, "He might have been my son. And now he has the place I have through the years tended, and this fine clever girl I've raised for him, and she hot-tempered, too, and good for him."

She smiled softly and at the same time pressed one arm close to her side. "I think hereafter I'll look down and watch and be happy."

"Whisht!" said Anne. "You'll be here with them to keep them in order."

Still smiling, Mairi shook her head. With her right hand she traced a line up over her left arm and shoulder and down into her bosom. "Something comes over me here that drains all the life out of me. Look, Anne! Be good to her, will you? If you can. And you, Felicity!"

"I'll do that," promised Anne. And, "Oh, yes," cried Felicity, her blue eyes soft.

The door opened on Katie and Fergus. He looked a little sulky, as if he had come under coercion. When the greetings and good wishes were said he crossed over to Mairi and sat down by her.

"He's truly fond of her then," thought Felicity. "And of Katie, of course. Still, he's a dark and glowering lad, and Meron's better without him."

Nevertheless, it was all hard on Meron. She was short and crisp in her answers these days.

"Have you been to see the new bride?" asked Lucretia smoothly, wiping the dishes as Meron washed them.

"No. Do you want to go?"

"I might. Perhaps I could find some small gift for her."

"As you like," indifferently, and a blue plate crashed to the floor. Meron stood looking at it. "One of the good ones." She glared at Lucretia, and the other laughed softly. "I'll give you a silver one."

"It wouldn't match."

"Child, child," cried Anne reprovingly.

Felicity went to her room and stood with her forehead against the pane, looking out. She felt restless and unhappy. She felt as if she were living in a great milling mass of people, and she not used to it. Her old home had been sparsely occupied. It had been a quiet, seemly household, gentle and composed in its manner of living. Here at Tulloch Ard the house was full of laughter and bickering and love-making and conviviality. It was for a while exhilarating, but one got tired. And Felicity was now tired.

Meron's bitter temper wore on her, and the subtleties of Lucretia, and the lusty life about her. Every night there was laughter and fiddling and singing about the big fire, and now and then drinking as well. Felicity, who had once been captivated by the heartiness of such gatherings, now found her head aching intolerably, and went quietly off to bed and was later joined by Peter who was sometimes a little unsteady from liquor. Once she turned away from him in a sudden, cold revulsion, and in the morning there was a wall of reserve between them, and she was all that day desperately unhappy.

Even her painting seemed to hold little interest for her. But Mathair Anne loved her picture of the crabapple tree.

"Let's hang it over the fireplace," she said. "Sure, it's spring itself, two months early."

Lucretia came and looked at it, and from it to Felicity and back again. The familiar opaque look came into her black eyes.

"It's pretty," she conceded, then continued meditatively, "Not long before I left the home I had with my brother he bought a painting. He was a hard, cruel man, and I hated him, but he knew about such things. So this picture he brought home. It was not pretty. It was savage, and proud, and strong. The man that painted it was an artist. Pretty! Bah!"

Felicity's eyes dropped to hide the hurt that was in them, but Mathair Anne turned straightly to Lucretia, "And why should she not paint a prettiness that is there to see? She in the springtime of her own life! Time enough for bitterness when she is old like you and me."

The Spanish eyes snapped. "I am not old."

"Old enough," Anne went on blandly, "to know better."

Felicity put the picture quietly away. She was hurt and angry, but deep in her mind was a more troubling and insistent thought. It was that Lucretia was right. The judgment given in malice was yet a true one. The picture was only an accurate and pleasing showing of a crabapple tree in bloom. To be an artist one must do more. "The seeds of greatness," old M. Barbin had said. Only the seeds. That meant only the awareness that there was something else to grasp. She strained to grasp it.

132

First something had to come plain in one's own mind. There had to be an idea, burning clear through the canvas and the paint. An idea that had been conceived in ecstasy and brought forth in travail, and that was one's own. She stood and looked out at the long blue shadows on the snow and the sky crimson behind the dark branches of the rowan trees. These rowans she had so often painted. But never, really. Could she do better now? Could she suggest on canvas what she had felt when she first saw them tossing their branches against the sky?

She pulled out her easel and arranged her canvas. She set out her old paintings to check on drawing and perspective. In her mind's eye she saw the finished picture in all its strange wild splendour. There would be in it that quality of her race that was strong in her, that fey sense of the unseen yet almost seen and any minute to be encountered. She felt as if she stood on the threshold of a great accomplishment.

She applied herself with fervour and complete absorption. She was even a little neglectful of Peter. Always before, when he came into the house his eyes sought hers and there was between them a quick, claiming look that warmed them both. Now, Felicity's glance was apt to be casual.

For three days she painted with ardour and with effort. Then she looked at the work of her hands and was not satisfied. She knew what she wanted to do, but alas! she could not do it. Not yet anyway. Her resolve stiffened, and she went back to work and gave it all her heart and mind and will. Then despair fell over her like a blanket, and she put her canvas away and wept secretly, her face buried in her pillow. Yet she did not entirely give up. Always there was

133

a hard inner core of resolve that told her she would yet do this thing to which she had set herself.

"How are you getting on at it?" asked Peter at night.

"Not very well."

"You shouldn't tire yourself, *mochree*.   There's no hurry."

She twisted her hands. But there was. A hurry and an urgency. This could not be tucked away in odd corners of her mind if it was ever going to amount to anything. Still, with her head against Peter's shoulder, that sense of urgency began to fade. His next remark pushed it further into the background.

"Red George is enlisting men for the Highlanders."

"Whatever for?"

Peter shrugged.   "The States are making a big row about the Right of Search and the blockade."

"They blame England?"

He nodded.

"More than France?   What of Napoleon's Berlin Decree?"

"The French have no fleet to speak of. So it's the British who do the searching."

"Would they try to take Canada?"

"Maybe. General Brock is now deep in preparations for defence."

"Who told you?"

"I had it from Abercalder, newly back from York."

"Would Canada fight?"

"Would she let herself be taken?"

"But they say the New England States are firm in their

friendship for Britain. So it will likely blow over. If not," she clasped his arm tightly with her two hands, "then I'm glad I married you. It will keep you out of it."

Peter said nothing.

CHAPTER

IX

MARCH came in like a lion. Storms swirled down over Tulloch Ard and the big pines gripped the earth against them. But when the clouds parted there was a deep soft blueness in the sky that meant that truly winter was breaking up and spring was on the way.

Hughie came home from Williamstown one blustery day and, as he stamped the snow from his feet and shook off his plaid, he pulled a letter from his pocket and gave it to Meron.

Meron fingered the seal wonderingly.

"Open it, child," cried Lucretia impatiently.

The letter crackled open, and as she read a flush crept up over Meron's cheeks. She slipped it into her pocket. "It's from Gavin Scott," she said briefly.

Later in the day she sought out Felicity. "He wants to come to see me," she confessed. "Do you mind?"

"Mind? Why should I? When is he coming?"

Meron looked a little distracted. "Soon. He's to be in Williamstown on business for Mr. Bethune and will drive on up from there."

Tulloch Ard was at its best when Gavin came. Magically the weather cleared, and the country was flooded with the exciting bright sunshine of early spring. And never had Meron looked better. She wore a gown of creamy linsey with a broad band of red and blue embroidery outlining the bodice, and her black braids were wound about her lordly dark head. She was beautiful in a high-coloured, barbaric, pagan way, and when Gavin came, she was like a strong wine on his palate. And Felicity, watching, was aware, not without a little inward pique, that what Gavin felt for Meron was a heady, potent something far removed from the kind, cool devotion he had given her.

But she was proud of the family which was now hers. Not at all were they overawed by Gavin, except perhaps David a little in his youth and shyness. Peter and Hughie and Rorie were easy and offhand in their talk. Angus was one man of the world with another. And Mathair Anne was just herself as she would always be. Nor was Meron over-impressed. She was the same laughing, downright, friendly girl she had been when Gavin first saw her.

"How is Charlotte?" asked Felicity in a pause.

"Oh, very well. And she sent her love to you."

"Take mine back to her," smiled Felicity. Her friendship with Charlotte had remained unimpaired, and she was glad of it.

After Gavin's visit peace settled down over Tulloch Ard. No longer was Meron sharp of tongue. She was now the loved and sought-after woman. Lucretia, in her turn, was impressed with this connection of her new-found kin and was well-mannered and respectful.

The men were working hard in the bush, felling the great trees, trimming and chopping them, against the time when the snow would be too soft for such work. The women prepared bountiful meals and, tired, they all went early to bed. Felicity no longer tried to paint. That was thrust into the back of her mind, temporarily ignored. And she was glad for a while to ignore it. One cannot continually strive.

Then came the day of the logging bee at MacFarlane's. Early in the morning the men left for it, all of them, and through the day the house was strangely quiet. Till on in the afternoon, when there appeared in the doorway Dougall MacKay and with him, John Bethune, the minister.

Felicity was more glad than she could say to see her father. The feel of his cold hard face against hers and the clasp of his hands filled her with happiness. The minister, too, was a welcome and honoured guest, for his office, and for himself. Soon they were all installed about a roaring fire and Anne had a hot drink to warm them.

Then when it came time for supper, and Felicity went to the kitchen to help prepare it, Anne said, "Bring out your own linen and silver, if you'd like, and you shall pour the tea."

And so it was. Felicity sat at the head of the table, her hands busy with cups and saucers and teapot, her lower lip caught in her teeth in her absorption, and her face bright with pleasure. Her father looked at her with pride, and the tired eyes of the old minister smiled kindly on this child of his flock now grown into a fine and lovely woman.

Lucretia was graciousness itself, with never a barbed word or glance. And conversation was mellow and friendly over the fried pigeon breasts, the scones and honey, the seed cake and the hot fragrant tea.

All at once Felicity saw a listening look on Anne's face. Then she heard it too, a sound of singing, far distant at first, now growing louder. Meron lifted her head. Now they all heard it. A sleigh swung into the lane. "*Horo mo nighean donn bhoidheach*" was flung lustily into the air by the voices of many men.

There was a complete silence about the table. They could now see the sleigh from the window, and the men leaping from it. Rorie, Angus, Peter, Duncan MacFarlane, Sandy Ban. The horses they tied to the gate post, and they all came stamping into the house.

Immediately the place was full of frosty air and loud voices and big men, all of them a little drunk, and some of them more than a little. Duncan lifted his hand in unsteady but courteous greeting. Rorie came striding through the crowd.

"Sure, your reverence," he cried jovially.

John Bethune and Dougall MacKay were on their feet now. Anne too. Rorie laid his great arm around the slender shoulders of the minister. "Once you gave me a wigging from the pulpit. But do I hold it against you? I do not. Here!"

He pulled a bottle out of his pocket, slopped the tea out of one of the good blue cups and filled it. "*Slainte!*" he cried.

They all crowded around him and bottles were raised high. "*Slainte!*" they yelled. "*Suas e*, and down with it."

142

Then Anne's voice cut through the din. "Sit down now, friends and neighbours. Sure, you're welcome, but sure, you'll behave."

There was a note in her voice that reached Rorie. He blinked uncertainly, laid his hand briefly on Felicity's head, then turned to her father. "You're welcome, Dougall MacKay," he said, and his voice was suddenly quiet.

Felicity's gaze never left Peter. But it was a new Peter. There was a reckless, hard look in his eyes when they met hers that she had never seen before. But then, she had never seen him drunk. A long quivering sigh rose from deep within her.

The men were now becoming a little subdued. John Bethune looked at them, his face hard. Then his glance veered round to Anne. Her eyes met his with a fine steady pride in them, and no apology at all.

"Our thanks to you for your hospitality," he told her courteously, and Dougall followed suit. He kissed Felicity as he went, and there was a steadying message in the firm grip of his hands on her shoulders.

No sooner were they gone than all eyes turned suddenly to Lucretia. She was laughing. Still in her place at the table, she threw her head back and her mouth opened on wild peals of mirth. It shocked the men into sobriety, and it seemed to Felicity the final indignity.

*   *   *

The next week was one of the longest in Felicity's life, and one of the most miserable. She was angry to the very core of her being. For Peter to have so humiliated her seemed more than she could bear.

It was not a happy household. Rorie and Angus were

subdued and vaguely apologetic. But not very much so. The simple statement, "Och well, we'd been drinking," seemed to them explanation enough. It even seemed so to Peter. But definitely not to Felicity.

As the week went on, her anger cooled a little and she had to keep reminding herself of the just cause of it, but the deep inner hurt remained. She felt sure she would never feel the same to Peter. She told him so. And he took her at her word and made no more effort to reconcile or placate her.

Sugar weather was now on them and the men were busy. The maples had to be tapped, and the sap, the sweet, cold, thin lifeblood of the trees, had to be gathered and taken to the pans in the big arch to be boiled down into syrup.

"The roads will be going," said Anne one day. "Why don't you and Meron drive over for a visit with your father and grandmother?"

Felicity was grateful for the suggestion.

When they arrived at the stone house by the water they found that sugar-making was going on there too. So, after the noon meal, Meron said, "I'll go to the bush with you. Sure now, I'm not dressed up at all. I'll love it."

So she kilted up her skirts and put on a stout pair of boots of Kirsty's, and was away. Meanwhile Felicity and her grandmother sat down in the pleasant front sitting-room and worked at a quilt that was on the frames.

They plied their needles in a companionable silence while the sunshine came in at the big south window and fell across the many-coloured squares that made up the quilt. Felicity felt that sunshine warm on her hair. The gray cat came and pressed against her ankles and she lifted it to her lap. It lay there, purring loudly and prodding her with its paws. It knew her and was glad to have her back. The whole place knew her, and she slipped into the familiar environment with a sense of peace and comfort.

The coldness in her heart melted a little. She looked up suddenly and met her grandmother's eyes fixed on her with such love and concern that tears stung behind her lashes. She tried to smile and managed it. "Did father tell you?"

"He told me of the fine visit he had, and of the jollification after."

"Jollification," bitterly.

There was a pause. "Are you angry at all of them, or just at Peter?"

"Only at Peter."

"Well, then, I think you'll just have to get over it."

Felicity stared at her, then laughed reluctantly. "I was coming to that conclusion."

"It's part of being married. Giving in and making up. You've been a lone child. Perhaps you haven't learned how."

Felicity quilted industriously for a while, then raised a flushed face. "This last week I haven't been very kind to Peter."

"Kind. That's not the word between man and wife. *Close* is better. No longer twain. One."

"I see." Felicity was thoughtful. "Then they'd never quarrel."

"I didn't say that. Of course they'll sometimes quarrel, if they're young and strong and have life in them. But no matter how angry they are at the moment, that closeness will remain, and beneath the wild words they'll know it."

145

Allison Munro's austere gray eyes met the young blue ones squarely. "It's a very interesting thing being man and wife, and when it's ended the one left is forever lonely." There was a moment of silence; then she rose briskly. "Come now, let's get a good supper for Meron and Kirsty and the men."

*   *   *

Sugar weather was at length over. The last run of sap had been boiled down from syrup into sugar, and that had been poured into receptacles to cool and harden. Then came the washing of the sap buckets, drying them well in the sunshine, and storing them, pushed one into the other in a long cylinder, far back in the attic to await another spring.

There followed then a brief breathing space before the time of the ploughing and the planting. Clearly a *ceilidh* and a bit of jollification was called for. So one night Sandy Ban and Duncan and a few of the neighbourhood lads drifted in when the evening chores were done.

Felicity was in her room at the time. She had been working in a desultory way at her picture of the rowan grove till the light failed her. Now she sat alone at the window looking out. It was a wild and lovely evening, with black branches tossing against a luminous pale sky. The wind was rich and boisterous with spring, and from the swampy hollow came the booming of bull frogs, a sure sign that sugar weather was over and warmer days were to come.

A lift of laughter drifted up from below. Felicity felt more and more desolate. Since that day at her grandmother's she was learning that once a coolness is established between two persons it is sometimes difficult to bridge the gap. Peter was still remote.

The thin sound of a fiddle now seeped through wall and floor. Would Peter come and call to her, "Come on down, Felicity"? A while ago he would have. Now, he would not.

Nevertheless, he is my husband, she thought, and so she tidied her hair and went down the stair. In the west room Anne and Lucretia sat working placidly in the candlelight, Anne at her mending, and Lucretia embroidering on gauze with purple wool. Felicity sat down with them and picked up a garment to mend.

Sounds of laughter and revelry came from the next room. Then a burst of song.

Felicity rose suddenly and, without looking at Anne or Lucretia, she laid down her work and went to the door. She opened it and stood for a moment and looked. The fire roared high on the big hearth. That was the only light in the room. But the warmth, the vitality, the colour of the scene smote her.

Meron leaned back, her hair loose, her cheeks flushed, laughing as she sang. Angus sat astride his chair, his cream-coloured mane tossed back, his shirt open over his great chest, his big fist beating time on the back of the chair. Rorie cradled his fiddle in the crook of his arm and now and then threw in a sliver of melody. Hughie. Duncan. Sandy. Peter? There he was, his back to her. One arm lay along the edge of the settle where he sat, and in his hand was a mug of whisky. The room was bathed in firelight, warm with laughter, filled with song. In the low light the figures loomed larger than human. They looked Homeric.

No one noticed Felicity in the doorway. Her heart pounded. She felt like a swimmer about to essay a high dive.

147

Then on a deep breath she stepped swiftly across the room. She took the mug from Peter's hand and set it on the floor.

"Make room," she whispered, and sat down close beside him. Surprised, his arm closed around her shoulders. She turned and met his eyes with a smile of pure friendliness. His arm tightened. Suddenly she could feel his heart beat against the back of her shoulder.

The song was finished. All eyes turned to Felicity. But Hughie swung promptly into The Skye Boat-Song, and they all joined in.

> "*Speed, bonnie boat, like a bird on the wing.*
> *Onward, the sailors cry,*
> *Carry the lad that's born to be king*
> *Over the sea to Skye.*"

Their voices rang out lustily in gay, fierce defiance. Defiance of what? Of the stern dull commonplaces of life, the hard unending toil, the drabness, the discomforts. A defiance that rejoiced in all carefree revelry, all gallantry, all laughter and delight.

Understanding slid into Felicity's mind as she sang with the others. They had worked hard, these men, they who were by not so many generations removed from a pastoral, hunting, warring existence, and on whom the drudgery of the pioneer farm at times wore intolerably. That was why they were sometimes drunken and over-hilarious. But Peter need not be. And would not, if she made him entirely happy. It came to her then that you can do nothing with an environment till you give yourself to it, till you submerge yourself in it.

But her thoughts were only half thoughts, and vague at that. All she was really conscious of was the warmth of Peter's arm about her shoulder, his closeness, and the knowledge that the barrier between them was quite swept away.

Later, when the neighbours had gone, and the back log had been fixed for the night, and the big clock wound, Felicity went with the rest for her candle to go up to bed. Hugh stood by her. He picked up a candle for her, lighted it, and as he handed it to her, his gray-blue eyes flashed for an instant into hers.

"Good night, Felicity MacAlpin," he said, and in his voice there was a sort of benison.

"Good night, Hughie, my brother," she answered.

When she came into her room she stood for a moment looking at her painting. "I'll come back to it," she told herself stoutly. "I'll make it come right yet." Then she forgot it entirely at the sound of Peter's step on the stair.

*　　*　　*

Later in the night she woke. It was very still. A shaft of moonlight lay across the bed. Peter was looking at her. In the ghostly light his face was withdrawn and strange. His eyes had a terrible intentness.

"What is it?" she whispered.

It was as if he reached down into the depths of him for the words. They came a little hoarsely, in the idiom of the old tongue.

"It's the man I am, looking at you and wanting to be good to you, girl that I love."

Her face broke up into tenderness, as she answered

gravely, "And it's I wanting to be close and kind to the man of my heart."

They kissed quietly, and lay side by side, hands clasped. It was as if a new sacrament bound them, as if at last their spirits had touched and fused.

CHAPTER

X

EARLY IN MAY David went to Dougall MacKay's for the
summer, and maybe for longer. At the time of Felicity's
wedding Dougall had first suggested his going, and later he
made a definite offer. David would for the first time have
money of his own earning, but his status would not be that
of a hired man. That, Dougall made quite clear. Indeed,
more was implied, and Felicity knew that David would be
as one of the family and might even have his future assured.
Dougall was much drawn to this quick, dark lad, the only
shy one of the lordly MacAlpins, and the gap in his life that
Felicity's marriage had made would now be partly filled.

Mathair Anne was a little pensive, nevertheless, getting
his things ready.

"Grandmother and Kirsty will look after him well,"
Felicity comforted her.

"Och, I know. It's just that I'll miss having him around,

my youngest one, and him never yet away from home."

Spring was coming on. The maple trees behind the house stood in a mist of small claret-coloured blossoms that clothed each twig and tiny branchlet. A green tide of grass covered the meadows, grass that was soon gold-dusted with dandelions. Mathair Anne sat in the sun on the west steps of the verandah, sorting garden seeds saved from the year before.

It was a lovely day. Felicity walked down into the ravine and up the slope of the hill to the west, with the birds swooping round her and the sun beating warmly down on her bare head. She sat down on a flat stone in the little clearing that was in the heart of the rowan grove.

Below, in the field to the south, Peter was ploughing. Crows followed him, cawing and flapping and lighting in the black upturned earth. The sky was blue, the fields green, and Peter with his black head and his blue shirt and the big white cattle straining in the plough made a fine, heroic, primitive picture. Felicity stood to look at him.

He saw her. She waved, and he left the oxen and came up the hill. They sat on the soft, short grass in the sunshine and talked.

"When are we going to build our own house, Peter, for you and me?"

He turned his eyes full on her for a moment. "Would you like that?"

She nodded. "Have you ever thought of it?"

"Many times."

"Why didn't you mention it?"

"Because . . ." Peter always took a while to put his

thoughts into words. "Because to live in your own house would mean more work for you. You might never have time to paint at all then."

She was silent. He had put his finger squarely on the issue, facing it more directly than she had. Yet she pressed the point. "But with just the two of us . . ."

"You're happy with the family?"

"Oh, yes. But crowded."

"Crowded! I know. Where would you like me to build?"

"Here where we are. In this little clearing among the rowans. On this higher hill."

Peter considered. "The wind gets the hill. But if we built of stone, with thick walls . . ."

Felicity's imagination kindled. "Tonight we'll draw plans."

He kissed her. An excitement that matched her own now shone in his eyes.

That night they discussed ways and means with the assembled family. Felicity brought out a sheet of foolscap and, with a newly sharpened quill, drawings were made, and the location of windows, doors and chimneys was gravely considered.

"How long before it is finished?" wondered Felicity.

"By the end of August?" Peter looked inquiringly at his father.

"Aye," agreed Rorie. Then, "We'll miss you."

"We'll not be far," smiled Felicity.

The next day Anne MacAlpin, with the help of her family, put in her garden. Peter ploughed, and Hughie spaded, and Meron raked, and Felicity helped to plant. But

155

Anne planned and directed and worked as well. Only Lucretia sat on the verandah and watched.

The peonies and the hollyhocks were already well above the ground, and the lilacs would soon be in bloom. The currant bushes and the gooseberries only needed to be spaded around, and the snowballs and the sweet-mary. But the long rows of onions and carrots and beans and peas had to be laboriously sown, and after that, in the bed in front of the house, pinks and portulaca and four-o'-clocks. A few love-apple seeds were planted in a sunny place and well marked.

"Is it true they're poisonous?" asked Felicity.

"They look it," grumbled Meron, straightening painfully. "Great red swollen things when they're ripe. But the leaves have a nice smell."

When the garden plot was a beautiful expanse of brown seeded earth they sat on the edge of the porch and rested.

"Nothing nicer than a garden." Anne smiled at them all in rich content.

"We'll enjoy it in the winter, if not now," admitted Hughie lazily.

In the winter. "Mathair Anne," said Felicity on a sudden thought. "Did you ever see flowers preserved in sand?"

"No. Can you do it?"

"My grandmother showed me."

"I'll get the sand for you," offered Peter.

Meron and Felicity gathered the flowers. In the creek that oozed brownly along the floor of the ravine they found marsh marigolds—smooth stems and round, waxy leaves and yellow flowers in shining clusters. Where the ravine spread out into a low meadow, there the wild blue flags grew. But the hepaticas bloomed in the woods. The tall trees stood in pools of them, blue, mauve and pink. Trilliums were like drifts of snow. The forest was full of a shy, fragrant beauty that belonged to it only in May.

The girls knelt on the mossy sod and loosened the earth away from the hepatica roots and took up a few perfect plants, strong leaves and woolly stems and delicate, pale blossoms.

Said Meron suddenly, "I've had another letter from Gavin."

Felicity smiled at her.

Meron was gloomy. "Look," she said. "You've been there. Can you see me in that house?"

Felicity thought for a while. "Yes, I can," she decided.

Meron heaved a sigh. "I'd miss this," she said briefly.

The sand was ready for them when they got home. They washed it, then baked it in a kettle and cooled it. They found an old pail with a convenient hole in the bottom, which they plugged. Then sand was poured in, to a depth of six inches or so. Into this the flowers were set upright in natural positions, and the rest of the sand was sifted in carefully till all was covered. The pail was then set near the fire, but not too near.

"This time tomorrow," promised Felicity, "we'll let the sand out by the hole in the bottom, and the flowers will be preserved in form and colour."

She dusted off her hands and all at once felt a little childish and embarrassed. She picked up her knitting and came and sat by Anne.

"That's all useless and foolish, I suppose," she ventured.

"Not foolish. Important." Anne pondered for a while, then went on as if feeling for words.

"When I was a small girl in the Old Country my father used to come in from work at noon, very hot and thirsty. And I'd run to meet him with a full cup of water. But would he drink it all? He would not. First, a small part he would spill out on the ground. One day I asked him why. He said he did it because his father before him had done it. And again I asked him why. And he thought hard and said it was to show that there is more to life than the needs of a man's body. That a man is more than his body."

She sat for a moment looking into space. "Strange, but it's real to me now, and it fifty years ago. I can hear him say the words. Anyway, what I'm trying to say is that it's the extra and unnecessary things in life that count."

She laid a hand on Felicity's knee. "So put up your wild blue flags in sand. And don't forget your painting either."

Felicity looked at her quickly.

"I know it's going to be hard, and you after a while with the care of a house and a bairn, but try, *nighean mochree*. Try."

*   *   *

These were busy days on the farm of Tulloch Ard, both within and without. Mathair Anne superintended the smoking of the hams. The pork that had lain in barrels in the cellar all winter was now taken out of the brine and washed and hung in the smoke house, where a fire of apple-tree wood filled the place with a sweet oily smoke that would both preserve and flavour the meat.

She also made the year's supply of healing salve out of

158

Balm-of-Gilead buds steeped in tallow. Fine for small wounds or chapped hands.

And every few days the tall churn was taken out and scalded and half filled with thick sour cream. Then Meron or Felicity or even one of the men plop-popped the long dasher up and down, and small spurts of cream oozed out of the hole in the cover where the dasher came through, and sometimes spattered on the floor. These, Phiseag Dhu, the little black cat, licked up with her quick pink tongue and then sat back waiting hopefully for more.

After a while the sound of the dasher changed. Instead of a thin spat there came now a muffled thudding. The butter was coming. Soon it was lifted out into the big wooden bowl, and washed and worked with the ladle and salted and worked some more. Then, smooth and yellow, it was moulded into rolls and these, wrapped in clean muslin, were stored in a stone crock in brine that was strong enough to float an egg.

Meanwhile the new house was going up. The cellar was dug and floor beams were laid—great cedar logs with the fibrous bark still on them.

"Last a hundred years, so they will," said Rorie. "And more."

The stone was quarried on their own place, on the north side of the hill where it fell away precipitously. The walls began to rise. Every hour Peter had to spare he worked with the masons, and in the evenings he and Felicity would cross the little ravine and come up the higher hill to the rowan grove and sit on a log and admire the slowly rising walls

159

and plan and dream. Never had Felicity been more quietly, deeply happy.

In June came the shearing of the sheep. On a bright, warm morning they were driven down to the creek and well washed and let run in the sunny pasture till dry. Then, as the trusting ewes crowded around, they were caught and flung on the shearing board, and the shears snip-snipped and their great white overcoats came off almost in one piece. They stood shivering for a moment in their nakedness, then bounded off to join their lambs.

And now indeed rosé a lamentable shrill bleating, the mothers anxiously seeking their offspring and the lambs fleeing in alarm. It was evening before serenity was restored in the sheepfold, and even then the silence was occasionally broken by the quivering little voice of a lamb, followed by a nuzzling sound that meant he had found his mother.

"Poor silly things," said Mathair Anne. "Look you, Felicity, let us take some of this new wool to make a small cradle cover. We'll dye it pale blue, then card it very soft and light, and enclose it in some fine white cheesecloth."

"Blue for a boy?" smiled Felicity.

"We'll tie it with pink yarn, and so be safe."

*   *   *

On the Sunday after, they picked up Sandy Ban on their way from church and brought him home for dinner. Then in the quiet of the afternoon the men lounged about on the grassy plot before the house, and the women came out and sat on the long verandah, talking of their own feminine concerns, but with an ear open for the more lusty masculine conversation.

"The flying-mare now," Angus was saying. "It's a good hold to know, but a man has to be quick."

"Peter can do it," put in Hughie.

"And can you now?"

Hughie got up. "Come on, Peter."

Meron called to them, "And who's to scrub the grass stains out of those white linen shirts?"

Hughie bent and Peter stripped the shirt over his head, and Hughie did as much for him, then threw the two shirts to Meron.

They were beautiful shirts, thought Felicity, fine homespun linen, carefully hand-sewn. She folded Peter's on her lap.

The two brothers stood face to face, and Peter caught Hughie's wrist and swung slowly as to demonstrate, and Hughie whirled across Peter's hip and over his shoulder and picked himself lightly up.

"Aye, that's the method. But losh, lads, put your backs into it." Angus lumbered to his feet. "I'll give the word. Ready. Go."

So they wrestled. Two bonnie long lads, one dark, one fair. Peter was heavier and taller and Felicity could see that he was holding himself in. Once he pressed Hughie's bare shoulders into the grass and bent over him grinning, but immediately let him up.

"Come on, fight," laughed Hughie. And they closed again.

Their mother watched them with quietly smiling eyes that were full of pride. They made a fine picture, their struggling bodies gleaming white against the greenness all around.

"After all, Hughie," remarked Sandy Ban, "he has ten pounds up on you."

"Sure he has," panted Hughie, then as they broke and flung themselves on the grass, "Anyway, I'm a good kicker."

"I'm not so bad at that myself," offered Sandy. He rose and Angus laid a hand on the top of his head and he walked out from under it and swung up a long leg and kicked the hand.

Then Hughie, rested, did the same, and Meron called out, "That's not so much. I can do it myself."

Whereat Peter leaped into the air, stiffened, and turned cartwheels across the lawn, and came up red-faced and grinning. "Let's see you do that, big girl," he called.

"It minds me of our young days, Rorie," remarked Angus. "What about a round between us now? For old times sake?"

Rorie half rose, then sank back. Felicity could see the working of his mind. He was remembering Angus' wound and the weakness in his chest. "Och, too old," he said.

Angus beetled his brows at him. "Tosh! How about you, Sandy?"

"I don't mind if I do," said Sandy promptly. And two more shirts came off.

Sandy was a sparely built man, though his shoulders were strong and square. His ribs showed. But those icy blue eyes of his were very steady. Beside him Angus was like a giant with his great chest covered with a gray-red pelt and his back flat like a barn door.

Said Lucretia in a tight voice, "Before he was hurt, Angus could lay any man in the regiment on his back."

162

Nevertheless across one shoulder lay now the blue seam of an old sword-cut, and that arm at least was not well muscled.

They closed. They strained. They sweated. The rest rose to watch. Angus enveloped Sandy, but Sandy like a lean eel slipped out of his grasp. They broke and lay side by side, laughing.

"I wouldn't have believed it." Angus blew his breath through his red moustache. "You're a good man, Sandy Ban."

"A tired one." His thin ribs went in and out.

Lucretia's breath came short too. Her face was pale and her nostrils tense. Was she troubled for Angus?

"Another round?" suggested Sandy.

There was a stress in the struggle now, as if each was anxious to see for himself just how good a man he yet was.

"Don't hurt yourselves, lads," called Rorie. Lucretia slipped into the house. They could hear the sharp tap of her heels on the stair.

When she came down they were again resting. Angus had rolled over on his back near the verandah steps and lay there relaxed, his chest heaving. Lucretia stood for a moment in the doorway, then stepped swiftly over to Angus and knelt by him.

Her hand slipped into his. For an instant Felicity saw something flash in the sunshine. A puzzled look spread over Angus' wide friendly face. Then a slow stiffening. Then a mounting fury. He sat up with a jerk, spilling Lucretia off her balance.

"Get away out of here!" he roared.

Her hand slipped back into her pocket, and she rose and

163

moved swiftly into the house and up the stair.

There was a complete silence. Angus got up stumblingly and came and sat on the verandah. He drew his hand down over his face and a red flush followed from his forehead down.

Sandy Ban reached for his shirt. "There's a chill by evening," he remarked calmly.

"Sure, you'll stay with us for supper," urged Anne.

"I'll be glad to." His voice was quiet and courteous.

One by one they drifted into the house. But Angus still sat on the verandah bench, and Felicity stayed with him.

After a while he said thickly, "Did you see what she was for giving me?"

"No," she lied kindly.

"Then maybe the others did not. It was a wee dirk. Like they use in Spain. It's her hot foreign blood. But she's a good woman." He looked sternly down into Felicity's eyes and she nodded warmly.

"I know she is. Don't worry, Uncle Angus."

There was nothing apologetic in Lucretia's attitude, however. To Anne she admitted freely what she had done.

"In my country when we fight, it's not for pleasure." Her lip curled scornfully.

"It wasn't fighting," explained Anne patiently. "It was just sport."

"I can't feel the same to her," she confessed to Felicity. "Do you think Sandy saw?"

"Maybe. He wouldn't let on."

Anne sighed. "I'm sorry for Angus. It's hard to see a man shamed for his wife."

The work on the new house went on apace. It was not

164

going to be a big house. But a sweet one. It was sturdy and four-square, and true of line and proportion. Two dormer windows broke the steep roof, and a narrow verandah low to the ground fronted the south wall. A wide chimney at either end anchored it firmly to the hilltop. The stone walls were two feet thick, with deep window openings.

From the upstairs especially there was a fine view. Over the tossing tops of the rowans one looked far out over a green and rolling and tree-shaded countryside. The darker green of the forest encircled it around, and through the fields the river ran.

"High land for a Highlander," said Mathair Anne. "We like to see what's coming at us."

One day Angus came home from a trip to Cornwall, riding Black Shanlan, and it was clear as soon as he came clattering into the yard and flung a leg over and dropped to the ground, that he had news.

"I've got me employment," he announced. "I have been to see my friend Collachie."

"Collachie?" Lucretia sat with her embroidery needle poised, and her eyes as sharp.

"Aye. The Honourable Alexander MacDonell, member of this Parliament of Upper Canada, called Collachie, because—well—because he *is* Collachie."

"His father's estate in Scotland," explained Felicity.

"Go on," impatiently from Lucretia.

"Well." Angus sat down, his knees spread, and mopped back his cream-coloured hair. "They're needing a new warden for the jail. And I'm to be the man. What do you think of that?"

"Will it be too hard for you?" asked Anne.

"Tush, no."

"We'll be sorry to lose you. Though you'll be happier, no doubt. But this house will be empty," she exclaimed, looking about her in alarm. "Peter and Felicity going soon, and now you."

"Oho," laughed Angus. "Hughie will be bringing home a bride some of these days. What of the small plump lassie he's aye with at the *ceilidhs*?"

"Tassie," sighed Anne.

* * *

In the month of July the community was saddened by the death of Mairi Dhu. But it was a gentle sadness that took cognizance of the fact that she had been well aware of the approaching end and went nonchalantly, almost blithely to meet it, happy in the thought that Fergus and Katie were settled and secure.

Felicity spent an afternoon with Katie shortly after the funeral, and on her way home she paused to rest under an elm tree on the west slope of the hill. All around her was a warm sea of clover, and gratefully she eased herself down into it.

The afternoon sun slanted through the blossoms. Felicity lay and looked at them. Looked at the firm jointed stems and the folded leaves and the heavy flower-heads—those dark red, honey-scented globes of bloom. Close to the ground grew the delicate pink clover, small and soft in its nest of leaves. Here and there yellow sorrel bloomed, or a drift of blue vetch, and now and then a tall golden buttercup. That was all.

What was there about this clover field that made it seem so significant? Was it the light? Each separate stem and flower bathed, as it were, in a sort of ineffable luminosity? Some trick of the slanting of the sun? Or something more? It was as if every sprig of clover, pink or purple, every nodding buttercup, every blue vetch vine, was filled with a vitality, a joyousness, a consciousness of itself. It was as if the secret of life and creation was there in the clover field.

Felicity's heart beat with a hard inner excitement. This, she would paint. And it would be as a field of clover was never painted before.

She would come tomorrow. But earlier. Much earlier. Then she could have the drawing blocked in before the light reached that exact heavenly pitch of incidence, from which came this unearthly splendour.

She lay still and drank in the colour and the line and the slanting yellow evening light over all. The warm, sweet perfume filled her nostrils. She marked the place exactly. Then she went home.

She said nothing about it even to Peter. She felt that to try to put her feeling into words would destroy that fine secret rapture. The next morning the sky was overcast and the clouds hung heavy all day. But the day after was fair. Early in the afternoon she took her canvas and paints and made her way towards the clover field.

But before she reached it she stopped. She stood a long time looking. Then she turned and walked quietly back to the house. The clover had been ploughed under. She thought, "This is something I can never tell anyone. No one would understand. There are so many clover fields, they'd say. How could they know that this was the only one?"

A few days later, as she and Mathair Anne were shelling peas on the back porch, she asked casually, "Why did they plough up the clover?"

"That piece of land wasn't so good. So the clover was planted, and when it was in full bloom they ploughed it under. There'll be a fine crop on that field next year. You'll see."

CHAPTER

XI

IN SEPTEMBER Peter and Felicity moved into their new house
on the higher hill. The rowan trees were then at their best.
Felicity liked to come out and stand among them. Immediately she was in a faery world where the light filtered down
through a screen of leaves and of thick, jewel-like clusters
of scarlet and crimson and gold. The vehement colours of
the fruit set over against the cool reflective green of the
leaves, and all held up like a roof by the smooth, gray trunks
of the trees, gave to the grove a strange bright beauty that
Felicity found both exciting and satisfying.

The house, too, seemed peculiarly her own place. From
the slant-roofed bedrooms above, with whitewashed walls
and snowy ruffled curtains at the deep-silled windows, to the
big kitchen–living room downstairs. Especially did she find
pleasure in the best room, whose windows looked out to the
west. No whitewashed walls here, but pine panelling already

rubbed to a mellow softness. For the hearth the mason had found smooth, flat stones from the bed of a creek. They were dark green, curiously veined with red, and they had a soft slippery texture when the hand was passed over them.

The wide boards of the floor were polished with beeswax and turpentine, and hooked rugs made pools of colour on it. Brass candlesticks stood on the mantel, and Windsor chairs and a long settle and a few shelves for books and a chest of drawers completed the furnishings. Simple it all was, but when the westering sun slanted in at the windows the room glowed like the inside of a jewel.

In November Felicity's little daughter was born. It was a night of sleet and wind but Felicity was not much aware of the weather. In the morning she lay in her bed, weakly happy, and watched Peter bending over the cradle and touching with a fearful finger a tiny shell-shaped ear that lay flat against the small dark head.

Anne came up with a bowl of gruel, and Meron knelt by the cradle to wonder and to adore. Both had been a comfort to Felicity. And so had Lucretia, who, on the very eve of her departure for Cornwall, had waited over for this event. She had been kindness itself, and the hard lift of her spirit had been a tonic and a strength.

The baby was a round sweet morsel, and grew rounder and sweeter every day. She had dark hair and blue eyes, not the deep challenging MacAlpin blue, but soft like larkspur. She was a pink rose of a baby, and so she was to be named. Felicity had planned to call her Barbara Anne after her mother and Peter's, but Mathair Anne had held her off at arm's length and looked at her and said,

172

"Why not Barbara Rose? I had once a small sister, *Rôs*. There's a likeness."

So it was Barbara Rose. And by a slurring of speech it became Barbary Rose, and that seemed even better and more like the small, sweet maiden herself.

*   *   *

The winter that followed Felicity was always to remember as an enchanted time, especially in view of all that followed after. Here they were, she and Peter and Barbary Rose, in their stout little stone house, warm and comfortable, with plenty to eat and drink, and time to enjoy each other's presence. What more could one ask?

On New Year's Day in the morning, Felicity's father, grandmother and David came. David appeared first in the doorway to give them the *Beannachad Urlair*, or the threshold blessing for the new year.

> "*Bless the house and all that are in it,*
> *Between stone and turf and beam. . . .*"

David had changed. He was taller. He was also more assured, more easy and adult.

Then the rest came in and, after the greetings, Mrs. Munro turned to David, "Go now to the other house, dark man that you are."

"We're all going there for dinner," said Felicity. Then she laughed. "But of course. It's good luck for the first one to come into the house on New Year's morning to be a dark man."

Lucretia and Angus were down from Cornwall. Sandy

173

Ban was there too. There were twelve of them in all for dinner, including Barbary Rose.

The table was beautiful with Mathair Anne's best dishes and her shining pewter and glass. There was an enormous roasted goose and one of the smoked hams, boiled, then baked, and basted meanwhile with spiced vinegar and maple syrup. There were mountains of potatoes and piles of scones and pats of yellow butter.

Rorie bent his lordly head for grace. His blessings at table were always private affairs, whispered colloquies with the Unseen. It was the only mark of shyness Felicity had ever seen in him. She remembered with a quiver of mirth how Meron had once said,

"I couldn't hear you, Father, when you asked the blessing."

And Rorie's eyes met hers in a full, hard stare. "I wasn't talking to you," he said. Meron had been for quite a while silent.

Mathair Anne's eyes played happily over the table. "I never sit down to a good meal with friends without remembering the hard times we had at first in this country."

"The hungry year!" Sandy Ban paused, his eyes thoughtful, then attacked his food with new vigour.

Anne turned to Lucretia. "We used to watch the cows in the forest to see what plants they ate, and then we dug and cooked them." She was silent for a moment on a bitter memory. Then her brow cleared. "But we all helped each other, and that way we got through."

Late in the afternoon Dougall and David went home, but Allison Munro stayed on for a few weeks' visit and to get better acquainted with her great-grand-daughter.

"I'm thinking, Peter, of a blessing to put on her," she said that evening, standing at the west window, holding the child in the crook of her arm.

"Any blessing of yours!"

"Och, but she deserves a special one." She cupped her hand over the small dark head. "I remember it now," she said, and looked out at the sunset beyond the pines.

> *"Oh, Thou up there, in the name of the Holy Three,*
> *of Michael and his angels,*
> *Put Thou clearness in her head,*
> *Honey-softness in her speech."*

She laid the small bundle in the cradle. "That should take her far, having beauty to begin with."

Barbary Rose lay and blinked solemnly at the ceiling and Peter, her father, stood looking down at her strangely as if she had been given a faery dowry.

*   *   *

Duncan MacFarlane came now to Tulloch Ard by way of business. He was making a year's supply of boots for the family, including a pair of fine, soft high ones for Peter.

Grandmother Munro enjoyed his presence. As did they all. He was full of old tales and songs and his mind had a debonair twist that was his alone. In his youth he had had a fair education and, thought Felicity, he might surely have become something more than a travelling shoemaker.

"Oh, I don't know," said her grandmother. "In the old days he'd have been a *seannachie* man, the one who kept in his mind and passed on the lore of the clan. This life suits him."

One cold afternoon when it was too windy to work in the bush, the men of the family gathered in Felicity's kitchen

175

about the cobbler's bench, and Mistress Munro sat nearby in the low rocker, placidly knitting. Felicity came into the room to hear Rorie say,

"Then you didn't like the minister's sermon?"

"Tush! It was a good sermon. But he made it sound like a hard duty when it was just plain common sense."

"What was it about?" Felicity sat down close to the fire to baste the joint of venison on the spit.

Duncan laid down his awl and lifted one hand and waggled it in the immemorial way of Scottish preachers. "If a man constrain thee to go with him one mile, go with him twain."

"Now that's a tricky text. You have to lay your mind to it. On the face of it it's plain foolishness. But let's see. The Lord lived in the time of the Romans. Short dark-complected men, they were, that overrun Gaul and England, but didn't get past the Highland line, thanks to the good God and to the fact that we were right handy with the claymore.

"Well, suppose it was Gaul. The fellows that lived there were cousins to the Gaels in Scotland and like enough to us, so I was taught in my youth. Now, here come the Roman soldiers, climbing a bit of a brae. Their packs are gey heavy and they're out of wind and short in the temper. It was the custom of the Romans, being cocks of the walk at the time, to press anyone they met into service to carry their packs.

"You can see the picture if you have the wit. Up the hill come the sojers, sweating and cursing. And halfway up and watching them is a tall fellow, a Gaul, blue eyes and black hair and a ragged bit of a kilt, but nobody's ghillie.

" 'Hi,' cry the soldiers, and lay hands on him. Does he

176

kick and swear and try to get away? Tut, he's a lad of parts.

" 'Sure,' says he, 'I'll lift your bit packs.' And he loads them on his broad shoulders, and on they go, the soldiers tump, tump, tump to the drumbeat, and he with his long countryman's stride. Bye and bye he lifts his voice in a bit of a song and then, forbye, he tells them a'yarn or two, and, laughing and joking, the mile is up.

"But will he leave them in the middle of the story of the fiddler and the tailor's wife? He will not.

" 'Sure and I'll go with you two mile,' he says. And on they go, and he'll be whistling now 'The Deil's amang the Heather,' or some such suitable tune for diversion. And they poor sweating Eyetalians, they laugh and sing too. A fair *ceilidh* they have on that long highway.

"Then at the two-mile mark, he downs the packs, and they part friends, so they do. Maybe he fishes in his sporran and drags out a bawbee and says, 'Here, boys, have a drop on me.' Then he walks home in a lordly way, and when he gets near his wee house, out come the wife and the bairns, crying, 'Och, fathair, we saw you going off with the sojers and were feared.'

"And he says, 'Tush, woman, get on with the taties and herrin'.' He sits himself down by the fire, and he's cock of the walk himself now and a good cut above those same soldiers."

"There's another text that has sometimes stuck in my throat," confessed Rorie, stretching his long legs out to the warmth of the fire. "It's the one about turning the other cheek."

"Well?" asked Duncan.

"What would you do if a man smote you on the cheek?"

"I'd do what the Good Book says. I'd turn the other one."
Rorie stared.

"And then?" asked Peter softly.

"Then?" Duncan pressed the awl firmly into the leather. He looked up and his face and voice were quietly happy. "Then with my hands I'd brek him in three halves."

*　　*　　*

It was borne in on Felicity at this time that her grandmother was not so strong as she had been. Once in the night she wakened to hear her stirring, and rose and came into her bedroom and lighted the candle.

"Are you ill, Grandmother?" she whispered.

"I felt a weakness. Then I couldn't get back to sleep."

"I'll stay with you a while."

"You'll be cold."

"I'll slip in by you."

"I've been thinking," Allison went on in a low, remembering voice, "of the time when I was a very small girl and visited my grandmother in Inverness. I slept with her. She used to get a cramping pain in her instep, so she'd rise and rub it on the nap of the carpet, and then come back into bed, and find it hard to get to sleep. 'Say me a psalm, Alsoon,' she'd whisper. She said my name in the old way. So I'd say 'The Lord's my Shepherd,' till I fell asleep or she did."

She herself now drifted softly into slumber, but Felicity lay for a while awake and troubled. In the morning, however, Allison seemed well and strong once more.

One afternoon Felicity walked across the fields to see Katie, leaving Barbary Rose asleep in her cradle and her great-grandmother watching by her.

The small, sturdy log house that had been Mairi Dhu's looked as trim as ever, and Katie greeted her heartily; yet there was a thread of unease in her voice that Felicity could not help but note.

The two girls sat about the fire, each with her knitting. There was a small pile of birch sticks near, and these Katie fed to the fire one by one, and the bark hissed and curled and flared up in crackling sheets of flame. It was a companionable fire.

"You're looking very fine," smiled Felicity.

Katie looked gloomily down at her moss-green frock. Then her mouth quirked into a smile. "I'll tell you about this dress."

She rose and filled the kettle and swung it over the fire and then picked up her knitting again. "You know I have some cousins in Glen Donald. A year or so ago I was there to stay the night. Peggy had a dress that I liked. So I said to her as I would to you, 'Lend me the pattern, will you?' And she said, 'And have you come out in the mate to my dress? Indeed I'll not.'

"So I said nothing, but when we had gone to bed together I lay awake, and there in the moonlight, lying over a chair was her dress. I got up softly and took it and went downstairs. I found a candle and some paper and shears. And standing there in my nightgown and my bare feet I cut a pattern and rolled it up small and came upstairs again and put back the dress and went to bed. She never wakened.

"Then in about a month there was a dance in Glen Donald. I went with Fergus. And I wore the dress. This one.

I met Peggy face to face. She said nothing. Nor did I. She only looked."

Both girls laughed. Then Felicity asked idly, "Where's Fergus today?"

"Oh, out somewhere." A shadow fell across Katie's face and she rose hastily. "I'll make the tea." She kept her face averted as she brought from the cupboard oatcake and a fat pitcher of cream.

"Now pull up your chair," she urged in a loud, firm voice, as if to call back her own composure, then suddenly her head went down on the clean, scrubbed table and her shoulders heaved.

In a minute she lifted her head and looked stormily at Felicity. "What are you thinking is wrong?"

"I've no idea," said Felicity calmly. "Drink your tea and you'll feel better."

"How is Meron?" asked Katie after a while.

"Oh, fine."

"A big, strong girl," muttered Katie moodily. "Stronger than I am."

Felicity shook her head. "I'm not so sure. Meron's so good-natured she's apt to be easy."

"Well." There was a humorous bright hardness now in the hazel eyes. "I'm good-hearted too, but I'm not easy."

"No, indeed," assented Felicity politely.

Katie laughed, then went on more naturally. "It's Fergus. I may as well tell you. We had a terrible big quarrel this morning and he didn't come in to his dinner. I put on my good dress and fixed my hair so I'd look nice, but he never came."

"What made him so angry?"

"He sold the young heifers that were just ready to be milch cows. I'd raised these calves myself. You know how crazy I am about him, Felicity, but he's not a good manager. Well, I am. My aunt taught me to be. But if I even ask about anything he is angry. And sometimes I get angry too."

"Is he drinking?" asked Felicity diffidently.

Katie nodded.

They drank their tea and ate the oatcake in thoughtful silence. Then Katie whispered suddenly, "I'm going out to the barn."

"I'll go with you," offered Felicity.

They made their way along the snowy beaten path to the log barn. At the door they paused and looked at each other, then Katie pulled open the door.

For a moment their sun-used eyes could see nothing. Then, there were the cattle in their stanchions, and the horses. And there in an empty stall, sitting on a milking stool, was Fergus. Red-eyed, sulky, defiant.

Katie cried, "Och, there you are, Fergus. Come away in with us."

He said nothing for a minute. Then, "What's she doing with you?"

"I came on a visit," put in Felicity mildly.

"You did, eh?" he sneered. And rose suddenly and kicked the stool at them.

They turned and went quickly out.

In the house Katie said, "I'm sorry, and I'm ashamed."

"I'm only troubled about you."

"Don't be. I'm not afraid. And I'm not sad any more.

I'm angry." She was, too. She was electric with it from the top of her red head down.

"You never saw my father," she said. "He was a little man and had to try himself to make his way among all these big fellows around here. 'But by ginger,' he used to say, 'I'll manage.' And he did. Though he died young. Well, I'll manage too."

"By ginger," agreed Felicity gravely, "you will."

Again laughter cleared the air, but as Felicity walked up the west slope of the hill towards home she thought, "Fergus and Katie will make up because they love each other in spite of everything, but he will never forgive me for being there today."

*   *   *

The day that Dougall came for Mrs. Munro, Mr. Bethune happened along, and they all sat talking for a while about the table. The minister had but lately made a journey from Montreal to Quebec and back again on Molson's steamboat.

He hitched one thin knee over the other and told them about it. "Remarkable! When I think of the slow, uncertain trips I've made by *bateaux*, or the times I've rowed from Williamstown to Lancaster and on up to Summerstown, Dougall, I marvel at this new age before us."

"What did she look like, sir?"

"The boat? Not a sail to be seen. A big smokestack, and black vapour pouring out. Chugging right along. What next?" He turned thoughtful. "You know, in the span of my life and of yours, Mrs. Munro, we've seen our people move from the days of the clans into this new country where life is travelling so fast and so perilously that no man can see what is ahead."

"Do you mean the threat of war, sir?" asked Peter quietly.

"That's one thing I mean. But not all."

"I look forward to the new day," contended Dougall. "But I should like to carry over into it some of the old ways."

"Such as?"

"Well, for one thing, we had unity in the days of the clans. One blood, one name, one loyalty."

"We helped each other too. I remember from the days when I was small an old woman who lived near and was in want. The neighbours brought food and money by stealth and left it inside her door by night, so that she might not be shamed."

John Bethune sighed. "Now, it's every man for himself. The old friendly days of the clans are gone, for good or ill, both in Scotland and here."

A log in the fireplace fell apart, and they turned to watch as a shower of sparks flew up the chimney. Then Peter spoke slowly, looking into the red glow on the hearth.

"I think there will come a time when there will be a finer and a larger clan than any yet. And it will not be the MacKay nor the MacAlpin, nor the great MacDonell that will be the name of it. It will be Canada. Not just Upper Canada either. Were not the French here first? We'll stand together then. And we'll learn how to look after our old and our poor in a careful and delicate way. We'll feel responsible for each other. That's what makes a clan. Or a country."

There was a kindling look in the old minister's eyes. "God grant you're right, Peter MacAlpin. Though none of us will live to see it."

★

★

CHAPTER

XII

WINTER EDGED once more into spring, and the snow began to
melt, and the March skies were blue and the winds full of
promise. But a new gravity lay over the countryside. The
talk of war that had seemed only an uneasy rumour now
took on a definite seriousness.

Dougall drove over to see Peter and Felicity while the
roads still held. There was about him a certain look of quietness and control that Felicity knew came only with the
facing of trouble.

"Some say that it will blow over," he commented. "And
well it may. Because neither of the countries truly wants war.
Does Britain, fighting for her life with Napoleon? And the
New England States are bitterly opposed to the opening
of hostilities."

Peter stood with his arm along the mantel ledge. He

looked tall and serious. "Nevertheless, I think war will come," he said.

"I can't believe it," cried Felicity. "It's outside our world. It's monstrous."

Her father looked at her with pity in his eyes. "So it always seems in time of peace."

One result of the unsettled state of the country was that Meron was married in March rather than in June as had been planned. Gavin wrote seriously of the threat of war and urged the earlier date.

"Sure, I'll marry him right away," cried Meron. "Something might happen."

In that downright easy spirit the wedding was carried out, with only the family and near neighbours to look on. Nevertheless, it was an exciting occasion, with Meron so tall and vividly beautiful, and Gavin standing pridefully beside her. When their eyes met after the ceremony, it was as if with a challenge to life and all its dangers. Indeed the very air held now the thin threat of war, not yet distressing but sifting over everything a vague, nervous brightness.

The big house seemed empty when Meron had gone. So said Mathair Anne to Felicity when she came over with Barbary Rose to spend an afternoon with her. The baby lay on her stomach on a quilt on the floor and crowed with delight as the small black and white kitten patted a spool across the floor.

"Sure you'll take the kitten home with you," cried Anne. "Spare him? And can we not? Phiseag Dhu had five this time. Yes, as I was saying, a year ago this house was full,

full of laughter and life and men and women. Today it is nearly empty."

"It will fill up again."

"Not with my bairns. Still, as long as they're well. As long as there's no war!"

"War!" echoed Felicity. "I can't believe it will come."

"I hope not. War's a hard thing for women who have men to love. And for the men themselves, God keep them."

Felicity was thoughtful, walking down the hollow and up the hill to her own place, with Barbary Rose under one arm and Tômas the kitten under the other. She laid the baby in the cradle and gave Tômas a saucer of milk on the hearth. Then she went out into the quiet April evening and sat on a bench by the door.

The sky behind the trees was pale yellow, and above in the cool green reaches of the heavens there sailed a sickle moon. From high in that sky came all at once a strange, faint honking. Felicity strained her eyes and saw far up a small dark wedge moving into the north. The wild geese were flying over.

Surely never was anything so lonely as that cry, all but lost in illimitable space. Lonely and relentless and strong, it was—a sound out of the wild heart of this new land. Felicity sat still, listening and following with her mind that cold, high journeying. Here on this April evening she got for the first time the very feel of her country and knew that she belonged passionately to it.

Peter came towards her from the barn. "You'll be cold," he said. And they went into the warm fireside, where Barbary

Rose slept in her cradle and Tòmas sat washing his face with an industrious black paw.

"The militia is being called out," Peter remarked casually.

"No!" whispered Felicity.

"Oh, just as a precaution. Your father will be busy. An old officer."

"You'll be in it?"

"Of course."

"It scares me."

"Don't be scared." He rose and loomed high in the shadowy firelit room. Like a spear he stood, tall and straight, high-shouldered, with square forehead and clustering black hair. He smiled down at Felicity, that arrogant, tender smile of his, and she came and leaned against him. She could feel the tenseness and excitement that he kept out of his voice.

He smoothed her hair. "I think that if war breaks out your grandmother should come here. Right on the water-front, they are."

"I doubt if she'd be willing to leave her home," thought Felicity.

As a matter of fact, she never had to.

David came driving over one day with the horse dark-streaked with sweat. "It's your grandmother. Can you pack a few things and come?"

Felicity went. With Barbary Rose on her knees and fear in her heart.

They found young Dr. Bradbury there from Cornwall. It was a congestion of the lungs, he said, and a fever. How old was she?

When they told him, he stood looking down at her with

190

a discerning look on his fresh, young face; as if he recognized an adversary who held all the cards.

"Keep her warm and comfortable. I'll leave some pills. She looks like a very fine person," he added in awkward, boyish tribute.

*　　*　　*

Allison lay still. Conscious, but with no strength to lift her lids and no desire to do so. She was not uncomfortable. The warmth of the fever made a gentle glow all through her. True, there was a great weight on her chest, but she ignored that, breathing shallowly, just barely breathing at all.

She was herself now. She was not the grandmother, nor the mother, nor the housewife, nor the refugee Loyalist dame. She was not any of them. She was all of them. She was all her selves, interchangeable and run together, now one and now another in the twinkling of an eye.

Scenes and places slid in and out of her mind. She was on the St. Lawrence. The rippling, wide blue water made a coolness all around. Oar locks creaked. Voices called. Her husband was with her, strong and well. They were near the end of their journey, and they were glad. Shining drops of water feathered from the long oars. Water. Someone was holding a glass to her lips. She drank.

She opened her eyes. They were all there. She made an effort and smiled at each of them. Dougall, that dependable, fine man, who was her son-in-law. David, whom she had not long known, but liked well. Kirsty, her handmaiden and friend. And Felicity, her chief joy. Her eyes rested on her as long as they could. Then, on a vagrant memory out of her own childhood, "Say me a psalm, Felicity," she whispered.

191

There was a pause, then in a voice tremulous but steadying, came

> *"That man hath perfect blessedness,*
> *Who walketh not astray. . . ."*

Inwardly Allison smiled to herself, a tender smile. The First Psalm. The only one the child could think of in the stress of the moment. It was a good psalm too. "Perfect blessedness." She had not thought of those words before. She said them over to herself and they unfolded in her mind like a flower. Perfect blessedness. All loveliness. All delight. She folded her hands and her breath came in a great sigh. And did not come again. It was over.

*   *   *

It was a subdued and saddened Felicity who came back home with her baby, and took up her life again. To her loneliness and grief for her grandmother was added the distress caused by the growing expectation of war.

Not long after her return Angus and Lucretia came down from Cornwall, and after supper they all gathered at the big house, and all evening they talked of war. There was nothing else, it seemed, to talk about.

Felicity's eyes moved quickly from one to another as each spoke. From Angus to Rorie, to Duncan, to Lucretia. But Peter and Hughie sat silent, gazing with smooth, expressionless faces into the fire.

Lucretia's knitting needles clicked viciously. "Of course there'll be war," she announced crisply. "And we'll show them. The soldiers of the line will."

"Soldiers of the line," echoed Angus impatiently.

"England is still busy with Napoleon. How many regulars are there in the country?"

"Between four and five thousand, I suppose." Hughie spoke quietly, impersonally.

"So." Lucretia's head came up, as if ready to take charge of the campaign. "Declare war first, I say. Attack!" Her black eyes snapped.

Anne MacAlpin straightened slowly, where she sat on the long settle facing the fire. Her eyes rested smoulderingly on Lucretia, and her rich slow voice, when it came, was smooth with bitterness. "Well said, O Mother of no sons."

There was an uneasy silence. Lucretia tossed her head. "Sons or no, it's good strategy."

Peter slipped along the bench till his shoulder pressed against his mother's. Hughie slid his stool back till he was on her other side, his head against her knee. Each of them leaned against her, comforting her, as she had so often in their childhood comforted them.

Anne sat unmoving, unspeaking. Then tears slipped over the edges of her eyes and ran down her cheeks. No one spoke. Peter and Hughie sat with set faces looking at nothing, but pressing hard against that strong, sweet woman who was their mother, and who was now in grief.

"What of the Glengarries?" came huskily from Rorie.

Angus hitched one knee over the other. "Red George MacDonell is whipping them into shape. The Glengarry Light Infantry Fencibles, they are to be called."

Rorie reared himself up impatiently. "I don't see why they won't take men like me."

"Too old, Rorie, you and me," put in Duncan kindly.

"Thunderation! Me that never turned aside from a tussle all the days of my life."

"Whisht, man. It's the regulations," spoke up Angus, the old soldier.

That night Peter said to Felicity, "I am now in the militia like the rest. But you must know that I may feel it my duty to join the Glengarries."

"I know," she answered stiff-lipped.

In July came the news that the United States had declared war.

That afternoon Hughie came up through the rowan grove and sat with Felicity on the steps. "I wanted to tell you," he said, "that I'm joining the Glengarries."

She looked at him. "Why?" she whispered passionately.

He shrugged. "It's in the blood, I suppose. The war-pipes shrill and the young men march. No, it's more than that, really. Someone has to do the fighting, and it is as if a hand was laid on my shoulder." He laughed softly. "A queer feeling. But an uplifted one."

"There's something else on my mind," he went on seriously. "I expect to marry Tassie before I go. Her mother is dead and her father has taken another wife. I'd like to know she was safe with Mother if anything happened to me. And with you for her friend. Will you be that?"

"I will, Hughie. All my life, I'll be her friend."

He looked at her for a moment with that heartbreaking bright smile of his; then he was away home.

The next day some squaws from the reserve at St. Regis came selling baskets. Felicity sat on the porch with them, listening to their soft musical voices and examining their wares. There was a work basket, dyed with bloodroot, garnished with twisted rolls of sweet grass. The perfume of the sweet grass reminded her of Mathair Anne, who kept her towels fragrant with sweet-mary. "I'll buy it for her," she decided.

She took it down to her at once. But when she opened the door there was trouble in the air. They were all standing. David was there. Mathair Anne's face was white.

"You too, David," she cried wildly.

"Mathair, what else could I do?"

"I know, I know, David *Og*." She swept him close with one arm, and tears and laughter were in her voice. "I knew all the time. Because it's men I've mothered, so I have. But whiles I'd rather them cowards, and they safe."

"You don't mean it."

"No. I don't. When do you go, long lad?"

"Two weeks I have at home."

"Good. Then we'll have a fine time together, so we will."

*　　　*　　　*

Strangely enough, the house seemed full again. Full of vitality and men's voices and laughter. And if there was a thread of tears in the laughter, what then? The word went around that Hughie and Davie were for going with the Glengarries. Not just militia, but soldiers of the line.

So the friends foregathered, and there was dancing and fiddling and the singing of songs. Never had this warm neighbourly companionship seemed so good, never the laughter so free, or the stories so rich in humour. Because underneath it all lay a poignancy and an awareness. In his heart each cried, "Shall we ever again see them just so? Will

195

Hughie do the sword dance for us again, or Davie finger the chanter so knowingly? Where shall we all be next year?"

It seemed that in this brief, bright interlude time was fore-shortened. Living had to be speedily done. So thought Hughie. Early in the allotted two weeks he brought Tassie home, a wide-eyed, bewildered child wife, in a daze of happiness and dread. Mathair Anne took her warmly to her heart, and Felicity remembered her promise to Hugh. And all of them contrived to give them as much time together as they could. Which wasn't much at best.

For irrevocably the weeks passed. Soon came the day when Hughie and David left. Two slender lads, one dark, one fair, walking smartly down the hill and along the river road. They watched them from the house at Tulloch Ard as long as they could see them, then turned aside, avoiding each other's eyes.

CHAPTER

XIII

ALONG THE RAIL FENCE to the east of the big house at Tulloch Ard, hops grew on sprawling vines, and one afternoon Anne and Felicity went out to pick them. It was an easy task. Felicity squeezed some of the hops in her hand. So light they were they were like nothing at all; yet they had a soft rustliness that was pleasant to the palm. Their colour was curious, too, a metallic yellow-green that seemed to glow a little. The scent was acrid, yet strangely agreeable. Surely no other blossoms were quite like this.

"Useful, too," agreed Anne. "What would we do for yeast without them? Here's Tassie."

She came through the garden towards them. She wore a short linsey dress, and her hair was tied back from her face. She had a serviceable, square-built little body, and she placed her weight firmly on her feet as she walked.

"Where have you been?" asked Anne, but comfortably,

with no hint of blame for inactivity in a busy household.

"I've been lying in the mow on the hay. Then I got up and gathered the eggs."

The three of them picked silently. The soft rustling hops fell into the baskets with no sound at all, and scarcely any weight. It was warm. Felicity felt her brow damp.

Tassie laid down her basket and sat on a low rail of the fence and looked out dreamily over the summery landscape. "You know," she said, "I think Hughie'll come home soon."

Anne looked at her sharply. "Why?"

"I have a feeling," simply. "I had it in the barn. And again now."

Anne laughed shakily and went on picking.

Tassie smiled at them both, that confiding smile of hers that was so young and yet somehow so old. "It might be today," she cried, her voice rising joyously. "I think I'll gather some flowers."

She ran towards the garden. They could see her sitting on the ground before the pink rose bush.

"She'll take the buds," said Anne uneasily, then laughed. "As if I should care about buds."

Soon after that news came of the taking of Detroit by Brock. With him had been his aide-de-camp, Lieut.-Colonel John MacDonell, young attorney-general of the province, and a near cousin of Katie's. Much-needed arms and ammunition had been captured, and Brock went back to Niagara full of plans to clear the frontier. Then came the proclamation by Governor Prevost of an armistice. The Orders-in-Council had been repealed by England before the declaration of war, but the news had not got through in time. Now, surely, the chief cause of war had been removed. Felicity's hopes for peace flared high.

But Peter shook his head. "I've seen dogs fight over a bone and, the bone lost, go on fighting. An armistice will keep Brock from following up his advantage. Still, it may mean peace," he added, smiling at her. But she knew he was only being kind.

Before Peter left for his term of training with the militia, he told Felicity what he could of the management of the farm. Together they looked over the establishment—the small stone house and the log barn, the stacks of hay, the sheep on the slope of the hill, the herd of red and white cattle, and the round-bodied little French-Canadian mare, Pegi, that Dougall MacKay brought over to be now Felicity's.

"How are you with a gun?" asked Peter, and handed her his musket.

She aimed at a knot in the bole of a pine tree and sometimes she hit it, and sometimes she did not.

"All you need is practice," said Peter, and took the musket. A flutter of wood pigeons lighted in the top of an ash tree. "Pot-pie?" he grinned, and a pigeon fell to the ground. He held it up, its bright iridescent breast all agleam. Plump it was after a summer's feeding, and it would make a fine supper against Peter's leaving in the morning for Cornwall.

It's not as if he were with the Fencibles, Felicity told herself. Nevertheless, she felt a weight at her heart as she prepared the small feast with her best dishes and the fine pieces of silver her grandmother had set aside for her. And a precious, quiet evening they had together, with Barbary

Rose asleep in the cradle and they sitting close and silent on the settle, holding their happiness between them.

When the grayness of the gloaming crept in around them Felicity stirred on a sudden thought, "Go now, and say good night to your mother."

"Will you come too?"

She shook her head. "Just you tonight."

So he went, and was soon back, and inexorably morning came and he was away. She cleaned the whole house with great vigour and diligence, lest, if she paused, loneliness should sweep down on her. Which it inevitably would, she knew, but she would fight against it as long as she could.

Peter in Cornwall that afternoon, drilling with his comrades of the flank companies of the First Regiment of Glengarry Militia, thought of Felicity and Barbary Rose and felt that somehow his life was already detached from them, though they were of all the world the most dear to him.

All about was a motley crew of militiamen awkwardly forming fours and with difficulty adjusting their long stride to a military quick-step. Some were in kilts of their ancestral tartans, others in homespun trews. No one yet had uniforms. They drilled under Captain MacMillan, but Major MacDonell, "Red George" himself, was in town.

"Is he not with his Fencibles?" asked Peter of a comrade, as they lounged on the grass in a rest period.

"No. They gave that post to Bayne. But he is officer in command of the St. Lawrence frontier. Here he comes."

They leaped to their feet as the major stalked onto the parade ground. Peter looked curiously at him. A fine, tense, red-headed fellow he was, straight-forward and uncompromising, but with a humorous twist to his mouth. He stood slapping his thigh with his sword and looking them over.

"We're about to have visitors," he announced without preamble. "So you'll need to smarten up. At ease now."

Hurriedly fingers were combed through unruly hair. Kilts were tightened at the waist and bonnets set firmly. On the order they snapped to attention. Every man held himself taut and steady.

A grim smile played over Red George's face. "There's a lot of pride in a Highlander," he said; then, "It's General Brock himself, and his aide, Lieut.-Colonel MacDonell, who is—as you know—one of our own, and his father, Greenfield, well known to you. When they come, raise a cheer."

"Aye, so, sir!" they answered in a companionable way.

Red George smiled again. "And don't be too familiar with me before the General. He's a good man, but a Sassenach, and doesn't know we're all clansmen here and brothers."

They smiled back at him with warmth and shyness in their eyes.

"For him a man would go anywhere," thought Peter.

Then the major's sword flashed up and they stiffened. First came a great white war horse. His feet pounded the earth; his mane tossed proudly. He had need to be strong. A large man bestrode him. A big, tall, kindly, inexorable man, red-coated, with fine cocked hat, blue-white breeches, and high shining boots. The General. A great cheer rose to greet him. And not only him. For with him rode one of Glengarry, John MacDonell, a slender young man with friendly brown eyes and sensitive nostrils.

"Horo, horo!" they yelled for the General, but a spate of Gaelic greeted young MacDonell.

Then Brock spoke to them. Spoke reasonably, steadily, explaining the situation and enlisting their co-operation. He spoke of the lack of uniforms and the lack of sufficient arms. "Get yourselves short, stout jackets that button well about the waist, and round felt hats that set firm on the head. Soon you'll have uniforms. And very soon you'll have arms. We got some at Detroit."

He smiled at their cheers. "You of Glengarry and Stormont are the sheet anchor of this eastern district. I depend on you."

Then he saluted and wheeled, and the great white horse pounded the hard ground of the drill yard, and MacDonell's brown charger fell in after him, and they were away.

Later in the day Peter was called in to see Major MacDonell.

Red George looked at him contemplatively. "Abercalder told me about you. And some of your Nor'-Wester friends as well. A clerk, eh?"

"I was, sir."

"You went down that big river with Simon Fraser?"

"Aye, sir."

"A trained man. And used to handling other men. We could do with you in the Glengarries. You see, the Glengarry Light Infantry Fencibles, to give them their grand long name, are going to be a very useful unit in this war. Regulars, but free and easy too, able to cope with those Kentucky Rangers they'll send against us. Natural fighting men. But a little short of officers just now. Are you married?"

"I am."

"Children?"

"One."

"Humph! Well, I'll leave it to you. If you want to transfer to the Light Infantry I'll put your commission through."

Peter looked steadily at the crack in the floor, then raised his eyes. "Sir," he said. "I have before me two weeks' training with the flank companies. Give me then a fortnight more to batten up my place for the winter and to make it as easy for my wife as I can; then I'm ready."

"Good man." Red George's hand came down hard on his shoulder. "I'll be seeing you then, many times and many places."

*   *   *

Tassie had been right about Hughie's coming. For, one day, he and David came walking up the hill just as their mother had so often seen them in her dreams. Grand they looked, too, in their scarlet coats and long-strapped trousers, but not really like themselves. So, in an hour they were back in their old clothes, Hughie in his green kilt and loose, linen shirt, which seemed his own rightful garb, and David in his homespun trews.

"So you're coming too?" Hughie smiled quizzically at Peter. "Well, it's a hard life and there are too many regulations, but it has its points."

"And the food?" asked Mathair Anne, laying out the cold meat. "Draw in now, boys. It's yet an hour to dinner."

"The food is not like this," grinned David. "But it does."

"A pound and a half of flour, ten and a half ounces of

205

salt pork, one half-gill of rum, per man, per day. Field rations!" supplemented Hughie crisply, and looked at the butter melting into his scone.

David smiled up at his mother. "Will you make curly-cakes?"

She laid her hand on his smooth, dark head. "And will I not?" she said deeply, and went quickly into the other room.

"I'll kill the small pig," cried Rorie, rising suddenly.

Hughie laughed. "Let it live. We'll not be long home."

He rose. He was thinner. So was David. But they were hard and well.

Hughie stretched himself out on the long settle. "Sit by me, Tassie," he said. She sat on a low stool and pressed her face against his outflung arm.

"We're all here," said Hughie suddenly. "Except Evan. In the far west where he is, maybe he doesn't even know there is a war. However, we have Tassie and Felicity to make up for him." He rumpled Tassie's hair. "Happy?" he asked, and she nodded speechlessly. "Are you?" he insisted, teasing her. Then she laughed, a low little laugh, so soft, so happy, so intimate that the rest flushed a little, listening.

Thought Felicity, "For one who speaks so seldom, she says a lot, even when she doesn't speak at all."

*   *   *

Not long after David and Hughie had left, Dougall MacKay came riding over. He was on brief leave from his duties as an officer in the militia, and knew of Peter's transfer.

He brought them chequered news from the Niagara frontier. The family gathered in Felicity's pleasant, pine-panelled room and they listened to his story of Queenston

Heights. He had a copy of the Gazette with him, to which he referred for corroboration of details. It had been a victory, but one plucked out of defeat, and too dear at that in the lives it took. Brock and MacDonell.

"The enemy had the height. Brock and his York Volunteers charged up the hill. 'Come on, boys!' he called, and he at the head of them. He was a big man, as you know. His scarlet coat, too. He was a perfect mark. An Ohio scout stepped out from behind a thorn tree, took aim and fired. Brock fell, a bullet through his breast. He whispered, 'This must not be noticed,' and died. It was half-past seven in the morning.

"His men fell back then to the far end of the village. Two hours later MacDonell rallied them. Dennis and Williams brought up their men too. 'Revenge the general,' they cried.

"Then MacDonell's horse was shot, and he himself wounded and thrown and trampled. 'Help me, Archie,' he called to young MacLean, who had been at school with him in Cornwall. They carried him from the field. He suffered a lot, poor fellow. Later, they took the hill."

There was a knock at the door; then it was flung open. Katie stood there. She looked at them all, then sank into the chair Peter placed for her.

"Then you've heard," she said. "I can see by your faces." She flung her apron over her head. "*Ochone a rie,*" she wailed. Then she wiped her tears. "You've heard how brave he died?"

"We've heard, Katie, and well may you be proud of your cousin," said Anne in her deep voice.

"But he suffered so," Katie went on pitifully. "Fergus

heard of it in Cornwall. Two feather beds the blood came through. And grieving to the last for the General."

"You'll want to read what is said of him in the Gazette." Dougall handed her the paper.

With her finger she traced the lines. She looked up. "*That brave and affectionate young man.* That's right. He was engaged to be married too."

"So was General Brock."

"When they buried them," went on Dougall, "and the minute guns boomed out, shot for shot was fired by the American commander at Fort Niagara. As a mark of respect."

Tears came into Felicity's eyes.

Anne frowned into the fire. "War is a black and senseless thing."

"Yet," put in Dougall, "never does the spirit of man burn brighter than in that blackness."

"Maybe so, but it's still senseless," came surprisingly from Rorie. "Now, in the old days, as I understand it, war was a simple thing. A clan rose against its enemy and there was a tussle, and a cracked head or two, and a few lads left cold in the heather. But they were men who were at odds with you, who wanted what you had, or the other way round. But in these modern wars a man fights those he has not seen, nor have they done him any wrong. It's not natural."

His fist came down on the arm of the chair. "Now if I cleave a man with my whinger, or pick him with my *skiandhu,* I want to say to him, 'You're a dom MacIlliskillen, so you are, and a red fox like your father before you.' Then a man has some pleasure in it. But shooting a bit bullet into a man who's done naught to deserve it but come at his country's call goes against my gorge. Much as I'd like to be in it."

For the first time Tassie spoke. She had listened wide-eyed to them all. Now she raised a great, bubbling sigh of relief and rose. "Anyway, Hughie wasn't there," she said, and walked towards the door.

Anne looked after her, shocked. But Felicity thought, "She meant it. She might as well say it. As for me, as long as Peter is safe, and my father, and Hughie and David, I can stand the rest, so selfish am I."

That evening after the others had gone, Felicity went out, as she so often did, into the rowan grove and stood beneath the bright, burdened trees. Without, dusk was falling. Within the grove, day was still imprisoned. The fading light fell through a screen of crimson fruit and yellow leaves. But tonight the beauty and splendour had no joy in it. There was instead a tautness, a rigour, as of pain pridefully and silently borne.

For Felicity, the coming separation from Peter and the knowledge of the danger into which he must go was like an actual physical pain. She came out from the rowan grove and sat on the doorstep and felt the weight of it at her heart. Night was closing in. Winds began to rustle the tree tops. Birds called sleepily. Then a new sound came eerily up over the shoulder of the hill. It was a lament played on the pipes. Softly, insistently, the notes slid one into another, floating out on the evening air in little whirls of sound, or soaring in long, lonely arcs of melody. There was sadness in it, but there was gentleness, too, and healing.

Listening, Felicity felt as if all her vague thoughts, her fears and yearnings, had slipped into place and made now a clarity and a strength in her heart. And a measure of peace.

Rorie had taken down his pipes and said to Anne, "I'm thinking of that red-headed slip of a Katie grieving for her cousin. I'll play a lament, so I will, for John MacDonell of the family of Greenfield, dead now at Niagara. And it will comfort Katie, his kinswoman."

So he sat by the door in the cool of the evening and played.

And Katie, listening, said, "Will you hear that now, Fergus? It's Rorie himself, kind man that he is. I wish you felt friendlier towards the MacAlpins."

Fergus listened, and shook his head.

CHAPTER

XIV

SHORTLY AFTER Peter had gone, Dougall came again to see his daughter and his small grand-daughter. He lingered all day, and in the course of the afternoon he asked to see Felicity's paintings.

"Any new ones?"

"Not many," she admitted ruefully.

But she got them all out. Those of the rowan grove. Floral studies—wild roses, a fuchsia plant with pendant red and purple bubbles of bloom. An unfinished portrait of Mathair Anne.

"It's going to be a *dreich* winter for you. You'd better turn seriously to your painting. It will pass the time."

"It seems unimportant now. With the war and all."

"Think of it as something to show Peter when he gets back."

Her eyes lighted at that and he looked keenly at her. "Tell me, have you any regrets?"

She met his gaze honestly. "Not a one. Sometimes I've wondered what it would have been like if I had married Gavin, but the idea seems so unreal, and this life so real, that I can't even think about it."

They came in to the fireside again. Barbary Rose sat in a pool of sunshine on the floor. When she saw her grandfather she rose and made her way unsteadily to him. He set her cosily on his knee and fished in his pocket for a lozenge.

"I'm glad you're happy and comfortable here, and at least a few miles back from the waterfront. Raiding will be common enough now, I'm afraid. Besides, I'm ordered further west. With the Canadian Fencibles."

"No!" she breathed.

He nodded. "You'll be all right? Not too lonely?"

"I'll be all right. But I'll miss you. Will you take care of yourself? Even a little?"

"That's quite a bit to ask of a soldier," he smiled. "However, during the winter months there's not much doing."

"Do you think the war will be over soon?"

"Not for a while. We've done not too badly on land. Though not so well on water. The Americans have built some good ships. At first the Royal Navy couldn't believe it. They do now."

*   *   *

When her father had gone, Felicity's life took on an unreal and dreamlike quality. Her household tasks she performed, hardly knowing that she did them. Every evening Rorie came and saw that she had a good fire that would last

214

the night, and that everything was snug at the barn. Then Felicity would carry the baby upstairs with her and tuck her in between herself and the wall. If Barbary missed her cradle she was philosophic about it, and her small, warm presence comforted Felicity as she lay in the darkness.

All over the country, she thought, there were women like her, and on the other side of the St. Lawrence too. Women whose men were away at the war. A dreary sisterhood.

She had work to do, fortunately. She kept her house meticulously clean. She worked at the small wheel and the air was full of the sound of her spinning. She wound the yarn on the clicking reel, and then she knit it into good warm socks for Peter. Never would his feet be cold if she could help it.

It was winter now. Every morning Felicity looked out on a world that was white and silent, the pines snow-laden and the rowans stiff and brittle with frost. Sometimes at night the wind whined about the eaves, and the pine trees began to breathe loud in their sleep, and then to murmur deeply, and then, when the wind took hold, their great branches rolled and twisted and the sound was a heavy booming like a surf at sea.

Felicity, lying flat on her back in bed, gave herself over to such a storm. It exhilarated her. The vigour and violence of it released the tensions within her. This was not that of which she was afraid. It was the long, still days that daunted her.

One bright, windy morning after a night of storm, she took out an oblong canvas and set it up on her easel.

Paint for Peter, her father had said. How, really, did

Peter value her painting? Only as it pleased her, and because it was another proof that she was rare and fine and clever. If she painted for Peter it would be to make him feel that still more. But for whom else, if not for Peter?

She would paint for herself. She would show this picture to no one. Only she would understand it. She would paint the hidden things in her mind for her own good.

Here she was, Felicity MacAlpin, born Felicity MacKay. What was behind this present life of hers? As well as she could, she projected herself into the past. Her grandmother was a link. Back as far as the sad year of Culloden she could see, when her grandmother had been a child and when that brother of hers had been done to death one sunny summer's day, rather than betray his Prince. There, Felicity felt, she in some subtle way belonged. With young Finlay whom she was like, as she had so often been told. The same smile, the same smooth quick walk, the same indefinable something that made a personality.

"Finlay!" her thoughts reached out. "Young Finlay Dhu, dead more than fifty years ago, yet part of me. You, I will paint. And how? When the soldiers caught you in the glen of white birches, and beat you, and you wouldn't tell? No. But as you came across the heather, your back to the sunset, climbing the hillside with your wounded father slung over your strong, young back. You for my past, young Finlay."

And what of the present?

Barbary Rose was awake now. Felicity gave her her breakfast of milk and oatmeal porridge dusted over with maple sugar. Then she washed the few dishes, and tidied the hearth, her mind all the time tense with thought.

What of Felicity MacAlpin in this bleak year of 1813? Where was the focus of her thoughts? Her house? Her baby? All of a sudden she knew. She saw another hill, and Peter climbing it. And with him were Hughie and David. They were in the habiliments of war, and death was on the slope of the hill. But they climbed strongly, bayonets set for the charge. David on one side, Hughie on the other, and Peter between.

With all the skill she had, and with all her heart behind it, she would paint Peter. His tall straightness, his square shoulders, his fine colourless high-cheek-boned face that could be laughing or tender or sombre. Peter, the very centre and core of her life. And beside him, David, slim and dark and shy, and Hugh, fair and lightsome and more beautiful than a man should be. Three brothers. Here, in this year of war, was the reality of the present life of Felicity MacAlpin.

And her future? Now that surely was a thought. She looked at Barbary Rose singing a small, unintelligible song to herself as she lay and kicked her bare legs in the warmth of the fire. Barbary Rose was part of her future.

She remembered her grandmother telling of her own grandmother in far-away Inverness, who used to say to her, "Say me a psalm, Alsoon," when she couldn't sleep at night. Had that great-great-grandmother of hers looked into the future and wondered about those who would come after? Well, she, Felicity, would look. Over a few half centuries and a quarter-century or so, and she would paint what she saw. But what would she see?

She laughed a little at herself. "I'm fey," she thought.

"I'm light-headed from being much alone." Still her mind clung to the idea.

The first two parts of the picture dealt with war. So would the third. But what would war be like in nineteen hundred and something? Would it be a matter of cannon and muskets, bayonets and swords? Strange and terrible weapons might by then be forged. They might push through water with great speed, like Molson's steamboat. They might even fly the sky. She laughed again at the foolishness of her fancy.

"Nevertheless," she thought, "if there is war, there will be men to fight it, and you—Oh, sons of my sons of my sons —will be in it. One of you may well breast a steep hill and climb valiantly against odds."

Then this would be her picture. At one side, young Finlay carrying his father up the heathery slope of Glen Morriston. In the centre, Peter, Hughie and David, mounting a hill of battle. And on the right, the young eager figure of a soldier of the future, shouldering gallantly into perils unknown.

That familiar inner excitement took hold of her, but no sense of hurry. She pondered long over every detail. Rules of painting, of balance, or composition, she cast aside when it suited her. This was for herself, for the clarification of her own thought. She was painting the pity of war and the waste of it, and the spirit of man shining through it. She was thinking on canvas.

She worked in secret. When Tassie or Anne came over to sit with her for an afternoon, or when Rorie paid his nightly visit, the picture was carefully covered and laid away in the big cupboard. Only so could she work unselfconsciously

218

and as she wished. She painted slowly. She had all this winter. This winter when she was reasonably sure Peter and the rest would not be in danger. Later her anxiety would hold her in a vise and prevent her.

She sketched in the three central figures as they bent to climb.

It would have surprised her, that bright February morning, had she known that even as she worked at her easel, Peter was climbing a steep and snowy and bullet-raked hill.

He had been with his company in barracks at Fort Wellington. Across from them was Ogdensburg, and the frozen river was between. The soldiers used to drill on the ice.

Brockville, nearby, had been raided by the Americans, and Major MacDonell had been sent across to remonstrate with the commander at Ogdensburg. Forsyth laughed at him. "Some time I'd like to meet you on the river," he said.

"Any day," Red George flung at him carelessly. All the way back his eyes were grim and his wrath smouldered.

It happened that in two days MacDonell was himself in command, and by seven o'clock of the next morning he was ready.

Nearly five hundred men started out across the river in two long columns, well spread out so as not to put too much strain on the ice. Two-thirds of the party were of Glengarry, either regulars or militia. One column under Major Mac-Donell himself was directed against the town of Ogdensburg. The other was thrown against the old fort on the upper side of the Oswegatchie on the enemy's left.

It was a long way across, a mile and a half, and the ice was not good. It undulated and cracked. Peter walked light-

219

ly, his blood coursing freely, his muscles fluid. His body was ready, a weapon forged for danger, like his bayonet. But his mind ranged free.

He remembered his minister whom he had seen but a few minutes before. John Bethune had grasped his hand in his own thin sinewy one, and there was gentleness and blessing in his dark eyes. Then his voice came hard and poured strength into him. "The power of God go with you, Peter MacAlpin, and bring you safe home." Nearby a fair lad knelt in the snow, while his priest laid his hand on his bared head to bless him. He looked a little like Hughie. It was a relief to Peter that his two brothers belonged to another company of the regiment.

He thought of Felicity and Barbary Rose with a tremor of tenderness at his heart. Then he put them resolutely out of his mind.

"Odd they let us get so far," said the man nearest him. It was the fair-haired boy who had knelt in the snow.

"Maybe they think it's manœuvres."

A ball whined across their path and crashed into the ice.

The boy laughed shortly. "Now they know."

The guns held the range fairly. Cannon balls smashed into the head of the column that wound warily across the lake like a long serpent. A serpent that writhed and broke as men fell in their tracks amid red patches widening in the snow.

The captain swung his sword and called out to his troops. He pointed to MacDonell's column now struggling up the bank. The men answered with a cheer and pressed on.

Grapeshot smashed the captain's left arm. He held it to him with the other.

They were like rabbits in an open field. Another ball got the captain in the right arm. It whirled him about and he went down. He was up again, but he plunged crazily through the snow and fell. Peter took command.

They were now in the lee of the shore. They stumbled through snow to their hips and over piled-up ice. Grapeshot and canister ploughed through their ranks. They mounted the ridge of the bank. Bayonets at the ready, they took the fort. Soon there were none of the enemy left but the wounded and prisoners. MacDonell joined them. His gray eyes were blazing with excitement. He smote Peter on the chest.

"Is this better than shooting the rapids on the Fraser?"

"Much the same, sir, as far as danger goes."

All this Peter told Felicity when he got leave in March. She sighed. "And I had thought you safe."

"Of course," he explained, "it wasn't like a real battle. It was more of a raid. About an hour's fighting in all. But it cleared our line of communication, and it will mean peace for a while along the river."

They had talked late. The fire glowed ruddily on the hearth. Felicity felt the heat of it in her hair. She shook it loose and it fell on her neck in tumbled curls. Peter buried his face in it, and parted it and kissed the white nape of her neck. Felicity felt heavy with happiness, drugged and drowsy with it. Surely the long loneliness would soon be over.

The days of his leave passed inexorably. Before Peter left he got her a dog for company and for protection. He was a shaggy, big, half-grown fellow, part mastiff and part

Newfoundland. Patrig Dhu they called him.

Peter was still uneasy. "It's hard to tell how close the war may come. Would you be better in the big house?"

"Not unless there's actual danger."

"Well, suppose there is danger. Could you use the musket if you needed to. Or even the dirk?"

She turned to him with a full, steady look in her blue eyes. She took his *skian-dhu* from the mantel shelf.

"If I had a brother you wouldn't ask him that," she said softly. She weighed the dirk in her palm and fitted her fingers close about the handle. "To protect the baby, or the place, or myself, I'd do my best."

He laughed. "*Dhia!* I believe you. You, who couldn't see me kill a chicken."

"This is different," she told him composedly. "The musket will be loaded, the *skian-dhu* will be handy, and Patrig Dhu will be on guard. Till you come. So you're not to be troubled about us."

Later in the night she said, "Peter, is it very dreadful in a battle?"

"In a way. But you're not alone. You're with men who are like brothers to you. And you're excited. You're out of yourself, yet thinking with all your might. There's a white-hot feeling all through you."

Felicity lay and thought. Then after Peter had left she went back to her painting. She tried to put into it that ecstasy, that absorption. To show Peter in battle, a face dead-white and blue eyes blazing and an ardent, headlong body. Then she flung her brushes down and sat on the floor before

222

the easel and wept. What was a painting, instead of Peter himself, whom she loved?

After a while she dried her tears and took up her brush again. David's face she had so far left untouched. Now when she came to paint it in, she found it very clear in her mind and full of meaning. This was David *Og*, the bairn of the family. Young and without guile. He stood for a great company of those like him. Those in all times who have been willing to lay down their lives in simplicity and devotion. The young, the brave and the innocent, who have offered themselves for a cause or a truth or a king or a country.

"God keep him safe," she prayed fervently. "And all of them."

CHAPTER

XV

EARLY IN JUNE Peter was in Montreal. He had come down from Kingston with despatches, and would soon be on his way back again with no time at all for even a quick trip to Glengarry. But he did have time to see Meron. So he made his way along the street that edged the first lift of the mountain, towards the house of Gavin Scott and Meron.

Just as he came near, a *calèche* clattered out of the drive-way. A middle-aged countryman slouched in the seat and plied a rawhide whip over the bony haunches of a roan mare. The countryman, whiskered and unkempt, puffed steadily on a short corncob pipe and peered vaguely at Peter as he passed.

Meron came quickly into the panelled front hall. She took his hands in hers and said, "Peter, Peter," in a shaken voice.

He bent and kissed her heartily. She was pale and her

eyes dark-shadowed. He looked at her with concern as she led him into the large and pleasant drawing-room.

A breeze stirred the looped damask curtains, and the air was sweet with white and yellow roses. It was a beautiful room, Peter noted in a brief glance, full of the satiny shimmer of polished wood and the richness of deep-piled carpets and the grace of delicate gilded brocade-covered chairs. It came swiftly into his mind that Felicity would look well in this room, and he felt a momentary queer compunction that he had prevented her presence here. But no regrets, he decided with a sudden imperious pride in himself, and with a sudden stab of longing for her.

"Where is Gavin?" he asked Meron.

She looked at him for a moment before she answered. "He has gone away. For a time."

"The militia?"

She shook her head. "No. On business. How are they all at Tulloch Ard?"

"I've not been there since March. They were well then."

"Barbary Rose?"

"Growing."

"Mathair?"

"Tired. I wish you could go up there for a little while, Meron. It's this month for Felicity and Tassie. You'd do them all good. I knew I had only to tell you."

Meron sat looking down at her hands in her lap. They were white hands now, and bright with jewels. Her gown was of fine silk, black with a deep blue satin stripe, and her hair was modishly coiffed. She looked like a great lady. She did not look like the Meron of old. Till she raised her eyes. They were honest eyes and full of tears.

"Peter," she said. I can't go."

He stared at her incredulously.

"I mean it, Peter."

"Why?"

"I can't tell you."

Wonder flickered in his eyes, then anger.

"Peter," she cried entreatingly. "Believe me when I tell you I'd go if I could."

He looked at her straightly. "I believe you, Meron," he said finally. "Can I help you?"

She shook her head. "Come and see the garden."

She took him out to the green and flowery lawns at the back of the house. A slim greyhound rose and licked her hand delicately. A peacock strutted and bent to peer at himself in a sunken pool. They sat on a bench beneath a drooping willow.

"How is Charlotte?" asked Peter.

"Didn't you hear?" Laughter bubbled through her words, and she was for a moment the old Meron. "I wrote to Tulloch Ard about it. She's married. To a French artist from the old land, a friend of M. Barbin. He's devoted to her and she's as happy as a lark. Really, it does you good to go there."

"Happy, is she? And you, Meron?" he asked bluntly.

She flushed. "As happy as anyone can be in wartime. How are Hughie and David?"

"They're with me now."

"And you're a lieutenant! How grand!"

He shrugged. "It's because of my years with the Nor-Westers."

"Were you at York when it fell?"

"No. But I was at Fort George and at Sackett's Harbour."

"That was a defeat too."

"It shouldn't have been. Prevost drew us off to the boats in the very nick of victory."

"What's the matter with the man? A coward?"

"Not personally. But as a commander, timid."

"It looks bad, doesn't it?"

"Aye. Bad. York burned. Fort George taken. But we turned them at Stoney Creek. That's one bright spot."

"Where next?"

"Probably they'll converge on Montreal. Fools if they don't." He looked at her with concern. "Are you safe here? With Gavin away? Your servants, can you trust them? I saw a queer character in a *calèche* coming out of the gate."

She looked down at her hands. "A peddler," she told him serenely. "Pins, needles, crimping irons, combs, awls, tacks, powder horns, condiments, thimbles and ink. All in a big box in the back of the *calèche*."

He laughed. "You'd think you'd memorized it." He rose and bent to kiss her good-bye.

She slipped her arm in his. "Do you know what just came into my mind? One day, when I was seven and you were thirteen or so, and we picked potatoes on the west side of the hill of an October morning. I was in my bare feet and the ground was soft and dry under them. A warm windy fall day, clouds sailing and the trees red. Peaceful, wasn't it? And now far away."

She rubbed her cheek against his shoulder. "Take care of yourself, Peter."

"I'll do that," he promised, his voice warm with affection. But when he was out on the dusty highway his brow creased.

"It's Gavin," he concluded. "On a business trip, and his country at war." His sword slapped against his thigh and his blood ran hot. No longer did he regret the fine house for Felicity, nor anything else.

When he came to the Recollet gate, a sound cut through the confused clatter of the city streets. Voices singing, full-throated and rollicking. It was a band of militia swinging down McGill Street. They wore *capots* and trousers of home-spun, and bright blue tuques. Muskets swung at their sides. They were easy, confident, full of high spirits.

Peter kept pace with them. Then he saw Jacques. Sure it was Jacques. Had he not sat in the same canoe with him over a couple of thousand miles of waterway? At the barracks the troops broke and Peter found his man.

"*Mon dieu.*" Jacques' eyes travelled admiringly up the bright uniform. "I had forgot you were so tall."

"Did you find Julie Rose?" asked Peter presently, their elbows on a tavern counter.

"Julie Rose? We-ell, no. But anoder one. Juliette. Now, *un bébé.*"

"Only one?"

"*Misère*, give me time. Now tell me, M'sieu Peter, how goes the war to the west?"

Peter told him. Jacques listened attentively. "Pretty soon we go to Kingston. Will you be there?"

231

"No. I hear I'm now for the Niagara country. But we'll meet again, I've no doubt. Before this is over."

* * *

In that same month of June two sons were born to the house of Tulloch Ard. Tassie's young Ian arrived first, a dark and lusty mite of manhood, and just a week later was born Felicity's blond and blue-eyed bairn.

"Boys in wartime. Strange that it is so. But it is," said Anne.

She had a busy time with two mothers and three children to care for, but soon Felicity and Tassie were up and about, and the babies could not have been better. While Barbary Rose hovered over the two small cradles and adored each impartially.

Mathair Anne looked thoughtfully at the three children lying warm and fed and asleep one evening. She turned to Felicity. "I want you to know now, Felicity *mochree*, that it is one of the best things in life to be able to make your children happy. It is possible for the most part only while they are young. Later you no longer have that power."

She looked bleakly out of the window. "What would I not give now for the happiness of my four sons or my daughter! And not one thing can I do that matters. But you're young and will have them by you for many a day."

Felicity felt for the baby's small bare feet beneath the blanket. Warm they were and smooth in her hand, with finely articulated ankle bone and instep. There was something infinitely pathetic about that smallness and fineness. What far paths might these tiny feet yet tread? But not for years to come, she thought jealously, clutching to her his

232

littleness and his need of her. Poor Mathair Anne, she thought, looking at her in sharp pity.

And looking at her so, she discerned the first signs of age and weakness. A sort of grayness was over her face and the hollows of her fine eyes were dark-smudged.

Felicity spoke to her about it. She was at the time washing a pan of greens. Tassie had brought in an apronful of lambs' quarters. As Felicity soused them up and down in water, Anne cut up some salt pork to boil with them.

Said Felicity, "Are you well, Mathair Anne? Is it the worry?"

Anne looked sombrely down at the sharp-slicing knife. "You know how it is. Any hurt or danger to your child is like a hurt or danger to your own body. And I have three in danger. That's all. Shall we have stovies for supper?"

"You make them. I never get them so good."

"It's all a matter of slow cooking. Two hours anyway."

She peeled four or five big potatoes and sliced them very thin, and two onions as well. She took a few tablespoons of good dripping saved from the roast of a few days ago and smeared it about the bottom and sides of a small iron pot. Then the potatoes and onion went in and salt and pepper and some more dripping. She poured on a cupful of water and covered the pot well and set it near the fire.

It was like a game they played to keep up their spirits, this interest in small housewifely wisdom. While all the time in their hearts they wondered, "Are they safe now? And now? Is there perhaps a battle raging? Is he warm and fed? Or does he perchance lie wounded?" The mind shuddered

233

away from the thought. So they pretended, did Anne and Felicity, and covered their fears.

But not so Tassie. If she was lonely she sat and rocked herself dolefully and looked forlorn. Sometimes round childish tears brimmed over and slipped down her cheeks. Unconcernedly she lifted the edge of her linsey skirt and wiped them away. She made Felicity feel old and full of responsibility.

Both girls helped Rorie with the haying. There was no one else to help him.

First came the cutting. Round and round the field walked Rorie, swinging his body to the long rhythm of the scythe, and leaving even, gray-green swathes behind him. A day or so of sunshine and they pulled the swathes into windrows with wooden rakes, and then with forks made them into coils. The hay was either stored in mows in the barn, or a stack was built in the field. This had to be cunningly constructed, with every forkful under Rorie's supervision, so that it would shed the rain and stand firm against the wind.

It was pleasant working in the hay, once the muscles of arm and back and thigh had hardened to the strain of lifting. Rorie was full of friendliness and good humour and was apologetic as well.

"I never thought," he told them, as they rested one day in the shade of a great harp-shaped elm, "that with four sons at my back I'd have to ask two fine young girls to help me with my hay crop."

Tassie lay flat, and the elm cast small changing leaf shadows across her face and her full young figure. "I like it," she said, "better than housework."

234

Felicity smiled at Rorie. "I like it fine, too, but I must go now and feed my baby. You, too, Tassie."

Tassie stretched. "Och, let them wait a bit."

Felicity shook her head and Tassie sighed and went.

In the house Anne was finishing a rag doll for Barbary Rose. It was stuffed with wool, and the face was of white linen with blue beads for eyes and a red, red mouth embroidered on, and the hair was of yellow wool plaited in two long braids. Felicity felt a rush of tenderness for her mother-in-law. She said to Tassie when Ian had been laid in his cradle,

"You go on out. I'll help with the dinner."

She washed the round brown potatoes and put them in a pot and slung it over the crane. She pulled some new carrots and set them to boil as well. Then she sliced some of the smoked ham and laid it in the long-handled frying pan and, sitting on a low stool, she held it over the fire. The grease crackled and sizzled and the good smell of frying meat filled the room.

Anne took Barbary Rose on her ample lap and rocked her. The dark curls spread out over her arm, and the little head was soon heavy on the softness of Anne's deep bosom. As she rocked she sang an old *cronan*.

> "*Cagaran, cagaran, cagaran gaolach,*
> *Cagaran foghainteach fear de mo dhaoine.*"

Felicity smiled at the two of them. Then Anne spoke softly in the very tone and tempo of the lullaby.

"Have you wondered, Felicity, that I have let you work

235

in the fields and you not used to it, while I stay sheltered in the house?"

"But not idle."

"Idler than you. I'll tell you why. I have sometimes a small pain at my heart. My mother had it before me at about my age. So I'm careful. I'd not like to leave you."

Felicity stared at her. "Mathair Anne," she whispered.

"Tut, child, don't you worry."

"A doctor?"

"I don't need one. I know. I've not told anyone."

Felicity felt as if the props of life had given way beneath her. Ever since she had come to Tulloch Ard, Mathair Anne had been there, close at hand, full of strength and loving-kindness. She was the bulwark of the place.

"Don't look so scunnered," she said with a smile. "All I need is to be a little careful."

"We'll see to that," cried Felicity fervently.

No longer would she stay in the big house giving Mathair Anne just so much more work. She and her two bairns would sleep and eat in their own place, and only when she went into the fields with Rorie would she leave them to Anne's care and tending. Anne was now to be protected. She would write to Meron.

Then she had a letter from Peter saying that Meron could not now come to Tulloch Ard, and she must not be urged. Which seemed strange to Felicity.

Between the haying and the harvest she re-established herself in the small stone house, and it was good to be in her own place with her children. But she missed Peter at every turn.

She was not the only lone wife in the countryside however. A knock at the door one bright morning, and there stood Katie. After she had admired the baby and Barbary Rose, she said, "I'm alone now too. Fergus is with the militia in Cornwall. They think the war is coming this way again."

"Really?"

"Yes. But that's not what I came to tell you. Blossom, the white heifer, has calved late in the bush and has gone wild. Will you help me bring her home?"

"Of course. How are you getting along?"

"Och, fine. I miss Fergus. But I'm getting a lot of things done."

There was a little sleigh at the corner of the wood pile, used to draw in wood. "We could take that," said Katie. "For the calf."

It was cool in the maple woods. The sunshine filtered down through the leaves and was pale like moonlight. The spreading fronds of tall green ferns made pools for the trees to stand in. Squirrels chattered, birds called, a fox barked. But there was no sign of Blossom.

Then they saw her, a nervous switching Blossom with lowered head and tossing horns. They came up to her cautiously. Katie spoke to her soothingly and laid her hand after a while on her smooth white flank, and rubbed behind the twitching ears. Blossom lowed suddenly on a note of content.

"She remembers me now," said Katie. "Look there in the bracken. Do you see the calf?"

It was a sweet little heifer with great glistening eyes, and all white but for one brown ear and a moist, pink nose. Its coat had dried curly where Blossom had licked it. She came and stood over it now, wild-eyed and solicitous. Felicity was a little wary of those swinging horns. But Katie spoke calmly to her and lifted the calf and tied it on the sleigh. The runners slipped smoothly over the grass once they were out of the woods. The calf struggled from time to time and mooed feebly and Blossom followed close, bawling and fearful.

It was an odd little procession, thought Felicity. And all of one kind.

Katie giggled and took the thought out of her mind. "Och, poor Blossom," she said. "Sure, we girls have quite a time."

*   *   *

It was not long after that that Rorie fell from the haymow and twisted his knee. With difficulty he managed to reach the house and, when Anne examined it, there was great swelling and pain.

"The ligaments are torn and strained," she said meditatively. "We'll ease it a bit for you, Rorie *mochree*."

She did that with hot and cold fomentations, and him flat on his back in his bed.

And there he would stay for some time, as she knew.

She told the others. What of the harvest now on them?

Tassie spoke up. "I have a young brother. They can surely spare him for a while."

So young Andrew came. He was like Tassie. Yet unlike. He was dark, self-contained and naïve; but unlike her he had a strong sense of responsibility. Life was real and earnest with Andrew, and he did not hold with clavering.

The three of them took off the harvest. They cut the

grain with sickles, and bound it in sheaves, and stored it in the mow. All through the warm, golden days of August they worked in the fields. Tassie turned even more brown than she had been. Felicity, whose skin never much tanned, had a drift of freckles across her nose. While Rorie fumed and fretted in the house to see them work so hard. But after a while he was able to hobble out to do the barnyard chores; then with the aid of a stick he went hirpling over the fields, supervising the work and doing all that he could.

In September the corn was cut and the pumpkins, planted in the same rows, ripened goldenly in the full light of the sun. Then the roots had to be dug, the carrots and the turnips and the potatoes. The potatoes and carrots were stored in a bin in the cellar, but the turnips were wheeled in barrows and dumped into the root house, which was a dark hole under the barn floor. With this, Rorie could not help very much because of his knee.

The storing of food had never seemed so important to Felicity. She felt a solid satisfaction in looking at the riches in her own cellar.

It was a dim, cool place with heavy ceiling beams of cedar, and flagstones for a floor. In one corner was the potato bin. Nearby was the barrel of pork in brine, and the keg of homemade vinegar. Two stone jars of butter too. And on long shelves were the precious preserves, grape, and crabapple, and wild plum, and black currant, and wine-red chokecherry jam, and a sharp golden jelly made of rowan berries. There was, too, a row of homemade cheeses. Mathair Anne had made these, but Felicity had helped.

But Mathair Anne was now concerned over her. "Look

at you. Your eyes so big and your face pale," she said. "Sure, you'd better wean Dougall, the bonnie bouncing lad! And you'll get back your strength."

Felicity held him fiercely to her. He was warm and soft, except for his hard little head that pressed into her breast. Barbary leaned against her shoulder on the other side. "These I have by me," she thought, "and these will I care for."

"He's doing so well. Let's wait a bit," she told Anne.

Her children were a comfort to her, but she missed Peter. Every day and every night she missed him, with an aching anxiety and an actual physical pain of loneliness. "Come home, come home," her heart cried.

But it was her father who came.

Fine and fit he looked in his uniform of the Canadian Fencibles, though thin. He was welcome for his own sake, and because he had recently seen Peter and David and Hugh. They were in good health, too, he said, which spoke well for their native constitution. For the troops in the Niagara country were mightily plagued with fever and ague.

"Do you mean they're sick?" asked Felicity.

Dougall MacKay's face was grim. "Many of them are. And ill-clothed and ill-fed. And some have not been paid for months. But they hold on. It's the devil of a country to fight in. Our lines straggling all the way from Montreal to Michillimackinac. With gaps, I'll admit." He smiled ironically. "Mostly gaps."

Felicity struck her hands together passionately. "How can our soldiers fight if they are not well clothed and fed?"

"You'd be surprised. When a man is fighting for his home. There was a skirmish at Ball's Farm near Niagara.

240

An eleven-year-old boy was missed by his mother. She found him on the battlefield, popping away with a musket and a box of cartridges. His mother ran in and caught him in her arms and carried him off the field, getting herself wounded in the process. He was unhurt."

"What else happened?"

He looked at her gravely. "We have suffered a grave defeat on Lake Erie and at Moraviantown. We've been out-generalled and out-fought. That is the blunt truth. Out-numbered, too, of course. The enemy hold all of Upper Canada west of Kingston except Michillimackinac and Burlington, where our troops are."

"They're staying there?"

He nodded.

"Won't they be in great danger?"

"Maybe. But I think the war will move eastward very quickly. In Kingston Major MacDonell is whipping eight flank companies of French-Canadian militia into a light battalion. I hear there's a large American army encamped up the Chateauguay. And sooner or later Wilkinson's army will come down the St. Lawrence."

★

★

CHAPTER

XVI

NOT LONG AFTER Dougall MacKay's visit, the war did move eastward as he had predicted. News of the battle of Chateauguay came through to the settlement, and the story of how Major MacDonell had brought his French-Canadians down from Kingston in record time and had combined forces with the great de Salaberry to win a decisive and badly needed victory, which had given security to the city of Montreal for the time being.

The news cheered and encouraged those at Tulloch Ard and lightened their spirits. On a fine sunny morning after a night of frost, early in November, Rorie announced at breakfast,

"The big butternut tree in the back pasture is fair loaded this year," and smiled at Tassie.

She looked up eagerly. "It's a beautiful day to gather them."

"Go you then," said Anne kindly. "I'll take young Ian and stay with Felicity."

Felicity said when they told her, "Come back here, all of you, for dinner."

The babies were tucked together into the trundle bed and went into their morning nap. Barbary Rose sat on the hearth rug, rocking herself back and forth, and singing a small lullaby to the yellow-haired doll in her arms. Anne took out her knitting and Felicity set herself to spin. Idly her glance swept down over the slanting hillside toward the road; then she stiffened into intentness. Anne, too, came to look.

A party of mounted men was coming along the road and up the hill. Behind them trundled a horse-drawn cart. A foraging squad.

"Patrig's with them in the back pasture," observed Felicity.

Anne picked up Barbary Rose, kissed her and put her on the settle, where she sat round-eyed and motionless.

A quiet anger began to burn in Felicity, quenching her momentary fear. Here, on their own place, was the enemy. Not one whit more than she could help would they get from her.

There was a sharp clatter of hooves on the gravel at the door. Then a knock. Felicity pulled open the door. A tall rifleman stood there, and beside him a shorter, older man. The others waited by the cart.

The tall man had a lean, humorous face. "Ma'am," he said, doffing his cap. "Have you any provisions for sale?"

"You pay for them?" asked Felicity coolly.

246

"We pay for them. Unless they're lying around quite unattached."

"Where now is your army?" asked Anne, standing by the mantel.

"Above Cornwall, ma'am, at the moment."

"You come a long way for your provisioning."

He smiled easily. "To tell the truth, we're trying to kill two birds. To get some provisions, and to locate a man of ours of whom we've lost track."

"A spy?" asked Anne bluntly.

He stiffened at that. "I never said so, ma'am. And if he were, it's all a matter of point of view."

There was a little silence. Then he repeated firmly, "We're looking for provisions. Pork, beef, grain, hay. And we're prepared to pay."

Felicity looked at him with an expressionless face. "We have nothing for sale."

His own face hardened at that and he shrugged. "So you've nothing for hungry men?"

"Hungry?" she repeated ironically.

Then Barbary Rose scrambled down from the settle and went to the low door of the cupboard and reached within to a secret corner of her own. For a moment she looked down at what she held in her hand. Then her own slow, sweet smile spread over her face as she went first to one soldier then the other. To each, she handed solemnly a small, sticky lump of maple sugar, and stood back happily to watch them eat it.

A sort of dull shame hung in the air. Felicity flushed and

247

asked in a low, uncertain tone, "Are you hungry, sir, really?"

He answered as softly, "What would you do about it?"

"The pot's on the fire."

He drew himself up and saluted. His eyes were now bright and kind. "Ma'am, I thank you for the good thought. But we all ate well an hour ago. May I hold the little miss?"

Barbary Rose leaped into his arms and patted his lean cheeks with her soft little hands, and talked in a swift spate of unintelligible sweet words to him. He kissed the top of her head and set her down.

"I have one at home," he said briefly.

"We'll be going down through the orchard," he went on. "I see one tree is still unpicked. May we help ourselves to a few apples?"

Anne laughed suddenly. "Sure, a half-dozen lads in an orchard. I'll be lucky if you leave me any."

But they did. They helped themselves only moderately as they passed beneath the sweet-apple tree. Soon the little cavalcade was around the corner and out of sight.

Rorie and Tassie and Andrew came back with the butternuts. Two big bags they gathered. Then they found a bee tree, and they made a smudge and smoked out the bees. Andrew climbed the tree and Tassie made baskets out of birch bark to hold the great dripping shelves and layers of comb honey. It was brown and sweet. It would be wonderful on the hot bannocks that Felicity patted out as she and Anne told of their eventful morning.

* * *

The story behind the events of that morning, Felicity got

about a week later from an unexpected source. It was in the evening. Rorie had looked in on her and had gone. Barbary was already asleep upstairs, and in a few minutes Felicity would lift young Dougall from his cradle and carry him up to bed. When Patrig rose suddenly, his hackles up, and a growl in his throat. There was a knock at the door.

Felicity hesitated for a moment, then opened it cautiously. It was Fergus.

"Come in," she cried hospitably. "You're home again, then."

He held out his hands to the blaze. "I came home this morning. I thought you'd like to hear of the battle."

Her hand went to her throat. "Yes," she breathed. "Do sit down."

He sat in the full blaze of the hearth. The firelight made points of red in his dark eyes.

"The battle?" she questioned fearfully.

"Yes," he said, and smiled. "But the Glengarries were not in it."

"Oh," she cried, and laughed in relief and happiness.

He continued, his eyes never leaving her. "Wilkinson's army left Ogdensburg, came down river and landed on our side. Morrison followed them as they travelled east, harrying them. They stood at Chrysler's farm. They fought there. The enemy had to retire. Then the men of the militia, we harried them too. To gain time to get the military stores out of Cornwall and hidden. After a while the Americans crossed the river. But they left a hundred horses behind."

"How?"

He laughed again. Was he a little drunk?

"Well, they tried to swim them behind the boats, holding them by the halters. We shot over their heads and the horses broke away and swam back to shore. Our shore."

Felicity heaved a sigh. "Then they're gone."

Fergus nodded. "They lingered for a while looking for a spy of theirs, I've heard. But they had to leave without him. We'll find him. We know what to do with him."

"What?"

"Ride him on a rail. Hang him. A spy is not like a soldier."

He was a *ghillie dhu* all right, a dark lad, within and without. She shivered. "How is Katie?"

He waved a casual hand. Moments passed. He sat looking at her. "A long time since Peter has been home," he remarked.

"Many months."

He laughed softly. "Do you remember the time you came home with Meron?"

"Yes."

"You were just a girl then. You're not now."

"We have all grown older," she said quietly, and got up and walked over to the mantel. He turned to face her.

Nothing was said for some minutes. His eyes, smouldering in the firelight, travelled over her, and when they met hers it was with an impact of meaning and intent.

In a swift movement he was beside her. Her hand flashed up, and in it was Peter's *skian-dhu*. And suddenly Patrig was beside her, pressing against her, a growl rumbling in his chest.

Fergus stepped back. Anger came down over his face, darkening it. Something close to hate was in his eyes.

"Very well so," he said stiffly, and picked up his cap.

At the door he shot her a look. "Some day you'll mislay the *skian-dhu*," he said, and went out.

Felicity bolted the door after him and sat down. She was trembling. She thought, "Shall I go to the other house and stay there, or will Patrig and Peter's dagger be enough?" She lay awake for a long time that night, thinking.

But something happened the next day that put Fergus quite out of her mind. Tassie came for her. Mathair Anne was ill.

"It came on her suddenly." Tassie was breathless. "Sandy Ban is there. We were talking after supper. A bad pain."

Anne was lying on the settle in the kitchen, a pillow under her head and a plaid thrown over her. Her face was a curious gray colour and drops of moisture were on her forehead, but her eyes met Felicity's in indomitable good humour.

"A silly old woman, that's what I am."

Felicity knelt by her. "The pain," she asked softly. "Has it gone?"

"Yes. But I'm afraid to move."

"Don't move. Where was it?"

"Deep in my chest. Squeezing."

Felicity straightened and looked at Rorie. "A doctor?"

"I'll go," cried Sandy.

"Take Shanlan then. He has strength in him. And don't spare him."

Rorie mixed a toddy and sat on a low stool and fed it to

251

Anne with a spoon. She gave him a comradely smile, and his face worked for a minute and then steadied.

"Sure now, Anna *mochree*, we'll have you well in no time."

Felicity heated some salt and filled some small sacks of it to lay at her feet. Then she got water and bathed her face and wrists. After a while Anne said, "I've been easy for quite a while. I'd like to get to my bed like a decent body."

The stairs! But they could knock down a bed and put it up in the west room. So they did that. Rorie and Tassie carried down the bedstead and slats and then the tick of corn husks and the big feather one. Felicity got out the sheets and made up the bed fair and soft, with blankets and cover of wool, all the work of Anne's hands over many years.

Then Rorie bent his broad back and slipped his arms about his wife and carried her to bed. She was a big woman and his brow was red with the effort.

She smiled up at him where she lay. "You're as strong as ever you were, my Rorie."

When Felicity was getting her into her nightgown, after she had for a while rested, Anne looked at her with the same loving-kindness in her eyes.

"Felicity," she said softly. "Peter's Felicity and mine." Her eyes crinkled into a smile. "You're like Black Shanlan. You have strength in you. You may need it. So it comforts me to know you have it. Another thing comforts me. Meron is safe, and Evan. Those of my children are."

She slept a little after that, while Rorie and Felicity watched. Tassie had gone up to the other house to be with Barbary and small Dougall. "I don't know what to do here," she said simply. "I'll tend the children for you." Andrew sat silent like a small old man by the fire in the kitchen, keeping watch.

Around midnight another attack came. A gasping sound, a huddling together of the figure on the bed, and sweat pouring down over the gray face. The breath laboured.

"*Dhia!*" Rorie kept saying, "*Dhia!*" between clenched teeth.

The spasm passed and Felicity wiped the wet brow, and Anne seemed easier. But her defences were down. The brave front with which she had covered her grief and anxiety had crumbled. She looked at Felicity and Rorie as if she did not see them, and out of her own heart's trouble she spoke.

In a sort of litany she said over and over again three words, wide-spaced. "Peter . . . Hughie . . . David." Each name stood out as though encased in pain. "Peter, Hughie," she said, and her voice was full of love and longing. Then, "David," and the tears ran down over the edges of her eyes.

She was for a long time silent. Then she raised herself. "My boys!" she cried loudly in grief and desperation, and fell back again.

They looked at her in a stunned silence. Her eyes opened again, and in a soft low voice, gentle as a sigh, she said, "David *og mochree*," and smiled and was silent.

Felicity hurried to the kitchen. Andrew took the kettle from the crane for her and poured the hot water into the glass. There was a sound from the other room. She hurried in.

Rorie was kneeling at the bed, amazement and dismay

in his face. "It's over," he said, and walked blindly from the room and out into the night.

It was daybreak when the doctor came.

"A little earlier and might you have saved her?" asked Rorie.

"It would have made no difference," the doctor told him kindly.

Later Felicity thanked him for his effort and his hurried trip over roads clogged with the first snow of the winter. And she thanked Sandy Ban, too, when he came in from rubbing down Black Shanlan and walking him up and down the length of the stable.

"Don't thank me," said Sandy, smiting his hands together. "It was Shanlan anyway. That's a great horse. He'd break his heart for a man."

The sun came up red over the new snow that covered the world. Felicity stood at the east window and watched it. She felt shaken, and she felt alone. The two women who had been for her a guide and a support were gone. It was as if a sapling had grown up in the shade of two trees, and first one and then the other had fallen, and the sapling stood bared and by itself to take the wind and the rain and the storm.

Friends and neighbours gathered for the waking and the funeral. Angus and Lucretia came at once. It was not possible to get word to Meron in time for her to come to the funeral, but she did come with all haste. And deep was her grief.

"If it weren't for the war I might have had this last summer with her," she said bitterly.

On Sunday they went to church and sat in the familiar pew, but not so many of them now as there had once been. After the service Meron went and looked down at the snowy mound that was her mother's grave, and stood for a long time with the wind blowing her cloak and the snow sifting white in her hair and her fine fur bonnet.

Mr. Bethune saw her so and came and took her by the arm. "You will remember, child, the life to come."

She looked at him straightly. "You're sure?"

He smiled at her, a serene smile that lighted up his thin face. "I speak as one who expects shortly to put it to the proof."

They walked through the snow to the waiting carriole, the tall girl in her rich clothes and in her prideful bright beauty, and the worn old man.

"Do you know," he said in a friendly low tone, "when I read the Scripture today and finished with the words, 'Here endeth the first lesson,' I thought that is true of life. That could be an epitaph. Your mother has ended her first lesson. And did well by it. Now the good Lord has promoted her."

Meron looked soberly at him for a moment, then gave him that wide generous smile of hers, and laid her hand in his.

"What of Evan?" Felicity asked of her when they were at home. "I haven't known how to get in touch with him."

"A letter in care of the Nor-West Company will reach him in time, in a few months perhaps. You have sent word to the other three?"

Felicity nodded. "But mail is uncertain. In wartime."

"It will be hard on them," Meron said sombrely. "Especially, I think, on David. He has no wife to cheer him. And he was her youngest, her latest bairn."

Felicity remembered those last whispered words, "David *og mochree*."

The day before Meron left, Felicity found her in her mother's room with her head on her arms on the old bureau, weeping quietly and bitterly.

"It's the things I might have done for her." She wiped her eyes. "I suppose it's always like that. Regret. I've been looking at her quilts, her hand-woven sheets, and her goose-down pillows, and the smell of sweet-mary on them all. Tassie has a good start."

CHAPTER

XVII

On New Year's Eve, Hughie came. The door opened quietly as they sat about the fire at the big house, and there he was. Tassie flung herself on him and laughed and cried. He kissed her in tenderness and gravity, and Felicity, watching, thought, "He knows about his mother." But she was wrong.

His eyes went searching about the room. "Mathair?" he said enquiringly, and there was for a moment silence. Then they crowded around him again, welcoming him. But he repeated gravely, "Mathair?" and waited.

Rorie looked sombrely at him. "Your mother died some weeks ago and is now buried."

Hughie sat down heavily and said nothing. Tassie tugged at his coat and he gave it to her, and sat still then with the snow from his boots making pools of water on the floor.

"Was she sick long?"

"Only a few hours."

"It was?"

"A pain at her heart."

"At her heart." He smiled a strange sad smile. "She was the one I dreaded most to see, with the news I bring."

They looked dumbly at him, fear flickering in their eyes.

Then, "What do you mean?" they asked together, their voices quick and high with that same fear.

"I mean," he said heavily, coming mercifully to the point, "that David has been killed."

There was a complete and terrible silence. The wind howled and snarled in the chimney and then was still. A shower of sparks broke from a smouldering log. The big clock ticked loudly. David was gone. No more his shy, dark smile. David, the latest born. David *og mochree*.

Hughie was speaking. "He was with a reconnaissance party, exploring the river's edge. They came on a small group of the enemy, but were themselves unseen. Some of them were for picking off the foe with the rifle. But David said, 'Why kill them? We'll take us some prisoners.' The rest humoured him because they liked him. So he advanced on the enemy, calling out cheerfully. And one of them threw up his rifle and shot him.

"He fell and died at once. Then indeed did his friends pick off the enemy without mercy. Donald Roy MacDonell told me about it. He was there. So was Murdie MacIntosh. They carried him back."

He paused for a moment, then went on. "We buried him at Fort George. The piper played a lament over him. That is all."

It was enough. Grief lay heavy on them. No one spoke. Then Rorie upreared himself and towered over them.

"Curse him." His voice was thick with hate. "Curse the man that shot Davie and him trying to save him. May his cattle die, and his sons be sickly, and his soul wander homeless in the night-time. That curse I now put on him, and you all to hear it."

He sat down. They looked at him uneasily. No one spoke. A great heaviness was on them, and a silence.

Into that silence came the young, matter-of-fact voice of Tassie. "Are you not hungry, Hughie?"

They got a meal ready then, and Tassie brought young Ian, sleepy from his cradle, and set him plumply on his father's knee. And the shadow lifted a little from Hughie's face, and on it was an odd shaken look of tenderness as his arms closed around his first-born.

"Peter is well," he said, looking at Felicity, "and grieved that he could not come with me."

"The war is going better with us now," he went on. "We took Fort Niagara. A surprise attack. An affair of the bayonet, and well carried out. The whole frontier is now ours."

Felicity had to swallow before she could find words to ask the question that was always in her heart. "Do you think it will soon be over?"

"Not for a while, I'm afraid. However, I hear that Napoleon was ousted out of Russia, and Wellington's doing good work in Spain. Next year, if all goes well, we should have some more help from overseas."

"Next year," thought Felicity desperately. "How can I stand it?"

*　　*　　*

It was a dreary New Year's Day at Tulloch Ard and hardly recognized as such. Felicity remembered the time David had been the first at the door to give them the *Beannachad* for the new year. Now indeed, "*Beannach So* to you, young David, forever and forever more, wherever your kind young spirit lingers."

Hughie was older and soberer than he had been. "I see you've been good to Tassie," he said to Felicity one day. "And I'm grateful. But what I can't forget," he went on gravely, "is that mother died in grief and anxiety. I'd like to have spared her that."

"Oh, but that was just at the last. Her grief and anxiety were real. But so also was her pride in you all. She said to me not long since, 'It's something to be the mother of brave sons.' And once long ago, 'All my boys are venturesome. I like them that way'."

There was a quiver of feeling in his face. "It's good to know that."

But David's death, coming so soon after the other, changed Rorie. The lusty humour and the kindliness seemed to dry up in him and gave place to a dark, harsh spirit of revenge.

He was morose. Even Barbary Rose failed to lighten his depression. She'd press against his knees and look quietly up into his face, the beginning of her slow sweet smile in her eyes. And he'd gaze down on her in gloomy affection.

262

"Poor wean," he'd say as though he knew that she, too, was born to sorrow.

As he went about his work, his face was slack and sullen, as if he was brooding on violence and revenge. Felicity remembered the time when she first came to Tulloch Ard, and he stopped the sleigh to put his plaid around her, the big dark MacAlpin plaid that had been like a mantle of love. Grief and pain were sore and sharp at his heart, she knew, and his ill-humour was but a froth rising from the misery within. Anne, only, could have exorcised that dark spirit, and Anne was dead.

Felicity herself felt an anxiety greater than ever before. While she had known with her mind that calamity might come, she had never in her heart felt it. Now death had reached out to tap young David on the shoulder and had become a terrible reality. And she was afraid.

The war was taking hold of the countryside in a new way. No longer was it a case of the Glengarries marching away to the skirling of the pipes, with the bright warm glitter of gallantry and daring bubbling in their blood.

Loneliness and anxiety had sobered the spirit of those who waited at home. Stark news had come to this family and that, and heart-numbing grief. Out of it grew a deep and sullen anger against their adversaries. It would go hard with any enemy stragglers found on this side of the St. Lawrence. Hate was sprouting from the dragon's teeth of war.

Felicity moved back into her house and thought, if she could help it, she would not again leave it. She no longer had any fear of Fergus. He avoided her. Drunk he had

263

probably been on that unlucky night. Her mind was too full of the perils of war to be much concerned with him.

She found comfort in her home. And in her children. And in the world of nature about her. A world that had been before her and would outlast her. The pine trees that sang a high sighing song on a day of wind. The sunset that struck red through the bare branches. And the starry skies by night. They spoke an impersonal but healing word that eased and steadied her.

Then came the day when she heard a sudden loud barking from Patrig at the barn, and went out to investigate, and found trouble for herself.

In the stable everything was as usual. The cows chewed contemplative cuds; the sheep were quiet. Pegi stamped companionably in her stall. But Patrig bayed furiously at the door of the mow, and when she came up, he flung himself before her and advanced growling into a shadowy corner under the eaves.

Felicity stood still, her heart thudding. Then, all of a sudden, a figure upreared itself from deep in the hay, a wild, red-eyed, shaggy figure, with a rifle held waveringly in unsteady hands.

"I'll shoot," he warned her hoarsely. The rifle pointed now at Patrig, now at Felicity.

"Put it down," Felicity heard herself saying sharply. "Here, Patrig."

Patrig backed reluctantly, and the man—he seemed more like a dishevelled and emaciated boy—let his rifle slip down, and then leaned heavily on the butt.

Felicity came forward, her feet sinking in the hay. "Who are you?"

"Who am I?" He laughed weakly. "I've almost forgotten." Then his knees folded and he crumpled in a heap.

He was ill. Felicity touched his forehead and it was hot. Beneath his ragged sleeves his wrists were very thin. He began to mumble incoherently. Something about a river. Then he gave a groan of frustration and was still.

Felicity took Patrig firmly by the collar, climbed down out of the haymow and closed the barn door carefully. Back in the house, she put a bowl of hot broth inside a pail and carried it out, looking uneasily to left and right as she did so.

The sick man was rational again. She fed him with a spoon and he looked at her with grateful, haggard eyes.

"How do you come to be in my barn?" she asked.

"Any port in a storm."

"You are from across the river?"

His eyes went evasive. "I have been many places." He lay back and his eyes shut drowsily.

She stood, looking down at him. He was very ill. He was also, she thought, a spy. The one for whom the enemy soldiers had been searching, knowing he was wounded.

As if he felt her thought, his eyes flew open. "Don't give me up," he whispered, his dark desperate eyes searching her face.

"You're safe for now," she told him and left him.

If she gave him up, what would they do to him? Tar and feathers, Fergus had hinted. Hanging. She shuddered, remembering the dark mood of the countryside.

Late that afternoon she went down the hill to where

Rorie was chopping wood. "I've watered the stock and fed them," she said. "You won't need to bother tonight."

He looked at her sombrely. "I see," he said, and went back to his chopping.

On her way back she met Fergus. She would have passed with a word of greeting, but he stopped her.

"I heard a terrible loud barking at your place today." His black eyes were intent.

"Yes. Patrig thought he had something under the barn." She moved as if to go on.

"We're still looking for that spy."

"Have you had any luck?"

"He was traced near."

"Indeed." And now she did walk on. But when she reached the house her knees were shaking.

She would have to act, either for or against. She would have to turn the boy over to his enemies, or help him avoid them. She had no one to consult. Had Anne been alive! Or her grandmother!

Her grandmother! She who had herself once been a refugee in an unfriendly country. She and her own mother. And a woman of that country had befriended them. She, Felicty, bore that woman's name. There was a debt there, still owing.

But she also owed a debt to her own country. Or was there an older, more elementary obligation that claimed sanctuary for any human creature, sick and helpless at one's door?

That night there was no moon, just a fine speckle of stars. Felicity waited till late. Then she put Patrig in the cellar and went out to the barn. It was very black in the haymow. Only a few thin pencils of light slanted in through cracks in the roof. She made her way to the far corner and felt with her hands till she found the huddled figure. He muttered uneasily. He was drowsy with fever, but she shook him awake.

"Get up," she whispered in his ear. "Get up."

He was silent, but she felt his mind working.

"You're no longer safe here. Come with me."

"My leg. A wound gone bad."

She got him to his feet. But the hay was loose and deep, and he fell and got up and fell again.

"Lie on your back," she told him. Then she put her hands under his arms and drew him backward to the door. Getting him down to the stable was difficult. They both fell eventually, and he lay for a while groaning, while the cattle tossed their heads in their stanchions and snorted in alarm.

Outside it seemed uncomfortably light with the snow on the ground and a bright filigree of stars in the dark sky. Painfully they made their way to the house, and he lay, spent, on the settle.

She went upstairs to fix the bed. When she came down there was a blaze of fire on the hearth. Papers curled and blackened in it. She whirled on him. "What were you doing?"

He was sitting up, his hands clutching the edges of the seat. He looked straightly up at her. "I was burning some papers," he said.

She eyed him hotly. Then the anger went out of her,

and a reluctant admiration took its place.

"Come now," she said quietly.

When he was at length in bed, Felicity brought water to bathe his wound. When she saw it she was for a moment ill. The leg was swollen large and was angrily red. The unhealed wound lay along the thigh.

"How did you get it?" she asked.

He said through clenched teeth, "A man tried to stop me." Then when she had it bandaged as well as she could, he added calmly, "I think it will be the end of me," and his eyes closed and he seemed to sleep.

The next morning when she came to tend him, he said, "My mother would thank you for this if she knew."

She looked at him. "Your mother," she echoed and thought for a while about her.

"If I give you her name and address, will you write her after the war and tell her about me?"

She took down the name. Mistress Nathan Russell, Glen Falls.

"My name is Nate too," he said drowsily, and drifted into that curious light slumber from which he wakened so effortlessly. It was as if there was no edge to his waking consciousness, and he moved in or out of sleep without knowing the difference.

But Felicity went about her tasks with an anxious heart. What if Katie came, or Tassie? Or if a loud delirium took hold of this man who was so surprisingly, when she came to think of it, in her bed upstairs.

Tassie did come that afternoon, but Felicity met her at

the door, and Tassie only said, "Come over and see Aunt Lucretia. She is with us for a visit."

Lucretia was full of news of life in Cornwall, and full of recriminations because of the incursions of the enemy the previous fall.

"A few of them came into town. Officers and men. Searching for arms, they said. Arms! Tush! Rummaging in trunks and cupboards."

"Were they short of clothing?"

"They were short of blankets anyway. At night they set fire to the log fences and lay alongside them. It was high time when they were harried out of the country."

"What a warlike thing she is!" thought Felicity. It occurred to her that the fierce and venomous ones were those who had none of their own flesh and blood in battle. It gave them a strange and vicious freedom. Not for them was the chastening consciousness that at any time might come news that would break the heart entirely.

They had supper together, and they were all conscious of the absence of Mathair Anne. "If ever I needed her," thought Felicity.

Then, to heighten her unease, Katie and Fergus came in the evening. The feeling around the fireside that night was not one of easy good-fellowship, as it had been of old. Now Lucretia and Fergus set the tone of the talk, and Rorie was in the same mood, and Katie added her own small, tight word of bitterness. Had she not a cousin dead on the slope of Queenston?

Lucretia brought up the spy hunt. She was like a hound hot on the trail. "He was traced to Martintown a week ago.

Some say he was wounded and died in the snow."

"I don't think he's dead. I think he's not far away," put in Fergus. "I've heard of them setting barns on fire and flushing out such vermin."

"Then set a few barns on fire." Rorie's voice was loud and defiant. He looked like a man who craved violence for the surcease of his own pain. He looked reckless and ready.

Fergus laughed softly, and Felicity took Barbary up on her knee and smoothed her curls, and hoped the candle-light did not show the paleness of her own face. That she was pale, she knew. She could feel the blood withdrawing from her cheeks.

"Aunt Lucretia," cried Tassie suddenly, as if she had not heard any of the foregoing. "Tell us about the time you eloped with Uncle Angus."

"Tush, child," said Lucretia, bridling and blushing.

"Oh, do," urged Felicity fervently.

So Lucretia told them. And the evening passed. Fergus and Katie walked home with Felicity and the children. Katie took Barbary's hand and they ran on a little ahead. And Fergus said in a low voice, "Is the *skian-dhu* still handy?"

She nodded.

"Or do you keep it just for neighbours?"

She looked at him speechlessly; then they caught up with Katie, and she was saying, "Come over for an afternoon, do."

"Some of these days," promised Felicity, and wondered if she would.

When she went in to look at Nate, she found him ill indeed. Red spots of fever burned on his cheek bones, and he was lucid only for brief periods. She bathed his face and then went down and sat by the fire.

She was in trouble now and she knew it. For some reason Fergus suspected her. He was bent on mischief. And she was without means to protect herself.

Or was she? To whom could she go? Then it came to her. The Reverend John Bethune. Minister and chaplain. A man of authority. But he was five miles away. If at home.

Her mind was quick with planning. There was Pegi, the little mare. There was this black night-time. There was also a long stretch of bush road. And sometimes there were wolves. She shuddered.

She went upstairs and looked long at the tossing figure on the bed. She went into the other room and held the candle to see her own two rosy bairns, little Dougall healthily asprawl and Barbary with her dark curls spread out like a fan on the pillow.

Then she came straightly down. She fixed the fire so it would burn long and slowly, and called Patrig and told him where he was to lie on guard, and went out to the stable.

Pegi nickered a welcome to her, and she flung a saddle on her and strapped it. Then she led her out to the mounting block, and was up, her feet firm in the stirrups. Pegi went quietly like a lady, the night was soft and dark, and Felicity felt sure that no one heard or saw. Nevertheless she was grateful when the hill hunched a dark shoulder behind her and she was shut off from view to the west.

The snow on the road was well packed and the going easy. But the night itself was awesome. It covered the earth like a blanket and lifted only a few feet at a time before them. From far, and then nearer, an owl hooted.

"Och, *cailleach oidhche*," murmured Felicity in reply. "Old woman of the night, put a good wish on me."

The sharp falsetto yelp of a fox came from the trees to the south. The bush was closing in on her. Soon, before her, she could see nothing at all. She now depended entirely on the wisdom of Pegi, on the sureness with which her feet picked out the firmness of the road and avoided the soft floundering snow beside it. She loosened the reins, and Pegi plodded on, her feet coming down firmly, and the muscles and tendons and joints of her sound, stout little body working consistently and well.

Tall pines now edged the road and the sound of their sighing was like a dirge. Felicity felt a shiver between her shoulder blades. A queer primitive fear slid along her blood, and she stiffened her neck against the desire to look back over her shoulder.

Then at last the road curved to the north and the trees fell away, and soon she could see the massed outlines of the roofs of the village. In a few minutes she was at the door of the manse, waiting for an answer to her knock, and praying meanwhile a small fervent prayer that the children were safe, that the boy Nate was still alive, and that Fergus had not set fire to the barn.

She told the minister her story. He listened intently, then went to the foot of the stair. "Veronica," he called. "Come on down."

"I am already coming," replied his wife, and she came down the steps with a candle in her hand. She wore a padded dark-red dressing gown and a lacy cap, and she looked comfortable and civilized and reassuring.

"You know Dougall MacKay's Felicity? A bite to eat will not hurt her."

"To be sure. And at once."

"I'll go back with you." The minister tugged thoughtfully at his lower lip. "But you need a woman too. What about Miss Jemima?"

"Oh," cried Felicity, "could I stir her up out of bed?"

"Well, you stirred me," drily.

Felicity laughed ruefully. "Really, sir, I was in great need." Tears slipped suddenly down her cheeks.

He laid a hand on her shoulder. "Child, to whom would you go if not to your minister?" His voice was mild and kind, but tired.

"Eat your meal now, and I'll send a boy over with a note to Miss Jemima, and we'll pick her up on our way. As for your little mare, Henri will ride her home tomorrow."

Miss Jemima was waiting for them. The three settled themselves in the carriole. Miss Jemima's arm came firmly around Felicity's shoulders. "Don't you worry, child. We'll sort them."

At home, they found the children sleeping peacefully and Patrig still on guard before the fire. But the sick man had sunk into a torpor and was motionless except for his fingers that plucked nervously at the edge of the coverlet. Mr. Bethune stood looking at him for a moment, then examined his wound briefly and drew up the covers.

"There is nothing you can do," he said. "It is now in other hands. Go you down, if you like."

He got stiffly on his knees by the bed and took the restless hands in his. "God, the Father," he prayed softly, and the two tiptoed out.

In a few hours it was over. They had a solemn breakfast together. Then the minister stepped outside for a minute. When he came in he said, "I saw a young lad out there. I sent him for Rorie MacAlpin, and Fergus, your neighbour."

Felicity waited in trepidation. When they came in, Mr. Bethune addressed them straightly.

"I have sent for you as two responsible citizens, one a member of the militia, and the other the father of a good family. To inform you of the fact that Felicity MacAlpin has found on her premises an inhabitant of the country with which we are at war, and presumably an enemy agent. As was right and proper and indeed her duty, she reported the presence of that man to me as an officer in His Majesty's forces. As a Christian woman she gave him succour in his sickness. He has gone now to a higher tribunal. I saw him die. Now I call on you to aid in his burial."

There was a thick silence. Fergus licked his lips and looked at Felicity. Rorie rose in his chair.

"Then the spy escaped us!" He turned furiously to Felicity. "Did he harbour here? Have I a traitor in my house?"

"Silence!" thundered the minister. He laid his hand on Felicity's shoulder. "This is the daughter of my friend, and a member of my flock. She is under my care, and everything she did has my approval. You will now get a conveyance for the burial."

He rapped out the words sharply, and Fergus' hand went reluctantly to the salute.

*

*

CHAPTER

XVIII

IN THE DAYS to come, life pressed heavily on Felicity, especially after Miss Jemima left. Not only life, but a sense of community displeasure weighed on her.

Rorie hardly spoke to her. He had been tricked, and his anger smouldered. When his eyes met hers they were hard with resentment. Felicity stayed entirely away from the big house now. Every morning young Andrew watered and fed the stock, and Rorie came in the evening to bed and feed them for the night. But no longer did he come into the house for a friendly few minutes by the fire.

One night he did not come at all. Felicity went out to the barn, tight-lipped, and tugged at the hay in the mow to put before the cattle and milked the two brindle cows. It was not too much for her, but it tired her nevertheless. And would have tired her more, were it not for the anger that ran through her veins, vitalizing her. Every night thereafter she went out early to the barn, lest she should seem to be waiting for help.

Katie stayed sedulously away from her. Lucretia went back to Cornwall without bidding her good-bye. Disapproval was thick in the air she breathed.

Not that her spirit showed any sign of breaking under it. A certain sombre strength took hold of her, a staying power. It was as if she drew back into herself and found herself adequate. She looked curiously at her reflection in the glass one day. She was not much different from the blue-eyed, bright-haired girl who had come to Tulloch Ard three years ago. She still looked sweet and a little fragile, except for her eyes, which had no more the misty charm of girlhood, but were the relentless blue eyes of her ancestry, the eyes of a fighter facing trouble.

Grimly she took over the supervision of her own place. She was with the ewes in March when they lambed. She cared for the small stumbling calves. She groomed the little mare, Pegi, and pampered her with lumps of maple sugar.

The care of her house engrossed her too. Dougall was now nine months old, and was full of life and laughter. When she took him up, he stood on her lap and bounced and stiffened and pranced, feeling the strength of his new-found muscles. He was a good baby and sturdy. Barbary Rose was like a small sweet woman. In her little full-skirted, ankle-length frock of yellow linsey, she pattered about her house-wifely duties. She swept clean the hearth with a turkey's wing. She jogged the cradle till the baby went to sleep and she played with him while awake.

One day Tassie brought young Ian and spent the afternoon. "We miss you," she said, and laughed ruefully. "I'm not a very good cook, I'm afraid."

"You'll learn."

"Perhaps." Then after a pause, "That time he didn't come over to do the chores, both he and Duncan were kept late in the bush."

"I see." But she thought privately, "He might have explained."

"I'm afraid you're working too hard," said Tassie.

"No. It passes the time."

There was a silence in which both were busy with their thoughts.

"One of them should have a furlough soon," said Felicity. "I can't understand why it is so long."

She rose to tend to the bread in the bake kettle on the hearth. She raked the coals away, then pulled the kettle out, tipped it, and took out and wrapped in a clean towel the big golden-crusted, sweet-smelling loaves.

Tassie looked at them enviously. Then she laughed. "Once after my mother died, I tried to make bread. The dough didn't rise at all. I thought it was no good so I poured it into a ground-hog hole behind the house. So no one would know. A warm rain came that night. And the next morning there was a big white mushroom of dough rising out of the hole."

Felicity laughed. "The ground-hog must have been surprised. Take home a loaf, won't you?"

"Shall I say it's from you?"

Felicity shook her head.

She met Fergus one day as he crossed the field near the barn. And such a wave of contempt and anger took hold of her that she wondered that she had ever been afraid of him. She was not afraid now and he knew it. She had no need of *skian-dhu*, nor of Patrig. She stood and looked at him in bitterness and pride, and he walked quickly on.

But her chief burden was her anxiety over Peter. That burden she carried day and night. Sometimes she got relief from it, and these times she treasured as her only real comfort. In those misty minutes just before sleep came, she stilled her mind, and held it so till it cleared and settled like a pool of water. Then she prayed. "Strength to you, Peter. Courage and keenness and comfort of body and mind. My love to you, Peter, forever and forevermore. In the name of the Father and the Son and the Holy Ghost."

Then it came to her, not always, but now and again—a deep inner flooding of tenderness and peace. A sense of his presence close and warm and by her. She felt she could put out her hand and touch him. Lest the edges of that feeling blur, she held it to her but a moment longer, then "Peter darling," she thought drowsily and slept.

Mr. Bethune came to see her when he could. He said to her once, "You're thinner. Are you well?"

"Quite well."

"Working hard, then?"

She smiled at him. "Aren't we all?"

"You're troubled, of course, over Peter and the rest."

She nodded, then on a sudden surge of feeling, "I'm angry, too, at the cruelty and stupidity of war."

"I suppose women have always felt that way. Yet wars there have always been."

"But there should not be."

"One nation alone cannot say, 'Let there be peace'."

"They could band together."

"Child, you over-simplify it. Nevertheless, if there were even four or five nations banded together for peace. . . . But these nations would first have to be both strong and righteous and reasonable, all of them. Which is quite a lot to ask of a people, or a person."

He sighed, then smiled at her. "Go get The Book now. I'll have a word of prayer with you and the weans, and be on my way."

One day Felicity looked out from the east window and saw Meron on the long verandah of the other house. She thought desolately, "I suppose she, too, will avoid me."

But she did not. She was at the door in a moment. She flung her arms around Felicity. She kissed Barbary Rose, and tossed up Dougall. She was like a fresh breeze of friendliness sweeping through the house. She was in high good humour, too, her eyes ablaze and very blue, and her colour high.

"Gavin's home," she cried. "And will be for a while."

"Lucky Gavin," thought Felicity, "and lucky you."

Meron sat down and took Barbary on her knee. "Tell me now all this nonsense about you helping the enemy."

Felicity told her.

Meron was for a while silent, looking down at Barbary's black curls. Felicity felt chilled and disappointed. Then Meron lifted her head and there was a queer tearful smile in her eyes. "I'm going to tell you something that I was afraid to tell anyone before. Gavin has been away on missions like that."

"Gavin?"

"Yes. A secret agent travelling through the states and reporting troop movements."

Meron laughed tremulously at the look of unbelief in Felicity's face. "You remember how interested he was in play-acting? You should see him. Dirty and smoking an old pipe. A peddler with a cart."

Felicity's hand went to her throat. "But if they caught him?"

"That's why I'm glad you were good to the man in the barn."

"Did you have anything to do with it?"

"His messages were sent to me and I delivered them to the authorities."

"That's why you couldn't come last summer?"

Meron nodded. "No one is to be told, you understand? I never told Peter, even. Everything depends on complete secrecy."

They looked at each other for a moment, their eyes alight with friendliness and fellow-feeling, but with that wary and alert look in them of women whose happiness is perilously poised.

Before she left, Meron said, "You'll have to forgive Father. His feelings run away with him."

Felicity thought of that later. Thought of a Rorie going off with his sons to a fracas in a tavern, light-hearted and careless and younger than any of them. A Rorie who could be generous and friendly beyond most men, but who could also be borne along on a dark tide of anger and vengeful thinking when life dealt him a hard blow.

Well, that turbulence she could understand. It was part of her own heritage. But she could see no way to scale the wall that was now between them.

Then one day Sandy Ban came to her door. He stood there smiling down at her with those icy blue eyes of his that were yet so kind.

"I came to go spearing fish with Rorie. But his knee is bad again. So I thought you and Tassie might go. Andrew will sit with your bairns."

Felicity hesitated.

"You'll like it," he urged. "And the fish are fine and firm now."

Tassie was waiting for them. They walked on down the lane and across the fields to the river. The air was cold and clean and sharp with spring. The sky was a sea of green with a sprinkle of stars in it. The trees were black along the shore.

They paddled silently down the river, and Felicity felt the tautness and strain going out of her. The beauty of the night soothed her. A breeze arose and it was as if wind and star-shine flowed smoothly over her. Her cares receded. She ceased to be herself. She was instead a small and unimportant part of a strange and lovely world.

Then Sandy passed back his paddle and took out his tinder box and lighted the pine torch in the bow. The blaze flared high, and in an instant the darkness retreated but was yet more black beyond the boundary of brightness. Felicity felt vulnerable and exposed, highlighted in a frame of gloom. Then she forgot about it as Sandy poised his spear.

"You've got to aim closer to the boat than you think,"

he remarked companionably. "They come fast."

They did indeed. The pronged spear plunged again and again. Soon the bow was filled with glistening silvery shapes. After a while, Sandy said, "The wind is coming up. Anyway we've enough."

He doused the torch, and immediately the night swept over them again, and the moon was bright once more and the stars.

When he was tying up the boat, Felicity said, "Thank you for taking us. It's been like a trip to a strange country."

"Tush," cried Sandy. "A gay callant I've been tonight."

Halfway up the lane they stopped, listening. "The chanter," said Sandy, "and played by one who knows. Hark to it now. It's the pipe-major himself."

It was indeed. When they came into the kitchen—and it was hard for Felicity to do anything else but come in—there were the two old men, Angus and Rorie, sitting by the fireside, and Angus had the chanter to his lips.

The air was full of soft little swirls of melody with grace notes warbling and twittering through them. It was an intricate yet friendly tune, and those listening smiled to hear it. Their faces were relaxed and easy. Even Rorie's was. The hardness had gone out of it.

*   *   *

May came in warmth and beauty. The maples stood clothed in a red mist of bloom. The marsh marigolds edged the streams with a line of clean bright yellow. And the trilliums, the white lilies of the forest, were like drifts of snow under the tall trees.

"Surely," thought Felicity, "Peter will come now."

Always he had contrived to be there in the springtime to plan with his father the planting of the crops. But the days and weeks passed and no word came.

An old saying from the Gaelic came into her mind. "Three things wear the heart: To pine for sleep, and sleep not. To wait for one who comes not. To long for death and die not."

The *dreich* words were running through her mind one evening, coming from the barn, a pail of milk in either hand and her eyes on the ground. So that she did not see Rorie till she was almost on him. And neither did he see her in the dusk. The defences of both were down. In her face and in his was the same loneliness, the same fear. There was no covering up or putting a brave face on it. Pain and distress were naked in their eyes, which met in complete honesty and openness.

Neither spoke, and in a moment they had passed on. But each felt that he now knew the other, even as he was known.

The next night Rorie did the chores at the barn. Afterwards he came in to see that they were happed for the night. And all was well between them again.

*   *   *

Then once again, Hughie came home. But not alone this time. Two friends came with him. Donald Roy Mac-Donell and Jacques Latourneau. Peter, unable himself to come, had despatched the three by boat from Kingston, Jacques wielding the paddle with Donald to help, and both of them tending and guarding and guiding Hughie. For Hughie was blind.

He was also quiet and steady and unobtrusive. That last seemed to Felicity the most intolerable. For Hughie, who had always been the very centre and pith of a gathering of people. Looking at him closely, at the lines and tensions of his sensitive, still handsome face, she felt sure that the quietness was only on the surface. Turmoil and distress seethed below. How could it be otherwise?

Tassie seemed hardly aware of his blindness. Or was it that she was deeply wise? She was happy to have him back. Her face, her voice, her whole person was vibrant with that happiness. The implications of his blindness seemed not to have occurred to her.

They occurred to everyone else.

On the evening of the day Hughie came, Felicity found Rorie sitting by himself on the bench by the back door. She sat down by him. He unwrapped the last fold of his plaid and laid it over her shoulders.

It was late and it was chill. Night birds swooped against the pale sky with strange calling noises. The full moon moved up over the black spruce-pierced edge of the horizon.

Rorie spoke then. He touched his eyes with his rough, work-hardened fingers. "These would I give him," he said heavily, and was still.

After a while he said, "I'll go up the hill with you, if I may, and sit for a while by your fire. Tassie is best with him alone."

It was some days before Hughie told them of the details of the battle. It had been early in May.

"Could they not have sent word before that you were wounded?" asked Felicity.

"Peter wanted to see what they could do for me. Doctor after doctor he brought. He had hope. At first. Then when he was suddenly ordered west again, he got these friends of his to take me home."

"It was at Oswego," he went on. "We went over from Kingston, a thousand of us. Made a reconnaissance in force to draw the enemy fire. Then on the morning of the sixth, the main party landed. There was a heavy fire and we lost quite a few. The Glengarries were ordered to clear the woods. That was where I got hurt. Peter brought me out."

Felicity thought of Peter working over Hughie, bringing doctor after doctor, dreading the moment when he should have to send him home like this. She felt in her own mind his anxiety and distress, and she felt, too, a great wave of longing for him.

Good food and rest filled out the hollows in Hughie's cheeks and gave him a better colour. But beneath that muted manner, that careful quietness of voice, what was he feeling?

Felicity had a hint of it when she came in one day to find him sitting alone by the west window.

She took a seat beside him. "Listen to the bobolink," she said. The liquid bubbling notes were like poured-out sunshine.

Hughie smiled a careful smile, but said nothing. His hands were tight on the arms of the chair.

Then, on an intake of breath, he spoke. "What shall I do, Felicity?" he asked in a low lost voice, a desperate, stricken whisper of a voice.

And then, hurriedly before she could find words, he went

287

on matter-of-factly, even with a twist of humour. "I'll have to learn to play the pipes. The blind piper!"

"A maker of music," she said unsteadily. "You might do worse."

He seemed not to hear her. He went on as before in that low, uneven voice.

"It's strange how it happened. The Glengarries were clearing the woods, as I told you. It was spring, you know. The sixth of May. Wild flowers and ferns. Mossy, rotted logs. Before me was a great bank of white lilies. Trilliums, you call them? In the midst of them a man was lying where he had fallen. One of the enemy. He was alive."

Hughie's hands tensed and twisted on the arms of the chair. Except for that, he was motionless, and his voice was now soft and singing. It had a saga note.

"Yes, he was alive. He looked up at me. I saw him clear. His eyes were gray. They were tired eyes, but calm. Then something like a thunderbolt hit me. There was an explosion of noise and light. I went down over the man among the lilies. The last thing I felt was that his arm went around me and drew me to him. My head was on his shoulder. When Peter found me, the man was dead, my blood all over him. Peter heaved me up and carried me away to the boats."

A sigh struggled from the depths of him. "The thing I can't forget is the look in his eyes. And the feeling of his arm around me. Like an elder brother."

His knuckles whitened again. "It wasn't, but it might well have been my bayonet that killed him."

"Don't think of it, Hughie. What's the use?"

"No use. But it troubles me. Why should he and I . . . ?"

He ended on a dull, fumbling note and Felicity looked at him in distress.

"Think of Tassie," she said.

The tenseness in his face and hands relaxed a little. "Aye. Tassie. Poor lass."

"And young Ian."

"Aye so. Young Ian. And not much of a father has he to do for him."

"Between us all I think he'll get along. Anyway, you're a great comfort to me. I can tell you all my troubles."

He laughed then in a natural way for the first time. "You're a lovely liar, Felicity. It's about my troubles we've been talking."

"Well, the next time then, Hughie."

So on a light and laughing note she left him, but when she was out of earshot her steps lagged and her face was bleak with pity.

CHAPTER

XIX

AT THAT MOMENT, miles to the westward, Peter with the little army of which he formed a part waited grimly for invasion. But his mind was not entirely occupied with the fortunes of war. He was remembering Hughie.

It had been a hard thing to send him home blinded. Never had he felt so sick at heart as when he saw him sitting in the canoe, the sun bright on his fair head and on his handsome, sightless face.

At the very last he had turned towards Peter and, with that heart-breaking sweet smile of his, said, "Take care of yourself, Peter. I'd like to see one man come back whole to Tulloch Ard."

"I'll do that," promised Peter huskily, and gave his final instructions to Jacques and Donald Roy. These were two good men to whom he was entrusting his brother. Jacques had been with him in perilous days on the Fraser, and Donald

Roy at Ogdensburg and other places. But at best it was heavy sorrow he was sending back to Tulloch Ard, that had already its share of sorrow.

It would have been better if he could havè gone himself with Hugh. But these were grim and bitter times and the officers of the little army of Upper Canada, one and all, shared the strain. No man who could help weld those war-weary battalions into an effective fighting force could be spared.

Disease had taken its toll in the spring and summer of 1814. Ague and fever and wounds not well tended. The soldiers were poorly fed. How could it be otherwise? The militia had been drawn off the farms, and the country threatened to be destitute of food from lack of men to till the land. The homeless fugitives of the Niagara frontier depended on the army commissariat. So did the Indians of Grand River and their families.

So General Drummond took measures. From the great body of ill-armed militia, he enlisted a Light Infantry battalion of four hundred able men and let the rest go back to their farms. The four hundred were well drilled and became known as the Incorporated Militia. Captured guns were fitted up for service and supplies were diligently collected.

In the midst of all the activity, invasion rumours filled the air. It was said the Six Nations Indians were massing against Canada, all but the friendly Mohawks. Drummond kept writing Sir George Prevost, Governor in Chief, of the importance of the defence of the Niagara Peninsula, arguing that the movement of troops towards Plattsburg was but a feint. And Prevost was pencilling petulant comments on the margin of the letters, as on one of June twenty-first: "Much

294

obliged to General Drummond for his opinion, but it is entirely without foundation."

Time was to justify Drummond, but in the meanwhile he had to rely on the troops he already had in Upper Canada.

Peter was with the Glengarry Light Infantry at York. He was there when the Americans came over against Fort Erie in force, and took it without a struggle. He was still there when, on the bitter day of the Battle of Chippewa, the enemy guns mowed down the Royal Scots and the men of the 100th, and at the end of the day General Riall's forces were reduced by one third.

They discussed the defeat in the barracks at York.

"Fool," chafed one of the young officers, sitting astride his chair and gazing gloomily out over the wide blue lake. "To take on a force so much larger."

"The point is," argued Peter, "that the Americans are better soldiers than they were at the beginning. Better trained. Better led."

"So are we, I hope." Young Cameron laughed shortly. "Some of these days we'll meet them when the odds are even, and it will be a bonnie battle."

"The sooner the better. Just so much sooner will the war be over and we'll be home."

"Home!" echoed young Cameron dreamily. "To sleep in a bed! To eat fresh food! To swing a lass in a reel!"

The door swung open and they stood to attention as Captain Fitzgibbon came in. He was smiling.

"Gentlemen," he said, rubbing his hands, "we join Riall at Ten Mile Creek. Warm work ahead for the Glengarries."

Cameron threw up his cap and caught it. Excitement ran

through the barracks as they prepared for embarkation. They crossed the lake, but Ten Mile Creek was not their final destination. They were part of the force that, under Colonel Pearson, took up the advance position at Lundy's Lane, while the enemy were three miles away at Chippewa, and battle imminent.

They were in an orchard. Apple, cherry and peach trees shaded them. Unripe fruit festooned the branches, and the gray-green leaves and gnarled trunks made a rustic and peaceful setting for the ranks of war.

Before each went to his position, Peter and young Cameron exchanged a word and a look, a hard, smiling, intimate look full of that comradeship that is between men who may in a few minutes die together.

The Glengarries were the right wing of the line of battle. There in the orchard they waited the first attack of the enemy and took it and held. Not so lucky was the left wing where the incorporated militia was attacked from the side and thrown into confusion. After some time they managed to re-form behind the British centre and regained their position.

The artillery held the hill stubbornly. Again and again, with complete abandon, the Americans charged, and many guns were taken, but eventually and with great effort the attackers were thrown back, and for a moment there was a lull. But not for long.

All afternoon the battle went bloodily on, with no sign of victory for either army. Even odds, young Cameron had asked for. This looked like a draw.

By nine o'clock it was dark. Whenever there was a lull in the noise of battle, the deep low roar of the Falls of

Niagara filled the air. The sound seemed louder and more pervasive with the coming of night.

In the darkness Canadian reinforcements arrived. Troops that had been marching and countermarching all day under a hot July sun. They came stumbling up the slope to the relief of their friends, and in the confusion blundered into the centre of the enemy force on the very lip of the hill.

The fight was now desperate and at close quarters. Indeed, the muzzles of the guns were often only a few yards apart. Men used clubbed muskets and bayonets and dirks. Officers barked orders and enemy officers replied. The field was flickeringly lighted by the constant gunfire, and in each sudden glow the faces of foemen flashed into view, their eyes gleaming and the buttons of their uniforms winking in the light. The scene had the lurid, sullen beauty of an inferno. And the sounds were in keeping.

The last hour was all confusion and effort and desperate bravery and bloody wounds and death. At midnight there was silence. The battle was over. The enemy had withdrawn. Each side had fought till it could fight no more. Again the heavy roar of the Falls filled the night with that mighty cadence of sound that has been since the world began.

But for more than an hour Peter had not been aware of the tide of battle. In the angle of a rail fence he lay, with the blood trickling from a hole in his thigh where a musket ball had gone through. He had managed to get a tourniquet on, and the full flood of bleeding stanched, but the wound still oozed redly and weakness came over him in waves. The crackle of musketry, the deep bark of the guns, the sharp, short shouts of battle, the mumbled groaning of the wounded, only vaguely was he aware of any of it.

He slept for a while, it seemed, for presently dawn was breaking, and he was being lifted into a cart. Young Cameron's face grinned down at him encouragingly and was gone. Then he was taken by stretcher into a long, low log building and laid in a bunk. This was a hospital.

The place was soon full. Bunks, in tiers two-deep, lined the walls, and men were lying on straw on the floor. There was a long table in the centre of the room where a tall, shock-headed doctor was operating with great despatch. There was no glass in the windows and flies came in, in hordes. They hovered over the table; they crawled over the wounded in the bunks; they kept up a constant steady buzzing that wore on the nerves.

A brawny red-faced sergeant helped the doctor. Once he brought water and towels and clean linen, and the doctor washed and changed on the spot. Peter watched him curiously.

It was afternoon before his own turn came. His leg had stiffened. The doctor swore companionably with him as they got him out and on the table.

"The fellows on the floor have the best of it when it comes to being moved," he said.

He examined and probed the wound, and fear caught Peter by the throat.

The doctor grinned down at him. "Thought we'd take it off, did you? Well, we won't. Not you. Thank God. Too many legs have I sawed off this day."

He continued to probe, then washed and bandaged it.

Pain went over Peter in billows of blackness. Then the indomitable pale face above him grinned down at him, and the wound settled into a bearable steady aching.

"Next!" called the doctor crisply.

The next was an enemy casualty. The surgeon had for him the same hearty friendliness. Here, it came to Peter, was one place where war was not so important as humanity. Indeed, war was in ill repute.

A messenger was at the door. A woman stood there with him.

"She has come under a flag of truce, sir," said the soldier. "To see her husband."

She walked through the ranks of the wounded, looking neither to right nor left. At the far end of the room a middle-aged man lay. He was hurt in the body, and was in great and terrible pain.

She sat by him on a stool the doctor placed for her. With her kerchief she kept wiping his brow. Her face was grave and controlled. For a while he tossed in agony. Then he quieted and they talked in low tones. In a half-hour he was dead.

She rose, curtseyed to the doctor, then stood for a moment, looking at the wounded men. Their eyes met hers in respect and sympathy. She spoke then in a quiet, bitter voice.

"Those who plan wars should be here," she said, and wrapped her shawl about her and went out.

The doctor heaved a great sigh. Peter looked at the enemy soldier who had just been treated. "The war's over for us," said the American. And it came over Peter in a great rush of feeling that it was.

Then they, that could, turned to look at the doctor. He stood for a moment, weaving on his feet, a scalpel still in his hand. He flung his arm around the post of one of the bunks and, still holding to it, he slipped slowly down to the floor.

"Asleep, by cripes," cried the sergeant, and stood staring down at him for a moment. Then he pulled over a *paillasse* of straw, pushed it under the doctor's body and threw a cloak over him.

He grinned pridefully at the men. "Hasn't been off his feet for a day and a night, so he hasn't."

For an hour the doctor slept heavily without turning; then he was up, blinking his eyes and smiling sheepishly at the men.

"Next," he said.

"This man," explained the sergeant, "was wounded three weeks ago at Chippawa."

"Ha-humph," exclaimed the doctor. "It's a queer thing that maggots in a wound seem to do no harm."

* * *

Peter convalesced in a little shack in the village of Newark. Less than a year before all the houses in the town had been burned by the enemy, so his quarters were not good. But in the clean air of that sunny, wind-swept place his wound healed healthily.

Dougall MacKay came to see him there. He looked older, yet fit enough. So far, he had come through unscathed.

"Where now are the enemy?" asked Peter when the greetings were over.

"They've fallen back on Fort Erie, from which it will be difficult to dislodge them."

Peter was for a few minutes silent. "I wish it was over and you, too, free to come home."

"It's not over, but I think there will not be much more fighting in Upper Canada. We've had our share. But with Napoleon in Elba, we can count on more regulars from overseas. For three years we have fought mainly a defensive war. Now we may take the offensive."

Peter's mind went back to the early days of the struggle. To Brock and MacDonell and Red George. "It's been a long pull. I wonder that we held. So few of us and so ill-prepared."

"We paid a price. I'm more sorry than I can say about David, who was to me like a son. And now Hughie. That's hard indeed."

"Aye. Hard." Grief darkened Peter's face.

"But Hughie will handle it. He has strength of spirit. I've often thought that those who carry well a heavy burden move on further than the rest of us. As they say in the old country, they're 'far ben.' Hughie will be like that. And he has his family about him."

"Not so many of us as there were."

"There will be more."

"I wish you could get leave and come and see your grandson."

"Perhaps I can soon. I've a silver mug for him at home. It will be in the chest that Kirsty buried. And I have with me a small gift for you to take to my grand-daughter when you go."

He unwrapped a china doll with black wavy china hair and a fixed sweet smile. Peter held it in his big hands, fondling it.

"I have, myself, a gift for Felicity," he said slowly. "Will you reach into my pack? A leather box."

It was a ring. Three opals in an antique, heavy setting. The jewels gleamed softly, rose and gold and green.

"One of the de Meurons gave it to me. When his young wife died in Switzerland he joined the regiment for foreign service. The ring was hers. I was able to do him a small service."

Dougall smiled. "You carried him on your back, I hear, for a long way under fire."

"But he died later anyway. When he knew that he would die he said to me, 'Are you married? Then give her this ring. A happy woman wore it.' Then he added, 'Some think an opal's unlucky. It's not. It means a light shining from within.' So I have this for Felicity."

He added after a moment, "It seems to suit her."

Dougall turned the bauble about on his palm. "You're right. It does suit her."

He looked thoughtfully down at Peter and remembered that he had not wanted him for a son-in-law. He knew him now and liked him.

"Give Felicity my love when you get home."

"I will that. I'm afraid she has had a hard time during the war."

"It will be better now," smiled Dougall.

CHAPTER

XX

IN AUGUST came word that Peter was wounded. Just that. Nothing more. When Felicity got the news she went to the other house to tell them and then came quietly home again. Her household tasks were there to do, and in a brittle calm she did them. Underneath that calm lay her grief and her fear. But the surface held. She went through the days with so withdrawn a look on her face that the others were loath to mention Peter.

But not so Hughie. She sat with him on the shady back porch one day, snipping off the stems and black blossom-ends of a bowl of gooseberries. Hughie's slim fingers were already deft.

He said presently, "There is no cause for despair, you know."

She spoke carefully over the stricture in her throat: "If

he were not badly wounded they would not have sent word."

"But he is not dead."

The thought in her mind was, "He may be blinded like you, or worse."

He picked up that thought. "It's probably much less than blindness. Don't tear yourself to pieces. There may be no need."

She was silent for a few minutes. Then, "I know you're right, Hughie. You see so clearly." She paused painfully and added, "You see so clearly with the eyes of the spirit."

Again there was a pause. His hands were still. Then, in a low, clear voice that was sweet with sadness, "Just now I'm not caring about the eyes of the spirit. I want to see with the eyes which I have lost." He gave an ironical quick laugh and picked up a handful from the bowl. "But I'm getting quite good with gooseberries."

She touched his arm. "Don't pretend, Hughie. With me say what you really feel."

He shook his head. "Not even with you, Felicity. This bit of fortitude I have acquired, I cherish. A small, shivering thing, but my own."

"Like my faith," Felicity thought later. "A small, shivering thing, but real too."

For she prayed. In the long night-time when sleep would not come, and in the daytime as she worked. She prayed in the complete sincerity of need. And as she prayed, her faith grew.

Surcease from anxiety did not come to her, but strength and staying power did. And a certain hard, harrying courage. It was as if she looked out over the miles that separated them,

306

and as before her heart called, "Strength to you, Peter, and health and good fortune." That rigour of spirit she felt she could in a queer way communicate to him, when God and her own indomitability had raised it up in her.

She felt her body tight-knit and taut with the turmoil and strength within. She seldom spoke of her anxiety, but she was aware of the support of them all. It was in the timbre of their voices, in the firmness of their hand clasp.

One day Duncan MacFarlane came rattling up the hill in his old *calèche*, looking much the same as when Felicity had seen him on her first visit to Tulloch Ard.

"A long time since I was here," he observed. "I've been making boots for the army. But look you what I have now in my pack."

He unrolled a length of soft red leather. "Says I to myself, that will make some fine fancy shoon for the little maid at Peter MacAlpin's. And sure Rorie himself will be wearing holes in his big boots by now. So here I am."

They were all glad to see him. When he saw how short-handed they were for the harvest, he took a sickle and went out into the fields with them. Then on rainy days or in the evenings by candlelight he worked at his last with awl and wax-end and needle. The little red shoes for Barbary Rose were soon finished, and her feet pranced with delight in them.

Duncan looked young Dougall over with interest. "See now the length from elbow to wrist and from knee to ankle. A tall chieftainly man he'll be."

Felicity laughed and laid her cheek against the yellow curls.

Duncan was good for Hughie. There was a natural likeness of spirit between them, a cool, crisp grasp of life and a courteous detachment.

"Many things you can do, Hughie lad," he told him with a kind casualness. "Both useful and pleasant. Piping and singing and the telling of tales. Sure a full-time job was that of the *seannachie* man in the old days. And some farm work too. Reaping and stooking you will yet manage. And many another task. Every day learn one new thing, however small."

He rose and laid a small log on the fire and turned the talk to other, less poignant matters.

"Have you seen these new things they call stoves? Big, black, high-stomached things spraddling out into the middle of the room. In place of a fire on the hearth. A footering idea!"

He took up his work again, pressing in his awl and holding it firm. "Well, Alec Jim Roy is now an agent for them. He was up Dunvegan way, getting orders, and stopped at Lauchie MacKelvie's. Now, as you know, Alec Jim Roy is a great talker. Almost he had Lauchie persuaded. But not Christie his wife. Christie was going about her business, making scones she was, and stepping light and keeping an eye on her husband.

" 'Look at the hard work you have now, getting the wood out of the bush every winter,' says Alec, all sorrowful and sympathetic. 'Buy one of these stoves, and half the wood you need now will be enough.'

" 'Is that right?' Lauchie scrapes his chair forward. Lazy he is, and that caught him.

" 'I'm telling you, Lauchie, the half will be plenty with this fine stove in the kitchen.'

"At that Christie looks over her shoulder at the two men, her eyes glinting. And in that soft, high voice that is on her, 'Buy two, Lauchie,' she says, 'and you won't need any wood at all'."

*   *   *

One night as Felicity was coming down the stair from putting the children to bed, Patrig barked once. Then there was a low eager whining. She ran to the door.

"Peter," she breathed, and could say no more.

But Fergus was there as well, and he half-carried Peter into the house. In a moment they had him on the settle, very pale, very haggard, but himself.

"I'm fine," he insisted. "I got a chance from Cornwall as far as Glen Donald, and I thought I could walk the rest of the way. I was weaker than I knew. But Fergus found me." He reached out a hand and laid it on the other's arm. "Sit down, man, why don't you?"

His eyes met Felicity's and clung, and in them was the sheer gladness and relief of reunion. After a moment he went on.

"Fergus saved my life. I well believe he did. My wound opened a little, and in the swamp where the wolves are, and with the scent of blood, well . . ." he laughed. "There was I, hirpling along, and the blood trickling into my boot! I was never so glad to see anyone. He helped me home."

"Why, Fergus!" exclaimed Felicity, and Fergus flushed.

"Better get him some toddy," he said brusquely.

"Of course." She stirred the fire under the kettle.

Peter's eyes closed drowsily. Fergus stood looking down

at him with a sort of awkward affection. Thought Felicity, "He feels that he has saved Peter's life. Now he has an interest in him. He's fond of him."

He turned to her. "See that you take good care of that wound."

"I'll do my best," she promised meekly.

"I'll send Katie over in the morning. She's good about sickness."

"Do," urged Felicity, and just as he went out their eyes met, and in that brief glance an incident was definitely closed.

That night Felicity lay awake from sheer happiness. She felt dizzy with it. Never had she felt more complete thankfulness. It was as if she had faithfully paid out a bitter price in anxiety and fear, and now it was by a generous God returned, full measure.

She was, in the days that followed, like a new person. Life fell suddenly into focus. It became real. It became full-flavoured and satisfying. Peter was home.

The children radiated her happiness and his. Peter's pride in them was enormous. Especially in his son. In young Dougall there was the MacAlpin bigness, and with it Felicity's fairness and her shimmering proud smile. A chieftainly lad, indeed!

Since Peter's return, Tassie and Felicity no longer shared their tasks, as each household now had a definite unity and pattern. Felicity thought a little uneasily of Tassie's casual cookery, so one morning she made a pile of buckwheat pancakes, covered them to keep them warm, and took them to the other house.

As she came near she heard young Ian's voice raised in

fretful wailing. She paused in the doorway. There he was, tear-stained and disconsolate, and there was Hughie feeling carefully with one hand through the shelves of the cupboard.

She made her voice matter-of-fact. "It's Felicity. Is Ian hungry?"

"He must be. I was looking for something for him." His voice was unsteady, and there was hurt and bewilderment in his sensitive face.

Felicity found bread and poured milk over it, then wiped Ian's face and hands and took him on her lap. The wailing ceased with the first spoonful. After each bite he bounced on her knee and looked up at her with a wide, ingratiating smile.

"He's a lovable bairn," she murmured companionably, trying to wipe the dark shadow from Hughie's face, and failing. While at the same time there flashed into her mind's eye the vision of a long line of lovable bairns, charming like their father and irresponsible like their mother, and she coming to the rescue to feed and dry-clothe them.

He took up her thought. "A lovable bairn," he agreed. "And there'll be others, I suppose. But there shouldn't be."

Felicity's mind agreed with him, but not her heart.

"I'd like to know why not," she answered sturdily, and set young Ian on the floor and put chairs to fence him.

Hughie laughed. "What would we do without you, Felicity? Who'd have thought that you'd hold all our lives in your hand?"

She shook her head. "I've enough to do to manage my own life. But look, Hughie, I brought you some buckwheat pancakes. And I was thinking, as I came, about the field where the buckwheat grew. There was clover there once."

She sighed. "I don't know if I can make you understand about that field of clover. I wanted to paint it. It was like no other field of clover ever was. I waited for a fine day when the sun would be right. Then, when I was ready to do it, the clover wasn't there any more. It had been ploughed under. To enrich the land. In due time buckwheat was sown. It was beautiful too. Shiny red stems like mahogany. Pink and creamy blossoms in clusters. And the smell of bees and honey over it all. And the pancakes from it are very good. You'll see. Nourishing."

"Is it a parable?" asked Hughie softly.

"I don't know. It's what happened to me, that's all. Here's Tassie now."

She came singing up the path from the barn, the sunshine bright on her dark head and her hands full of flowers.

"*Tha mi gu math*," she cried cheerfully, and sat down close to Hughie. "I was looking for an old turkey hen's nest along the fence," she explained to Felicity. Then she turned to Hugh. "I brought you a flower from the pumpkin vine. Not much smell, but a nice shape. Yellow. And some wild morning-glory. Very trailing. And elderberry flowers, and sweet-mary from the garden. And a big pink cabbage rose." She flattened it against his face. "Lovely, isn't it, the feeling and the smell?"

The strain was going out of Hughie. His arm tightened around his wife. Her complete naturalness loosened the tension in him.

She rubbed her cheek against his shoulder, then rose, stretched and yawned and looked at young Ian who sat quiet and bright-eyed, watching.

312

"You've fed him," she remarked with satisfaction. "That's fine." She looked around the room and sighed. "I'll have to scrub the floor," she decided gloomily. "With him crawling."

Felicity tried not to look too closely, not to remember Mathair Anne's snowy curtains and clean-kept floors.

Tassie's eyes had followed hers. "Perhaps I should wash the curtains too," she said uncertainly. Then, with relief in her soft voice, "But I'll have to set bread tonight, and that will keep me busy."

"I'll be baking. I'll send you down some."

"Now, isn't that kind of you! And your bread's so good." She rubbed her back against the frame of the door. "The linsey gets itchy when it's hot."

"If you'd wear something under it," suggested Felicity mildly.

"Why?" came idly from Tassie leaning against the door, her full young figure comfortable in the blue linsey.

Felicity felt assailed with inner laughter. "I might have kept the bread," she thought on the way home. "She won't wash the curtains anyway."

Nevertheless she knew well that, lacking as Tassie might be as a housekeeper, as a wife to a man in trouble she was more than adequate. The simplicity of her nature was full of healing. So was her kindness. She was a child of Mother Earth, and full of deep, instinctive knowledge.

From the stable door Rorie called to Felicity. "Come and see what I've got here."

It was a new horse. A big dappled gray that would with Shanlan make a fine team.

313

Rorie led him out into the sunshine. He was a handsome animal. His mottled coat was like satin, his long tail swept the ground. He snorted and rolled a white-edged eye, and curvetted proudly at the end of the halter.

"I'm going to hitch him up this afternoon and take out a load of gravel."

"What's his name?"

"Rex, they called him."

He was a kingly brute, indeed, and full of pride; yet he seemed amiable too, reaching out to the wisps of grass that Felicity offered him.

"He's handsomer than Shanlan," declared Felicity, peering with a sort of jealous affection into the dark stable where Shanlan stamped in his stall.

"I doubt if he'll be as willing, though. How is Peter's sore leg?"

"It's healing so fast," cried Felicity with thankfulness in her voice. "It aches only when he's tired."

"Aye so. Well, he's lucky." And their eyes met understandingly.

Then Rorie said something that surprised her. Still with his fingers in the mane of the horse, Rex, he said, "Felicity, are you going to make any more pictures?"

"I don't know. Why?"

"Well, Anne used to hope you would, that's all."

She smiled at him, touched.

Back in her own home and alone, she reached into the big cupboard and took out that last painting of hers. "Young Men in Uniform, Climbing a Hill," it might be called, if it had a name.

314

It was still unfinished. The face of the last young man was vague and incomplete. She looked at the others. Finlay long since dead. David also dead. Hughie blinded. Peter by a blessed chance safe and at home. And that last lad, who would fight in battles yet to be, what would he be like? Like Dougall, that chieftainly young son of hers? She thrust the thought from her. One war in a lifetime was enough. Yet her heart reached out in boding, protective love to that young lad of the future whose face she could not see.

She squeezed out some paint and took up her brush and made a few tentative strokes. She frowned. Then she set up a small bare canvas and set to work. But not for long. She laid down her brush and looked curiously at her fingers.

They were stiff. As tools they were no longer serviceable to her. And even if by patient effort they regained their skill, where would she get the time to paint?

She was through with her painting. In her heart she had long since known it, but she had never brought it up into the open spaces of her mind. Really, the issue had been decided years ago when she had chosen Peter instead of Gavin. Her father had known it. But she in her young arrogance had thought she could reach out with greedy hands and take from life what she would.

She sighed deeply but she was not unhappy. Why should she be? For a long time women had been throwing their special gifts back into the common pool. Like the clover field ploughed under for the enrichment of the future yield. She thought, "When I am an old woman I shall remember not that I once painted a few good pictures, but that Peter came home from the wars and we were together again."

That afternoon Rorie went by on his way to the gravel pit with Shanlan and the new horse Rex. Felicity came to the door to watch them.

Down the steep slope the team stepped cautiously, the harness taut against their great haunches, their strong legs moving rhythmically. Rorie stood, feet wide, braced. The sun was bright on his gray head and on Shanlan's shining back and on Rex's coat of dappled satin.

Felicity followed them down into the gravel pit. She laid a hand on Shanlan's shoulder and offered him a wisp of clover. Rex stamped and crowded, and she held some out to him. She smiled to think how variable horses were, and how like human beings.

Shanlan, now, that fine and faithful horse, did not encourage coddling. A courteous word or a pat in passing was all that seemed indicated with him. While the small mare, Pegi, whinnied with delight when anyone came into the stable, and poked her head into the kitchen door when she was at large, and because of her ingratiating ways was much pampered with lumps of sugar and attention. Rex, also, would like to be petted, thought Felicity, watching him roll a black, white-edged eye at her.

The load was now on. Rorie thrust his shovel into the gravel and climbed up. He clutched the reins and the horses' heads swung up.

"Giddap," he yelled cheerfully, and the wagon lurched into motion. The traces tightened, the shoulders of the horses hunched forward, the whiffletrees were taut and even.

"Good lads," cried Rorie. "Up you go."

The incline steepened. The horses were scrambling now,

low to the ground, their bodies queerly elongated.

"Oh," thought Felicity, "it's too heavy."

Then it happened. Rex, the big and beautiful and mighty, stopped trying. His muscles relaxed. The whiffletree swung sideways. The gravel in the wagon box began with a curious slithering sound to slip back.

With a leap Rorie was down over the front of the wagon, his feet on the pole. He paid no attention to Rex.

"Shanlan," he yelled. "Shanlan Dhu."

Shanlan heard. The sods flew back as the great feet clutched and held. The head went low. The muscles played along the mighty back and haunches.

"Shanlan," whispered Rorie, leaning over him.

He went down on his knees then, did Shanlan, for the last steep yard or two. He strained and crawled and scrambled like a cat. Then up over the lip of the rise, and there he was on level ground, the wagon behind him, and Rex standing by him, slack-traced and unconcerned.

Rorie leaped down and flung an arm around Shanlan's neck. The horse leaned his head against him. His flanks were wet and he trembled. They stood so for a moment, the handsome gray-haired old man and the big raw-boned black horse.

When Felicity came up, Rorie was gazing sadly at Rex. "He can't help it," he explained. "He hasn't got it in him."

"This is another parable," thought Felicity. Those who are willing and able, they carry the load. Her mind went back to Mathair Anne, who had said on the night she died, "You are like Shanlan. You have strength in you."

317

It was clear to all, though no one mentioned it, that the burden of the two households would in the long run fall inevitably on Peter and herself. And why should it not? Peter was able. And with him by her, so was she.

* * *

That evening some of the neighbours dropped in for a friendly hour by the fireside. Many such gatherings had been held in the big house in Mathair Anne's day. Now the nerve-centre of Tulloch Ard had moved to the new house on the higher hill. And Felicity was the one to give welcome and hospitality.

So a small fire flickered on the hearth in the pine-panelled west room and the tall candles were lighted. Rorie and Hughie and Tassie were there. So was Duncan MacFarlane and Sandy Ban. Fergus and Katie too. And a scattering of lads too young for the army who hung on Peter's and Hughie's every word.

Inevitably the minds of all turned to those who had been of their company and were now not with them. Yet it was as if they were truly there, and their presence should be recognized. Sandy raised his chanter.

"I will now play a small tune for those we love, no longer with us," he said softly.

With his fingertips he seemed to be feeling for that which would heal and not hurt. The lonely music of a lament was twined into a lullaby, and they thought of Mathair Anne. That in turn slipped into one of the songs Dark Mary used to sing, and again into the young, reckless, yet somehow

318

wistful measures of a marching song, and it was as if David had looked in on them briefly with his shy dark smile.

Sandy tapped out his chanter and raised it again, and Duncan lifted his hand to beat time, and they sang. Hesitatingly at first, then one by one joining in, till in "Over the Sea to Skye," they were full-throated and relaxed. Hughie's voice rang true and clear, Tassie singing with him, her head against his shoulder and his arm around her. Katie's small soprano fluted away like a bird in a brake.

Felicity's eyes moved from one face to another around the firelit circle. Here in a time of war and trouble were once more gathered together those of the house of Tulloch Ard and their friends. Since the last time they met, they had known loss and heavy grief. The rigours of war were still with them. Before them lay a future stark with toil. But rich, too, with friendliness and high-spirited living. Life was at full tide again on this higher hill beside this bright fireside.

When they had all gone, Felicity went out into the rowan grove. Even in the dim light the place was quick with life. The branches stirred restlessly and the red berries shone black against them. A wind that was full of the dark ecstasy of the night swept through the grove and flowed against her.

She thought of the friendly gathering just past. She thought of this home of hers and her children asleep in it. She thought of her husband, her lordly and lovable Peter, so blessedly home from the wars. She had that familiar sense of the beauty and significance of the present moment, as if it should be limned on canvas, or caught in deathless words. But it was not to be held. It was life itself marching

319

on in power, and she for a moment seeing it with unbound eyes. It was to be lived, whether or not recorded.

A swath of light cut through the darkness. She turned, and Peter loomed tall in the open door. Limping only a little, he came down the path towards her.

THE END